Dare to Love a Duke

She sensed someone's gaze on her like a velvet glove stroking down the back of her neck.

Lucia looked around to find the source of the sensation. Her breath stuttered and her pulse came in a quick flutter when she saw its origin.

A rangy, dark-haired man in a blue mask strode purposefully toward her. He moved with fluid, masculine grace, his body muscular and strapping. The direct way he approached captivated her—as though nothing could keep him from being near her.

Lucia's pulse leapt again.

She shook her head, trying to dismiss her reaction to the guest's approach. Clients often turned their interests toward her. Yet there was a palpable sensuality to the way he walked and the interest in his gaze. It held frank erotic intent, and the confidence that he could give her extraordinary pleasure.

Even at a distance, his eyes said, *I. Want. You.*

By Eva Leigh

The Wicked Quills of London
FOREVER YOUR EARL
SCANDAL TAKES THE STAGE
TEMPTATIONS OF A WALLFLOWER

The London Underground
FROM DUKE TILL DAWN
COUNTING ON A COUNTESS
DARE TO LOVE A DUKE

Eva Leigh

Dare to Love a Duke

❧ The London Underground ❧

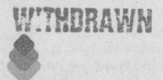

AVONBOOKS

An Imprint of HarperCollinsPublishers

DARE TO LOVE A DUKE. Copyright © 2019 by Ami Silber. All rights reserved. Printed in the United States of America. No part of this book may be used or reproduced in any manner whatsoever without written permission except in the case of brief quotations embodied in critical articles and reviews. For information, address HarperCollins Publishers, 195 Broadway, New York, NY 10007.

First Avon Books mass market printing: January 2019

Print Edition ISBN: 978-0-06-249945-5
Digital Edition ISBN: 978-0-06-249946-2

Cover design by Patricia Barrow

Avon, Avon & logo, and Avon Books & logo are registered trademarks of HarperCollins Publishers in the United States of America and other countries.
HarperCollins is a registered trademark of HarperCollins Publishers in the United States of America and other countries.

FIRST EDITION

18 19 20 21 22   QGM   10 9 8 7 6 5 4 3 2 1

To Zack

Acknowledgments

First and foremost, I would like to thank my editor, Nicole Fischer, for her boundless patience and her belief that Tom and Lucia would get their HEA—despite my conviction that I couldn't make it happen.

Thank you to my agent, Kevan Lyon, who continues to support me.

I toast the staff of Avon Romance with many cupcakes, and much gratitude for the tireless efforts of Caroline Perny and Pam Jaffee—the hardest working women in Romancelandia.

This book was also a group effort, and without the assistance of many kind souls, I would still be wandering around, confused, searching for answers. Thank you to Laurie London, Justin DiPego, Rose Lerner, Katharine Ashe, Aleksei Moniz Mirov, Peadar O'Caomhánaigh, Maitú Ó Coimín, Stephanie Patterson, Kelly Maher, Michele Sandiford, CJ Lemire, Cassandra Carr, Caroline Linden, Laura Lee Guhrke, Fran Strober Cassano, Sarah MacLean, Erin Satie, Tessa Dare, HelenKay Dimon, Megan Frampton, Victoria Dahl, Erin Pollaro, and Marisa Escolar.

And thank you to readers everywhere. I would not have the privilege of writing my stories of love and acceptance without you.

Thank you to the women who fiercely champion women's work.

DARE TO
LOVE A DUKE

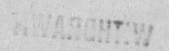

Chapter 1

A droplet of sweat rolled between the shoulder blades of Thomas Edward O'Connell Cúchulain Powell, Earl of Langdon, as he steadied the cocked dueling pistol and took aim. He looked down the weapon's barrel, his concentration fixed on his target twenty paces away. His exhalation misted in the chill midnight air as he fought for calm.

He inhaled, held his breath, then pulled the trigger. There was a flash and a cloud of smoke as the weapon's concussion split the night's stillness.

Twenty paces away, glass shattered.

The hushed crowd burst into applause and cheers of "Bravo!" as Tom lowered the pistol and grinned. He kept his footing as people swarmed around him, offering their congratulations and hearty thumps on the back. Numerous women, scented heavily with perfume, kissed his cheeks—so many that he imagined it looked as though he wore rouge.

"The hero of Regent's Park," George Mowbray declared.

"Not to Culver, I'm afraid."

Tom looked over at his opponent, Lord Culver, who sulked as he handed his dueling pistol to a footman. Culver had missed when taking aim at the bottle of claret. Perhaps if Tom had been more virtuous, he would have deliberately missed so that there was no winner and no loser. Though Tom was an earl and the heir to the Duke of Northfield, no one would ever call him virtuous.

"Ah, shag him," Mowbray said magnanimously.

"I'll leave that to the professionals."

Tom smiled ruefully as Culver's hired companion for the evening attempted to soothe her client. When Culver shoved her away and she stumbled, Tom immediately strode through the crowd and jammed his fist into his opponent's sternum.

"You may have lost, but you're still a gentleman," Tom said in a low, warning voice. Gently, he took the woman's arm to make sure she kept her footing. "Apologize to the lady."

"She's just a whore, Langdon," Culver said.

"Apologize." Tom's jaw firmed as he held up the pistol. "Or else the next time I fire this, it will be at your worthless heart."

Culver scowled, but said in a grudging voice, "I'm sorry." Under his breath, he muttered, "You Irish son of a bitch."

Tom narrowed his eyes. "Repeat that."

"I . . ." Culver gulped. "It was a jest."

"A poor one." Since the age of twelve, when he'd been brought from his mother's Irish home to be educated in his father's country of England, Tom had heard some variation of Culver's insult. Why anyone thought Tom ought to be embarrassed about his Irish blood, he'd no idea. But he wouldn't tolerate slurs. "Must I ask for another apology?"

"My sincere contrition," Culver said. After casting Tom a wary glance, he hurried toward his waiting carriage.

"Hope I didn't cost you your night's earnings," Tom said to the woman.

"Ah, no." She gave him a dry smile as she eyed the throngs of young, wealthy bucks passing bottles back and forth as they caroused. "There's plenty of pickings in this crowd." She glanced at him and her smile turned more genuine. "Happens that I'm free right now, my lord. If you're interested."

"Perhaps another evening." He wasn't ready for bed yet.

One of the rakes came forward with a substantial bundle of cash and jammed it into Tom's hand. "Your winnings, Langdon."

No sooner than the cash was in his hand than Tom turned and handed it to the woman. "For putting up with Culver."

"I couldn't, my lord," she said as she tucked the

money into her bodice. She gave him a wink. "'Night, love." She pressed a quick kiss to his cheek, then strode off into the darkness.

"That was near seventy pounds, Langdon," Mowbray said in shock.

"She'll have better use of it than me."

There was no shortage of funds in Tom's coffers, between income from his earldom as well as his generous allowance provided by his father, the duke. Other lordlings and bucks swam in seas of debt, hounded constantly by tailors, club proprietors, and wineshop owners. Tom made certain to pay everyone on time, for no other reason than the fact that he could.

"I'd do it again for free if it meant humiliating Culver. Bloke's had it coming since he refused to cover his mistress's bills."

"You're a daft bastard," Mowbray said with a shake of his head.

"I'd agree," Tom said affably, "except everyone knows about my parents' celebrated fidelity. Bastard in deed but not blood."

Someone handed him a bottle of whiskey and he took a drink before passing the spirits along to a trio of bucks who looked in dire need of refreshment.

"Good Christ, *here* you are!"

The throng opened up just enough to allow Christopher Ellingsworth to emerge, looking slightly bedraggled despite his military bearing. Since returning home from the War a year ago, Ellingsworth had renewed the friendship he and Tom had begun at Oxford, and from that point forward they had been nigh inseparable, with the exception of tonight.

"Missed the excitement." Tom handed his pistol to the footman, who returned it to its polished mahogany case.

"Not for want of trying," his friend said. "I've been to the opera, two gaming hells, and a phaeton race. Everywhere I went, I'd just missed you by ten minutes." He shook his head but his eyes gleamed with reluctant admiration. "Good thing we're not competing for the title of Most Scapegrace Gentleman in London, or else you'd best me."

"That trophy isn't much sought after, anyway. Why such urgency to find me?" Tom lifted an eyebrow. "My father's not looking for me, I hope."

The duke periodically got it into his head that Tom would somehow reform and conduct himself with the dignity and sobriety of a ducal heir with a family history of deeply traditional beliefs, but that was *precisely* why Tom spent his days asleep and his nights in endless rounds of revelry. One day, hopefully in the far distant future, Tom would inherit the title, and with it, the morass of responsibilities and duties that came with being one of the most powerful men in England—and a voting record dedicated to preserving the ancient systems of power.

Life as Tom knew it would end. He'd say goodbye to nights entertaining opera dancers, midnight swims in the Serpentine, and behaving like the kingdom's veriest rogue, with his equally dissolute companions keeping him company.

As a marquess's third son who had recently sold his commission, Ellingsworth had considerably less money but shared Tom's appetite for running riot. There wasn't one corner of the city they hadn't explored in search of amusement and pleasure.

Ellingsworth hooked an arm around Tom's neck and led him several paces away from the celebrants.

In a low voice, he said, "I've heard about something that I knew would interest you. A place in Bloomsbury called the Orchid Club."

Tom groaned. "I've grown weary of clubs. Same games of chance, same people, same wine, same everything."

His friend's grin flashed. "This club is different. For one, it opens its doors only once a week and it just so happens to be open tonight."

That wasn't enough to snare Tom's interest. Many clubs did what they could to cultivate an air of mystery in order to ensure steady business from those eager to discover its secrets.

"What else makes it so special? Is it a brothel?"

"It is most decisively *not* a brothel. You'll need this, however." Ellingsworth unhooked his arm from around Tom's neck. He reached into his coat before producing something, then slipped the item into Tom's hand.

Tom held up the object so he could study it better. It was a half mask made of midnight blue satin.

"What the devil . . . ?"

Ellingsworth chuckled. "You're intrigued."

"You've gotten my attention."

Tom had torn all over London tonight, but still edginess and restlessness pulsed just beneath his skin. He needed diversion. Surely there had to be something in the city he hadn't already done.

"Excellent." Ellingsworth clapped his hands together. "I left my horse with the boy watching yours."

He headed toward where the animals waited, and Tom quickly followed.

"Won't you tell me more about this mysterious Orchid Club?" he asked.

"I wouldn't dream of ruining the surprise."

They reached the horses and after tossing coins to the lad holding the reins, Tom and Ellingsworth swung up into the saddles.

"Not even a hint?" Tom pressed.

In response, Ellingsworth put a finger to his smirking mouth, then wheeled his horse around.

Together, he and Tom rode off into the night.

BLOOMSBURY slumbered peacefully as Tom and Ellingsworth rode down an avenue lined with prosperous-looking homes. It hardly seemed the environment where a club—of admittedly unknown character—might thrive. The street was empty, while lamplight glowed warmly on the houses' facades.

Ellingsworth pulled his horse up outside one genteel but ordinary home that boasted several stories and a colonnade, with potted plants flanking the front door. Heavy curtains had been drawn in all the windows, keeping the activities inside hidden. Not a sound emerged from the structure. No human voices, no music. Nothing.

"Still as the grave." Tom eyed the building doubtfully. "You're having me on. There's no club in there."

"I'd never feed you poor intelligence. Not when it came to finding new pleasures." Ellingsworth looked affronted that Tom even suggested such a thing.

"My most sincere apologies." Tom inclined his head. "What do we do with our cattle?"

"We take the mews to a stable in the back, but everyone enters through the front door." Ellingsworth clicked his tongue as he guided his horse toward the narrow alley beside the house, and Tom followed.

A considerable brick stable awaited them, staffed by three smartly dressed grooms. A few carriages were parked outside, dozing coachmen sitting atop the vehicles. But within the stalls, there were horses of varying quality and age. Some were sleek, pampered animals clearly purchased from Tattersall's, while others had seen years of hard service to their owners. There was even a donkey.

As he handed one of the servants the reins, he studied the groom's face for some indication as to what kind of place this might be—a knowing wink, or maybe a sneer of disgust. Yet the servant seemed to deliberately school his features so that he gave nothing away.

"Be needing a mask, sir?" the groom asked.

Tom frowned at the servant's use of *sir* rather than *my lord,* but he surmised that any club requiring a mask seemed to want anonymity for its patrons, insisting that he be called by his proper title might be ill-advised.

"I have one," Tom said, patting the inside pocket of his jacket.

"You'll want to put it on now, sir. Before you go inside. House rules."

As Tom donned his blue satin mask, he saw that Ellingsworth did the same with one made of bronze silk.

"We're to play at being highwaymen?" Tom guessed.

In response, his friend smirked. "Badger me with as many questions as you like, but I'll answer nary a one until we're inside."

Tom heaved a sigh. "You're enjoying my torment."

They walked back up the mews to the front of the house.

"The trouble with you, Langdon, is that you're far too indulged. That's what comes of being the heir. Whatever you want, you get, and if anything is denied you, you insist it's worse than the sufferings of Tantalus."

"I am *not* indulged. I merely dislike delaying gratification. Waiting is unsupportable."

Ellingsworth snorted. "You may be able to wield a sabre, and you can shoot, but you'd make for a terrible soldier."

"I'll leave soldiering to more desperate blokes like you."

His friend's expression darkened. "Those days are behind me."

Tom fell into troubled silence. Since returning home from Waterloo, his friend's temperament shifted and altered rapidly from moment to moment. Ellingsworth might be full of quips and jests, and in a trice, he would grow moody and withdrawn. Though it worried him, Tom never asked about these abrupt changes in humor, held back by a concern over his friend's masculine pride. He sensed it had something to do with the War, something that, as a ducal heir, he would never experience.

How could he offer Ellingsworth a listening ear when he couldn't begin to understand all that his friend had seen and done, all that he'd survived? Perhaps someday, Tom might bring the subject up—delicately. Until then, he'd be Ellingsworth's companion in revelry.

They emerged back onto the street, and Tom held the gate that opened to the walkway leading to the front door. As if sensing the new experience that lay just steps away, his heart thudded with excitement as he approached the club's entrance. Distantly, the bell at St. George's proclaimed it to be one in the morning, straight in the middle of a rake's day. While the good people of London slept and rested in anticipation of their labors, he and people of his ilk prowled the streets in search of adventure.

Ellingsworth stepped to the door and knocked. *Tap. Tap-tap. Tap.*

Tom's lips pressed together as he suppressed a laugh. A secret knock? Truly? How trite.

The door opened, revealing a masked young black woman with closely shorn hair. She wore a coral-hued mask, and she gazed at Tom and Ellingsworth expectantly.

"I've come for the plums," Ellingsworth said.

"We haven't any," was her answer.

"Peaches will suffice."

Tom frowned, dimly recognizing the exchange from someplace, but he couldn't quite recall where he'd heard it. A moment later he realized the phrases came from *Alone with the Rogue*. He'd read the erotic novel—penned by the mysterious and wildly popular Lady of Dubious Quality—cover to cover, and then reread it almost immediately after turning the final page.

For all its pretense at secrecy, the Orchid Club certainly had good taste in literature.

The masked woman opened the door wider. "Come in, friends."

Tom and Ellingsworth stepped into the vestibule and the woman firmly shut and locked the door behind them. A single candle burned in the candelabra on a small table, but Tom could still make out the details in the entryway. It resembled any other in a well-to-do home, with nondescript but well-rendered paintings of exotic flowers hanging on the walls, and a large unlit chandelier hanging overhead.

"Is this your first time at the Orchid Club?" the woman asked.

"Yes," Tom replied.

Ellingsworth said, "My name's—"

She held up a hand. "No names here. The club abides by a code of strictest privacy. All are equal within these walls."

Tom's brows lifted. An egalitarian club was astonishingly progressive. Clubs were supposed to be strongholds of elitism, or so White's would have anyone believe.

"The only person at the Orchid Club who is permitted a name is our proprietress, Amina. But you are not to ask anyone else for anything that might identify them. Is that understood?"

Both Tom and Ellingsworth nodded.

"There is one other rule which must be obeyed," the woman said. "Everything must be consensual. No one shall be persuaded, coerced, or bullied." Her voice firmed. "Whoever does not submit to this will be summarily escorted out and banned from returning." She snapped her fingers and two brawny men emerged from the darkness, their faces impassive behind their masks. "These gentlemen are here to enforce the rules. I pray you do not make me summon them. Do I make myself clear?"

"You do," Tom said. His mind spun, trying to determine what exactly transpired at the Orchid Club that required these rules.

"How much to enter?" Ellingsworth asked.

The woman spread her hands. "That is at your discretion. We operate on the largesse of our guests and ask that you pay as much as you are able."

Tom took a crown from his pocket and held it out to the woman. She plucked it from his fingers and dropped it into a pouch at her waist, then turned her gaze to Ellingsworth, who shot a wry grin in Tom's direction.

Chuckling, Tom dug out another crown and gave it to the woman. Ellingsworth's allowance as a third son was comfortable, but his friend went through it at an alarming rate. It hardly mattered to Tom, as he had more than enough to cover their nightly expenses, and then some.

After the woman tucked the second coin into her pouch, she waved toward the hallway branching off the vestibule. "You may enter, friends. Enjoy yourselves."

His pulse hammering, Tom strode down the dark corridor, Ellingsworth at his heels. A low hum of human voices flowed out of a room ahead, and beneath that came the lilting strains of music. Then came the unmistakable sound of a woman moaning in pleasure.

"What in God's name have you gotten us into, Ellingsworth?" Tom asked lowly.

The possibility of a brothel had already been ruled out, and Tom was something of an expert in the noises women made when in the throes of passion. He could tell when they were feigning pleasure, and when they were sincere. The moaning coming from ahead was most assuredly genuine.

"Patience," his friend said. "All shall be revealed."

They both stepped into the doorway of a large parlor. Tom's heart jolted in his chest, and blood rushed straight into his groin.

Everywhere he looked he saw exposed flesh. Women's bared breasts, men's upright cocks, abdomens, arses, limbs. It was a bounty of people barely dressed, or completely nude save for their masks. Men and women tangled together on low sofas, sprawled on thick carpets, or leaned against walls in groups that ranged from couples to quintets. A man in laborer's clothing fucked a genteel lady from behind as she bent over a table. Three women formed a complex knot as they lapped at each other's quims, while a gentlewoman unbuttoned the falls of a man's breeches so that another man could suck his cock.

Sex. Everywhere, sex. The humid air was thick with the smell of it, and with the sounds of unrestrained sensuality.

Meanwhile, masked servants bearing pitchers of wine or platters of sweetmeats walked between the couplings, calm and disinterested. Clearly, they were quite used to the spectacle.

Tom wasn't. Though he was no stranger to small parties that evolved into group sex, he had never before witnessed so many people from such an array of classes all engaged in public displays of carnality. He'd seen and done everything that London had to offer, but the Orchid Club was entirely new. And entirely wonderful.

"Bless you," Tom said to his friend. "How did you learn of this place?"

"One of my old comrades in arms told me. It's an open secret. Been around for years, actually, but it manages to stay hidden." Ellingsworth's lips quirked. "I see it pleases you."

Tom watched as a man reverently stroked and kissed a woman's arse while another man fondled her breasts.

"This is Paradise," Tom said reverently.

Ellingsworth grinned. "None of the thoughts I'm entertaining are at all angelic."

"Shall we explore the rest of the club?" Eagerness hummed through his body—at last, after years of exploring all of London's most thrilling facets, he'd found a new experience.

A brunette reclining on a divan in nothing but her shift and a white mask crooked her finger at Ellingsworth.

With a grin, his friend clapped him on the shoulder. "I leave the investigation to you. A pressing matter has come up." Ellingsworth walked quickly toward his waiting lover.

Less than a moment later, a blonde dressed as a dairymaid swayed over to Tom's side.

"Shame you being on your own," she said as she trailed her fingers down his waistcoat. Her accent held the rough consonants of East London. "Shame that I'm on my own, too."

His body answered with a quick throb of lust, but he softly took her hand between his and pressed a kiss to her rough fingertips. So her garb and accent weren't disguises. She truly was a dairymaid.

"Forgive me," he said with a smile. "I'm still getting my sea legs."

"Don't need balance if you're lying down." She winked and glanced toward an unoccupied chaise.

"I'm truly tempted, love," he said with genuine regret. "But I mean to get the lay of the land first." When she frowned in disappointment, he said, "You'll have no trouble finding a willing friend. If I return in quarter of an hour and you're still on your own, I promise to make it up to you."

She looked at him, her expression considering. "Sound awful sure of yourself."

"There's much in this world that defies my understanding," he said. "Yet if there's anything I do understand, it's fucking."

"Anybody can fuck," she said, her hands on her hips. "But can you do it *right*?"

"Oh, yes," he said with complete confidence.

She looked him up and down, and she smiled, liking what she saw. "Come find me then. A quarter of an hour."

She ambled away toward a servant pouring wine, but before she'd gotten halfway across the room, an elegantly dressed man stopped her with a kiss. Given the enthusiastic way in which the dairymaid responded, Tom was certain she would be quite busy in fifteen minutes.

After grabbing a sugared cake from a platter and then following it up with a glass of wine, Tom moved from the parlor to an adjoining room. It was considerably larger than the previous chamber and looked very much like a ballroom, complete with parquet floors below, two sizable chandeliers above, and substantial framed mirrors on the walls. In the corner, a group of masked musicians played a waltz. At the farthest end of the ballroom stood what appeared to be a stage, currently empty. Tom could only speculate what sort of performances might happen at the club.

The dance floor was full of more guests in various stages of undress. Some of them actually danced, though their bodies were far closer than any Society function would permit. The rest swayed in couples or trios, kissing and caressing one another. Even a Cyprian's Ball could not compete for unalloyed sensuality.

A man and woman paused in the middle of their heated embrace and beckoned for Tom to join them. Despite his stab of desire, Tom politely waved a decline.

This was precisely the sort of diversion he normally relished. Yet here he was, sticking close to the perimeter, content merely to observe rather than participate.

An unknown force held him back. He merely watched everything unfold around him and could not quite bridge the distance between himself and what he saw.

Perhaps he should leave. Leave Ellingsworth to his debauchery and then . . . and then what? Go back to his bachelor lodgings and spend the rest of the night reading by the fire? What a truly gloomy thought. He hadn't spent a quiet evening at home in nearly a decade. But if he wasn't going to avail himself on the Orchid Club's bounty, maybe it was better to beat a retreat.

With a frustrated sigh, Tom turned to go. But he stopped when he caught sight of a woman standing alone by a table that held a potted orchid.

She was fully dressed in a sophisticated white-and-gold gown and wore a mask of gold satin. The light in the ballroom was dim, yet even from this distance he could see the olive hue of her skin, and the long line of her neck revealed by her upswept black hair. She possessed a bold splendor, her features strong and striking. She had a beautiful, generously proportioned nose like a Mediterranean goddess, and full, ripe lips. Like him, she watched the proceedings in the ballroom, but did not move to participate.

She held herself with the kind of poise that came only with complete self-assurance. As if she refused to believe anything could hold her back. That, even more than her beauty, made her magnetic. Once Tom's gaze fell upon her, he could not look away, not even if the building had fallen down around him.

Who was she? What kept her from joining in the activity all around them? He ached to know her every secret, and burned to hear her voice—would it be high and musical, or low and husky? Anything and everything about her he ached to discover.

He couldn't remember a woman affecting him so strongly, so quickly. He knew desire, certainly, and the quick pull of attraction, but this immediate fascination was unknown. Until now.

Every part of him craved to be near the woman in the gold mask. Overcome with staunch determination, he moved straight in her direction. Whatever tonight's outcome might be, he could never regret coming here, because it brought him to her.

Chapter 2

❦

*E*xcitement and anxiety pulsed just beneath the surface of Lucia Marini's skin as she surveyed the Orchid Club's belowstairs kitchen.

"We'll have enough cakes?" she asked Jenny, the cook.

"For the fifth time, yes," Jenny said with an exasperated smile.

She placed a candied violet atop one sugared confection and set that on a silver tray. Immediately, a masked female member of the staff whisked the platter away.

"Circulate three times through each room," Lucia called after the girl.

A pair of hands settled on Lucia's shoulders and gently squeezed. "Breathing's not so difficult, once you get the hang of it."

Lucia turned and smiled at her friend Kitty. Kitty's ash-blonde hair fell loosely about her shoulders, and her hazel eyes regarded Lucia with fond amusement.

With her coral freckles scattered across ivory skin, Kitty looked more like a country girl from Devonshire than a London woman of experience. She had once been the former and was now the latter.

At the sight of Kitty, a fraction of the tension knotted in Lucia's chest loosened.

"I'm being ridiculous, aren't I?"

"A little," Kitty said. She rubbed her hand over her exceptionally pregnant belly in habitual movement. "But a bit of ridiculousness is perfectly understandable. Tonight's your first night as the club's manager. Only an escapee from Bedlam would be calm about it."

"I may need to be committed to Bedlam after the night's over." Lucia couldn't keep still, and, despite a glower from Jenny, adjusted the placement of miniature tarts on their platter. They looked good, but were they *good enough*?

Jenny pointed a cook's knife in Lucia's direction. "Hands off, or I'll chop them off and make them into mincemeat pies."

Hands raised up, Lucia backed away from the sweets. "It's not that I doubt your skill in the kitchen—"

Kitty laid her fingers on Lucia's arm. "Stop right there before you say something that'll make you cringe later."

She tugged Lucia out of the kitchen. In the corridor, Kitty stroked a few strands of hair from Lucia's face. "Be at ease, love. Everything will go swimmingly."

Despite all the encouragement Lucia had given herself earlier, her composure fell away and she fought to keep from twisting her hands together.

"Mrs. Chalke entrusted the Orchid Club to *me*. All the souls that work here, they all rely on me to keep our doors open. I fail, and we starve." The magnitude of Lucia's responsibility nearly crushed her, yet this was what she'd yearned for—a place of her own, and the means by which she could create a better life for herself and those she cared about.

"Not so dire as that. True," Kitty said with a nod, "we need the extra blunt the operation gives us, but nobody's going hungry, no one's sleeping on the steps of Christ Church. You needn't ride yourself so."

Lucia stepped back to allow passage for a small convoy of male staff members carrying crates of wine bottles.

"Remember, *ragazzi,* new rule—each guest gets a maximum of two glasses of wine." Wine and spirits clouded judgment, and she wanted to ensure that every guest acted from a place of lucidity.

"Yes, miss," they called over their shoulders as they moved up the stairs leading to the ground floor.

"And what of the girls' home?" she continued to Kitty. A swell of anxiety rose up within her. "It won't come to pass if the club sinks. All those girls will be left on the streets, without roofs over their heads, unable to read a letter or write their own names."

Kitty exhaled. "Before you set sail, you've got to first build the boat. A step at a time, love."

"What if—"

"Enough fretting now." Kitty smiled warmly as she tapped a finger on Lucia's chin. "You proved to our dear former manager, Mrs. Chalke, that you deserved to take over her job when she retired. No one doubts your ability—not even you. So go on upstairs and oversee your new empire, Your Highness. As for me," she continued with a small grimace, "my feet are swollen as melons, so I'll be retreating to my room. But I'd rather be down here, helping."

Affection swept through Lucia in a soft tide. She enfolded Kitty in a quick embrace, though she bent into a concave shape to make room for Kitty's round stomach.

"Never doubt that you help," she said sincerely. "Between you and Elspeth, I have more than my share of better angels."

Kitty laughed. "A winged angel big with child, that's what I am."

"Now fly, *piccolo angelo*," Lucia said, swatting Kitty on the arse. "I'm a busy woman."

Shaking her head, Kitty waddled toward the servants' stairs, leaving Lucia briefly alone. She swallowed hard. Dark and ravenous for more of her flesh, the fear that always lurked climbed out from its pit.

She shut her eyes as she drew in a deep breath.

Cara Mamma, she implored the spirit of her mother, *wherever you are, send your girl the spirit of good fortune and even better business.*

Quickly, Lucia crossed herself. Now was the time. This was her moment.

She climbed the stairs, drawing strength and composure with each step. No matter how much fear or uncertainty she felt, she could never allow her guests to see any hint of apprehension. The Orchid Club relied upon its aura of unbridled sensual freedom to attract visitors again and again. Guests wanted to feel safe as they indulged their erotic desires. If there was any hint of the proprietress's anxiety, the fantasy would shatter like brittle sugar sculpture.

By the time she reached the top step, Lucia had swathed herself in the cool serenity of her professional persona. She was a queen, benevolent but untouchable.

She hadn't gotten this far in life by giving up, by being afraid. Poverty hadn't stopped her, nor had losing her only parent, or undertaking a long, perilous voyage to a foreign land. Again and again, she'd pushed onward, as she would continue to do so. Until breath left her body.

Some might consider her achievements dubious, but to her, they were triumphs.

She opened the baize-covered door that stood at the head of the stairs and stepped into the hallway. Sounds of sex encircled her, as familiar as the sounds of seabirds over the Golfo di Napoli had once been. There was also the warm ripe scent of sweat-glossed skin, and the heat that came from dozens of bodies engaged in vigorous activity.

Bypassing the two main rooms in the club, she neared the entryway, where Elspeth stood awaiting the subsequent knock on the door from the next arrival. Tall and lean, Elspeth wore her peach-hued gown to perfection, and with her short hair, she looked every inch the noble gatekeeper.

Before Lucia said a word, Elspeth's smile flashed.

"Fear not, Amina," Elspeth said, using Lucia's alias. She held up a pouch that jingled, heavy with coin. "The take's as good as it's ever been. Better."

Lucia permitted herself a small exhalation. Perhaps this might work out. Perhaps she could allow herself a moment's satisfaction.

She envisioned herself donning an invisible cloak that gave her strength and poise, standing straighter as its folds swathed her body. "Any troublemakers?"

"I turned away a pair of drunken Mayfair louts. Other than that, it's been smooth as a dish of milk."

"So long as no bothersome cats come along to tip that dish."

The coded knock at the door sounded, and Lucia moved on as Elspeth went to admit the guests.

For the first time, she stepped into her empire as its rightful ruler. No cornets heralded her arrival, and no rose petals scattered across her path. It was, in all ways, unremarkable—except to her. She drew confidence from each footfall, rising up taller and taller.

This is mine because I fought for it and won it fairly. I belong here.

Within the two main rooms of the club, everything appeared satisfactory. The sight of people fucking in full view of others had long ago lost its ability to shock or even arouse her. It was simply business. So long as her guests were happy and kept returning, the spectacle remained merely a component of her work and nothing more.

The staff moved through the chambers with smooth efficiency, offering refreshments, righting any overturned furniture, and monitoring their guests. Lucia exchanged attentive nods with Will and Arthur before proceeding on to the ballroom.

Before this evening, there hadn't been music, but now musicians she had personally selected for their ability and discretion played music that graced the finest assemblies in London and the Continent. The melodies provided an elegant background as guests gave free rein to their most primal desires in full view of everyone.

Lucia herself had never attended a fine assembly. This would be the closest she'd ever get to hearing the music meant for the elite, and she smiled to herself to think that what a *conte* or *principessa* heard in some august ballroom was currently performed for people of every rank as they fucked one another.

Surveying the room, her gaze lingered on the female guests, looking for signs that they were being coerced or pushed into doing things they didn't want to do—a man's hand gripping a woman too tightly, or a woman literally backed up against a wall. But her female guests seemed willing and eager to participate.

She released a long breath, permitting herself a moment's relief. Fears that her first night as manager would result in disaster began to dissolve. Everything seemed attainable, and that potential rose up within her like the bubbles in sparkling wine.

I can do this. It's possible. Everything is possible.

Her thoughts abruptly silenced. She sensed someone's gaze on her like a velvet glove stroking down the back of her neck.

Lucia looked around to find the source of the sensation. Her breath stuttered and her pulse came in a quick flutter when she saw its origin.

A rangy, dark-haired man in a blue mask strode purposefully toward her. He moved with fluid, masculine grace, his body muscular and strapping. The direct way he approached captivated her—as though nothing could keep him from being near her.

Lucia's pulse leapt again.

She shook her head, trying to dismiss her reaction to the guest's approach. Clients often turned their interests toward her. Yet there was a palpable sensuality to the way he walked and the interest in his gaze. It held frank erotic intent, and the confidence that he could give her extraordinary pleasure.

Even at a distance, his eyes said, *I. Want. You.*

Rather than walk away, as she normally did when a guest took interest in her, she stayed where she was.

The distance between them closed, bit by bit, her heartbeat picking up speed the nearer he came.

And then he stood less than two feet away. He bowed, pressing a hand to his chest. She nodded her head in acknowledgment.

This close, she could see that his garments were exceptionally well made, clearly the work of an expert tailor, because only the finest needlecraft could create a suit of clothing that fitted his athletic form with such grace. His shining boots also had to be custom from Jermyn Street. Yet in contrast to this elegant appearance, dark stubble covered his cheeks and angled jaw, and he smelled slightly of gunpowder.

That, combined with his roguish grin, made her think of a buccaneer.

"Madam."

"Sir." She gave him a polite but shallow nod.

"You keep to yourself."

He had a faint Irish brogue, making his words gently musical. She had learned many years ago to repress her own Neapolitan accent. There were many in Britain who viewed foreigners with suspicion, and it had been a matter of survival to sound as English as possible.

"I choose to," she said.

He moved to stand beside her. His nearness was an intoxicant, making her slightly dizzy. Together they watched the swaying mass of bodies on the dance floor.

"I do as well, it seems," he said, as if faintly puzzled

by his own behavior. "This is my first time here and I find myself more content to observe than participate."

"Some prefer it that way. They derive sensual gratification from watching." She nodded toward a man who stood by himself, his eyes fastened on the spectacle of two other men kissing passionately, while his hand was down the front of his breeches.

"Usually," the buccaneer said wryly, "I choose *doing* rather than *watching*."

His grin flashed again, and her stomach gave a quick jump. She could imagine that he wasn't the sort to sit idly by and let someone else devour an experience.

"What makes tonight different?" she asked. "I hope the establishment meets your expectations."

"I had no expectations," he said. "The friend who brought me here kept the nature of this place a secret until I stepped inside."

She turned to him. "And now that you are within its walls, what are your thoughts on the place?" It was always a good idea to talk to guests, learn what pleased them and what they didn't care for. Yes, that's why she kept talking with him rather than moving on to other duties—to ascertain whether or not the club satisfied him. That was the only reason.

He looked thoughtful. Interesting that he would turn pensive, when, not several yards away, people engaged in acts of unrestrained eroticism.

After a moment, he said, "What's here is joyous exuberance, a celebration of bodily pleasure and letting go.

Aside from the code of conduct outlined in the vestibule, rules have no place in this establishment. People can fully express themselves without fear. That's something to celebrate."

She looked up at him in surprise. His eyes were the blue of the skies above Napoli, and they gleamed not just with sensuality, but sensitivity and intelligence, as well.

"Uncommon to hear a man articulate himself so well," she said, "particularly when it relates to the act of fucking."

His smile was genuine and devilish. "Madam, I can wax rhapsodic about fucking. But," he added, "this place is about more than sex. It's about . . ." He searched for the right words. "Living without limitations, liberated from censure and disapproval. That's something that everyone desires. Even you, I'd wager."

Instinctively, she stiffened and mentally reached for her unseen shield, protecting herself from any man's attempt to delve beneath the surface of her carefully crafted persona.

"A moment's acquaintance, and you feel you know me," she said drily.

Undisguised fascination gleamed in his eyes when he looked at her. "You're clever and aware. Always assessing the situation. But that's merely one part of who you are. There's passion there as well, though you try to keep it at a distance."

Her mouth went dry, and she tried to swallow. How

could he discern all this about her? From head to toe, she was swathed in her professional identity. She might be a different person with Kitty and Elspeth, but here on the floor of the club, she was Amina the Untouchable.

She pushed out a laugh. "Mercy," she said, "you ought to set up a booth at Bartholomew Fair and tell fortunes. People would pay good money to have their characters delineated so incisively."

"Learning about other people doesn't interest me." His gaze held hers. "Learning about *you* does."

Her breath caught as they stared at each other.

He stepped closer, and warmth radiated from his body into hers. "Will you join me for a dance?"

There was no mistaking the intention in his low, seductive words, especially as almost no one on the dance floor was actually dancing.

Could I? More to the point, should *I?*

Guests propositioned her nearly every night the house was open, and that clearly hadn't changed since she'd become proprietress. Her breathing had never quickened with those guests. When she'd fielded their offers, she hadn't felt the heat of the room pressing against her sensitized flesh.

She had never been tempted, not enough to neglect her duties.

But this buccaneer—with his Irish accent and his wicked lips and his burning blue eyes—he enticed her. To hell with all her rules and caution. She could lose herself in heat and sensation. Without a doubt, he could give her an abundance of pleasure.

But the club, and her dream, came first. Entangling herself with a guest led to complications, and any complication—such as an importunate or jealous lover—would throw yet more obstacles in her path. He would demand her time, her attention, and neither could be spared. She couldn't afford to be distracted by a man. And *this* man would assuredly be a distraction.

She struggled to lock away her reaction to him, like a keeper of wild beasts trying to urge a tiger back into its cage.

"There are so many available partners," she said.

"I want to dance with *you*."

Her heart took up a fast rhythm. "I cannot." Regret tinged her words. She held out her hand. "I'm Amina, the manager."

His brow above the mask creased with surprise, but like a gentleman, he took her hand and bent over it. Instead of kissing the air above her knuckles, his lips touched her skin.

Fire shot through her body. From the simplest, smallest contact.

He murmured, "I'd introduce myself—"

"But you can't." Her voice was breathless. She withdrew her hand, though her skin continued to radiate with his warmth. "For the safety of my guests, I know nothing about them, not even their names."

"A good precaution."

"Policy dictates that I don't get involved with guests."

His full lips shaped into a frown, and she braced herself for him to ask for an exception, or cajole her, the way other clients had done. Men did not like to hear a woman tell them *no*.

A moment later, he said, "Understood. I must respect your choice. Everything here is consensual, after all."

She relaxed slightly. "So it is." She offered him a smile. "This being your first time, I welcome you. My hope is that everything is to your liking."

"Everything but the manager's policy regarding her involvement with guests." But he smiled as he said this. "This is a wondrous place. We can be our truest selves."

Much as she wanted to, she couldn't speculate on his background. Anonymity stood as one of the central tenets of the Orchid Club. Yet he was well dressed, even more finely than a banker or brewer. The artful way he'd bowed revealed a privileged background. She inhaled his scent of gunpowder and spice, taking it deeply into herself, tucking it away for later.

A thousand questions assailed her, wanting to be given a voice. What brought him here tonight? What was he seeking? What responsibilities weighed so heavily upon him that he took delight in the establishment's offer of freedom?

She could never ask, and never know the answer. "You paid the entrance fee," she said, "so I urge you to take advantage of what there is to offer."

She waved toward the dance floor, which had evolved

into a mass of sweat-slick flesh. Moans and grunts competed with the music.

Damn the distance she put between herself and the guests. If nothing else, he'd give her several hours of pleasure. Touching her deeper, realer self—that was an impossibility. Letting someone get truly close led straight to disaster and misery.

The buccaneer's gaze never left her. "The most fascinating and intriguing thing here is you."

She made herself laugh. "Sirrah, you are fulsome in your blandishments."

He didn't laugh or smile, his expression utterly serious. "When I set foot outside these doors," he said, "I don't need to flatter anyone. What I want, I get. So believe me when I say honestly that I'd much rather talk with you than fuck a stranger."

Her heart thudded. "Because, unlike everyone else, I tell you *no*."

"Because you intrigue me beyond measure."

She could only stare at him. The part of herself that she'd locked away, the part that longed for comfort and affection and all the things lovers shared, ached with want. Oh, she'd taken men to her bed over the years, but other than physical gratification, she'd made certain those encounters never touched her heart. She had been forged through hardship and loss, treading a solitary path. If sometimes her body throbbed for want of someone to hold her all through the night, if she ached for someone to whisper into her hair that she was to be cherished . . . she tamped it all down.

Think of Mamma. Her pain and loss.

Yet here was this man, this guest, a person unknown to her. Her buccaneer. Offering a taste of what could never be.

"I must go," she said. "My duties can't be neglected."

His mouth turned down, but he nodded. "I will be back soon. To see you, Amina."

It wasn't her real name, yet the sound of it on his lips sent a dark thrill through her. Oh, to hear him call her Lucia as he joined his body with hers . . .

He gave another bow before turning and striding away. She watched him, her gaze riveted to the width of his shoulders and how beautifully his breeches fit his long, muscular legs. Compelled to follow, she trailed several paces after him, observing him as he walked. He didn't join any of the couplings but went straight for the door.

Lucia did not follow him any farther. The threshold was where her dominion ended.

Taking a deep breath, she straightened her shoulders and adjusted her mask.

The club's policy was to be open every week. Perhaps the buccaneer would return then. Perhaps she might see him once more, and they could talk, as they had tonight.

Her breath came faster.

In all her time here, he was the only guest who ever

truly caught her attention, the only guest she'd wanted for her own selfish pleasure.

Doesn't matter. Flirtation is all we can ever share. The establishment—and the profits it generated—was too important to her to throw anything away on a casual encounter.

Drawing herself up straight, she continued on with the rest of her night. There were responsibilities that needed tending—keeping the refreshments circulating, ensuring the staff's well-being and the guests' safety, maintaining the club's spotlessness—a hundred tiny tasks she had to supervise. Yet, like a child sneaking tastes of her parents' wine, she permitted herself brief thoughts of the buccaneer.

It would be a struggle not to grow drunk on him.

Chapter 3

One year later

$\mathcal{T}$om waited at the foot of the back stairs, his body both heavy with grief and impelled into motion.

For six weeks, he'd kept vigil at his father's bedside, barely sleeping, eating only when forcibly urged to by the physician, and hardly stirring from the ducal bedchamber. But for all that, for all the physician had bled Father and applied every technique that modern medical science had devised . . . the old duke had died anyway.

Tom could still hear the rattle and rasp of his father's breath stopping. It was that dreadful silence that heralded the end. The man that had both berated and coddled Tom had departed the earth, leaving behind a chasm that might never be filled. That chasm yawned open within Tom. Its emptiness threatened to devour him whole.

Feeling his shoulders bow beneath the weight of grief, he struggled to straighten them. Today was for Maeve, and he had to have strength for both of them.

Only that morning, news of his father's death had been printed in the pages of the *Times* and *Hawk's Eye,* revealing to the world the loss of one of England's most staunch defenders of traditional values. They had said nothing about how the late duke preferred roast potatoes every Tuesday, or that, despite the fact that he continually bemoaned his son's carousing and wildness, he used to give Tom books of adventure stories on his birthdays, even into adulthood. On Tom's bookshelf in his private study, he had a copy of *Guy Mannering,* with a typically terse "To My Son on His 32nd Birthday—Yr Father" inscribed on the inside cover.

None of that had been in the papers. There were aspects of the Duke of Northfield that no one but those closest to him would ever know.

But in the *Times,* there had been a paragraph that, hours later, Tom could recite from memory. It had burned itself into his mind, and into his heart.

We cannot help but speculate whether or not the new duke will take up his late father's ideology and principles. His Grace, the previous duke, has left a sizable void in the nation's political landscape. Further, it is a known truth that the younger gentleman in question has led a somewhat undisciplined existence. Many await his next steps with bated breath. Shall he continue in his riotousness, or will he take up the mantle left behind by his father, and preserve England's established institutions?

We cannot foretell.

God above, but if that wasn't a burden to carry. The eyes of the country were on him. And all he wanted to do was run.

But now that he was duke, he could use his might in the advancement of progressive causes, as he'd longed to do when he was only the heir. Others might expect him to be a duplicate of his father, but he didn't have to be. He could be his own man with his own beliefs, his own goals.

A step quietly creaked. He glanced up, and saw Maeve, dressed in mourning black bombazine with a jet broach at her throat, a veil covering her face and a black handkerchief twisted in her fingers.

His heart plunged to see his sister, a girl of just nineteen, so somberly garbed. She ought to be dressed in bright, springtime green or the yellow of daffodils, with a coral necklace about her neck and her pretty face rosy from the heat of a ballroom.

He smoothed a hand over the dark band encircling his arm and ran his finger along the length of his black neckcloth. Unlike Maeve, his mourning was limited to smaller signifiers—in every way.

Ballrooms were forbidden to her, as were color and

joy. As if she, or Tom, could ever feel joy again in the wake of their father's death.

Maeve's steps were slow as she descended the stairs. When she reached the bottom, she paused, holding the newel post. Her veil stirred as she let out a long exhale.

"Are you certain about this?" Tom asked. "You don't need to tax yourself."

"I need to go," his sister said. Her words were steadier than her gait. "I need to see him."

"As you like." But Tom wrapped a sheltering arm around her shoulders as he guided her toward the back door.

Tenderness and protectiveness rose up within him when she leaned against him. He was rocketed back to when he'd been a lad of thirteen, cradling his newborn sister in his arms, frozen with terror that he might drop the delicate thing and have her shatter into tiny fragments at his gangly feet.

His mother hadn't been able to keep any other baby she'd conceived. All his siblings had either died in utero or within a day of their births. No one had been certain whether or not Maeve would join her departed siblings in the churchyard. Yet she'd made it through the first week, and when Tom had finally been allowed to see and hold her, he'd vowed then—just as he vowed now—that he would safeguard her for the rest of his days.

They reached the door that opened to a narrow, walled yard, and Tom pushed it open to escort Maeve out. Thick gray clouds smeared across the sky, and a cutting wind blew into the yard.

Maeve tilted her head back and inhaled deeply. "I missed this."

"The dreadful weather?"

"Being outside. I haven't set foot outside the house in three weeks and five days."

He'd had to report back to her about the funeral and burial, as she and their mother had been obliged by the rules of polite society that such a sorrowful ordeal would tax their fragile emotions overmuch.

A corner of Tom's mouth lifted in a humorless smile. *He* had been the one who could barely stand beside the open grave as the casket had been lowered. *He* had swallowed countless tears, trying to manfully force them back rather than permit himself the luxury of open grief. His throat still burned with gulping back sobs. Maeve and their mother, Deirdre, were free to show their sorrow—so long as they did so within the confines of Northfield House. Open displays of anyone's emotions, be they male or female, were distressing and gauche.

No one seemed permitted to indicate that they had feelings, especially not messy, complicated feelings that threatened to rip one apart from the inside out.

But he had to be strong. For Maeve, for their mother.

"How does it feel to be in the open air again?" he asked.

She was silent for a moment. "Cold."

"We can go back."

She shook her head. "I don't mind. It proves that I'm still alive."

The unspoken words *but he isn't* hung in the air.

"And," she added, "Hugh's expecting me." Though her veil obscured her face, there was a hint of brightness in her voice as she said Lord Stacey's name.

"The carriage is waiting for us." Tom helped her out of the yard and down the gravel path that led to the stables. "I told John the coachman to draw the curtains so that no one could see you."

"My thanks."

Tom bit back a warning about the possible damage to her reputation if she was seen outside of her home so soon after her father's passing. It was her decision to make, and he trusted her judgment.

It was a cruel thing to permit men the release and freedom of leaving their homes in the wake of a family member's death, while women were trapped within the walls, barely permitted a visitor other than a consoling clergyman. How could anyone survive the crush of grief if they could not take in a little air or be given even a moment's reprieve from their sorrow?

So Tom had agreed when Maeve had proposed this sortie. He would give his sister anything, if she asked.

"This way," he said, guiding her along the path.

"I can't see a thing behind this blasted veil," Maeve grumbled. "It's like my eyes are full of smoke."

"I'll be your eyes."

"Again, my big brother champions me," she said warmly.

"As a big brother, I am contractually obligated to champion you."

They had reached the stable yard, where the carriage and driver awaited them, while a groom held the horses. In a show of respect, the coachman wore a black caped coat, the footman standing beside the vehicle was attired in inky livery, while horses had been draped with black fabric.

Tom and Maeve approached the carriage.

"Your Grace," the coachman said, bowing. "Lady Maeve."

Tom suppressed a grimace. *Wrong,* he wanted to shout. *My father is His Grace, not me.*

His whole life, he had known that one day he'd assume the title. But that had been a purely intellectual exercise and easy to dismiss. Yet to finally *be* the Duke of Northfield felt like trying to breathe underwater.

I'm not ready, damn it. Not for any of this.

"You know where we are headed?" Tom asked the driver as the footman helped Maeve into the carriage.

"Broom House Farm, Your Grace. In Fulham."

"And?" Tom prompted.

"And Her Grace isn't to know of it," John recited.

"*No one* is to know of this excursion. Make sure your grooms keep their silence. You'll all see yourselves handsomely rewarded for your discretion and punished for any indiscretion."

It was a fact of life that servants and staff gossiped, and if word ever got out that Tom helped Maeve break her mourning to see Lord Stacey, she would be the one suffering the harm to her reputation. Lord Stacey and Tom might receive sidelong glances of disapproval, but they'd still be admitted into drawing rooms and dining chambers throughout London.

A carriage kitted out in mourning might attract moderate interest, but Tom could move about the world freely without consequence. If someone recognized the vehicle, it would be a simple enough matter to explain that Tom was attending to his newfound responsibilities—alone.

"Yes, Your Grace."

"Grand." For good measure, Tom slipped a guinea into John's hand before he climbed into the carriage.

Once the door had been closed, and the curtains in the windows secured, Tom rapped on the roof to signal they were ready to depart. The vehicle jolted slightly as it surged into motion, but it was excellently sprung, and as they drove down the mews and onto the street, he hardly felt the movement. The sound of the wheels was dampened by the straw that had been laid out along the street during the late duke's illness. Soon, though, they had driven past Northfield House, and the rumble of the wheels and the clop of the horses' hooves formed the background noise of their journey.

Fulham was some four miles away from Mayfair, a journey that took them through Belgravia and Chelsea. At a decent pace, he and Maeve would reach their destination in three quarters of an hour.

"Don't peep through the curtains," Tom warned Maeve as she attempted to do exactly that.

She flopped back against the seat, making a sound of frustration. "I wish I could look outside and see the world again."

"It will still be there when you're out of mourning."

"Months from now." She sighed regretfully, then clicked her tongue. "You think me a callous chit for thinking of my own comfort and amusement at such a time."

"I think," he said, his voice gentle, "that you can mourn whilst also longing to live your life. It's a hard burden to be locked away from all company, and doubly so if one is a girl barely into her second season."

"A *young woman*, not a *girl*."

"My apologies." He pressed a hand to his chest and gave a slight bow. "And if you are a *young woman* with an ardent suitor, six months of deep mourning might seem like an eon."

"So it does." Maeve leaned forward, reaching out and taking Tom's hand in hers. "Hugh and I haven't seen each other since Father took ill. Your kindness in facilitating this is remarkable."

His brows lifted. "Shall I be a cad, and stand in the way of my sister's happiness?"

"Don't be flippant, Tommy. This is a risk for both of us."

"A moderate one for me, but an extraordinary one for you."

"One I *have* to take." Urgency and youthful conviction throbbed in her words. "Hugh is everything to me."

What would that be like, to believe in something so strongly? To have faith and purpose?

In the whole of his thirty-two years, Tom had never experienced that. It shamed him to feel a pulse of envy for the girl—*young woman*—that had once gazed upon him with pure idolization.

He shouldn't, couldn't, begrudge Maeve her happiness. But out of all the experiences he'd had in his life, never had he known what it was to care deeply for anything or anyone not related to him. Somehow, the little sister who had tried to run after him on her stubby toddler legs had grown into a woman who loved, and was loved in return.

Her brother could not say the same.

"You are certain that Lord Stacey will be waiting for us in Fulham?" Tom asked.

She nodded. "His last letter spoke of nothing else." She patted her heart, and Tom could only guess that was where she carried Lord Stacey's missive. "He's made all the arrangements that we might see each other, if only briefly."

Foolish, romantic girl. How he coveted that for himself.

"We'll be unable to stay long," he cautioned.

"*Any* time with him is a gift."

He snorted. "Now you sound like one of Shelley's poems."

She made a soft scoffing noise. "As though I would attempt to emulate that histrionic, overwrought scribbler. Everyone knows that Keats is far superior."

Tom didn't hide his grin. It was never difficult to solicit an opinion from his sister, a fact which bedeviled their mother but delighted him.

"I'm partial to Byron, myself," he said. "Except for that bit about sleeping with his sister."

"Half sister. But still, that does tend to color one's enthusiasm for his work."

The constriction around his chest eased. For all that she was thirteen years his junior, he never felt the divide of their years. They could always talk and jest freely, and while he never detailed his dissolute exploits to her, she was one of the few people that accepted him as he was.

I'd kill for her.

The words formed in his mind as firmly as if he'd spoken them aloud. It was an oath he swore to himself.

"Talk to me of anything but the past six weeks," Maeve pled. "What was the last play you saw?"

"An excellent work by the most esteemed Viscountess Marwood. It involved a kidnapping and three assumed identities." Riveted by what he saw on the stage, Tom had barely stirred in his seat, not even to flirt with a few daring widows.

Maeve clapped her hands together. "Ah, splendid! And was there a swordfight?"

"Between the heroine and the villain."

She chuckled. "Even better."

For the remainder of the journey to Fulham, they spoke of subjects unrelated to death and loss—a relief. They carved out a space for themselves in the midst of grief, where Tom could set aside the fact that now, he was the duke, shouldering the title's massive responsibilities, and he and Maeve were merely themselves as they had been. The scapegrace elder brother and the sardonic but adoring younger sister.

The carriage slowed to a stop, far faster than Tom had anticipated.

"We're here, Your Grace," the coachman called down.

In short order, Tom stepped out from the vehicle and helped his sister down. They had stopped in the front yard of a tidy farmhouse that was surrounded by trees. At another time of year, the garden might be abundant, but within the chill months of late autumn, all that clustered around the house were bare hedges. Beyond the farmhouse was a little barn and an enclosed pasture. Smoke rose in a column from the house's chimney. Someone was inside.

"My assignation spot?" Maeve asked, looking around.

Tom grimaced. "*Assignation* has carnal associations that I'd rather not consider in relation to my baby sister. Let's call it an *appointment,* instead."

"If that's what helps you sleep at night."

He shook his head. To the best of his knowledge, Maeve and Lord Stacey had never been fully alone together. They weren't officially affianced, and even if they had been, it was the unfortunate custom of the *ton* to prohibit intimacy between gentlemen and young women of good breeding.

A stolen kiss was the best any of them could do. No wonder Tom had so little interest in polite society. He'd moved past mere kissing nearly two decades ago.

The door to the farmhouse opened, revealing a man's silhouette. Tom barely had time to consider the identity of the man before Maeve cried out, flinging back her veil as she ran toward the house.

Tom followed at a deliberately sedate pace. He feigned interest in the autumnal garden as Maeve and Lord Stacey embraced.

"Oh, Hugh," Maeve said, "I am so glad to see you."

"There, my darling," Lord Stacey answered in a soothing voice. "We're together now." In a slightly louder voice, he said, "Your Grace."

Tom stopped his sham of investigating a pruned rosebush. "Lord Stacey." He bowed slightly to the younger man.

Hugh Gillray, Lord Stacey, was considered by people of estimable opinion to be one of the best catches in London. He was handsome, in an amiable and approachable manner, with waves of sandy hair, bright hazel eyes, and the athletic form of a true Corinthian.

Even more significant, he was the heir to the powerful and influential Duke of Brookhurst, possessing the allowance to match.

But clearly none of that mattered to Maeve, who had her head on Lord Stacey's shoulder.

Maeve and Lord Stacey had met at a regatta in May and had been nigh inseparable ever since. It was merely Lord Stacey's relative youth—only twenty years old—that prevented him from asking for Maeve's hand. The Duke of Brookhurst had made it clear that only when his heir had reached the mature age of twenty-one could he propose.

But Lord Stacey's birthday was in a month, within Maeve's period of full mourning. Fielding an offer of marriage during mourning was uncouth. And so Maeve and her beloved would have to wait to even begin their official courtship.

A fact which was made clear by the way she and Lord Stacey had plastered themselves together today. They stood side by side, hands clasped, as though unable to permit even the smallest distance between themselves.

"Thank you so much, Your Grace, for permitting this," Lord Stacey said with all the fervency of youth. "The owners of this farm have been generously compensated for providing the venue as well as their discretion."

Tom made himself look as formidable as possible. "Don't betray my trust by taking undue advantage."

"Tommy!" Maeve exclaimed, sounding mortified.

Yet her embarrassment meant less to him than safe-guarding her reputation. Perhaps it was hypocrisy to protect her virtue when Tom himself enjoyed the standing as one of the *ton*'s profligates, but that was the double standard that guided most of Society. He might not support that double standard, but he wouldn't gamble his only sister's happiness on his own opinion.

"I won't, Your Grace." Lord Stacey's gaze was earnest.

In all of Tom's dissipated carousing, not once had he crossed paths with the lad, leading him to believe that Lord Stacey truly was an upstanding—possibly virginal—young man.

"How fares your father?" Tom asked.

"He's quite fixated on passing an upcoming bill," Lord Stacey said. "Something to do with increasing the punishment of transients." The lad's eyes grew somber. "The passing of the late duke came as a blow to him."

"That, I don't doubt." In addition to sharing a friend-ship of over three decades, the Duke of Brookhurst and Tom's father had been longtime confederates in the political scene. Together, they had formed one of the most dominant conservative syndicates in Parliament.

When Maeve and Lord Stacey had shown a marked preference for each other, Tom had witnessed the Duke of Brookhurst and the late duke at White's, toasting the continuation of their alliance and the marriage of the two bastions of England's utmost traditional, upstanding families. It would be a union that pleased everyone.

"He, ah, mentioned something this morning," Lord Stacey said, his face reddening. "About you. About . . . needing your support in Parliament. He's relying on it. For, ahem, *our* sake." He glanced down at Maeve, before looking back at Tom. "Might I…speak with you in private for a moment, Your Grace?"

Tom frowned. "As you wish."

Maeve made a sound of exasperation but didn't stop Tom or Lord Stacey when they moved a small distance from her.

Tom gazed at the young man in a silent prompt to speak.

"Forgive me, Your Grace," Lord Stacey said, a touch of stammer in his voice. "My condolences on your loss. But I have to tell you that I overheard my parents speaking just this morning. My father . . . he hasn't fully decided whether or not he supports my marrying Maeve."

Only when Lord Stacey backed up a step did Tom realize that he scowled fiercely. "Why the deuces not?"

"Because you were a bit wild. That's what he said to my mother. He didn't know if he could trust you to uphold the line's reputation—and he wants your vote."

"My vote," Tom ground out.

"Yes, Your Grace." Lord Stacey ducked his head. "He said to Mama that if you didn't support him in

Parliament . . ." The young man coughed. "The marriage wouldn't happen."

Tom stared at Lord Stacey. "What?" he said in disbelief.

"I'm sorry, Your Grace. That's what he said. And I would never impose myself on you in any way, only . . ."

"Think of Maeve."

"Yes, Your Grace."

Tom gave a clipped nod. It was in the papers, and now this. Expectations. Pressures. And this threat.

"Hugh," Maeve called. "Stop making my brother scowl."

Her suitor coughed. "Yes. Right. Sorry."

With Lord Stacey following, Tom walked back to Maeve. His head rang. Lord Stacey's words, and the column in the *Times* cemented a reality he did not want to face. Did not but had to.

To preserve unity between his family and the Duke of Brookhurst's, Tom had to follow the path his father had walked. It was a path that stuck to England's most revered traditions and ancient institutions. Many a time Tom and his father had argued over the late duke's firm stance against progressive policies. But his father had remained obdurate.

As the new duke, Tom could choose to abandon his father's staunch beliefs. But that meant severing ties with alliances that went back to the time of the Restoration, including the tie between the Northfield and Brookhurst dukedoms.

It was clear in Lord Stacey's awkward confession the

Duke of Brookhurst would forbid his son from marrying Maeve if Tom did not fall into line. The duke would surely cut off Lord Stacey's allowance. The young man was a good lad, but Tom wasn't certain he'd choose noble sentiment over realistic poverty.

"I'll leave you two to your *chaste* rendezvous," Tom said to Maeve and her suitor. "You have fifteen minutes before we must return home. Mind, you'll keep yourselves to this front yard, and I shall keep you in my sights at all times." He fixed Lord Stacey and his sister with a sharp look. "I make myself clear, aye?"

Maeve rolled her eyes, but Lord Stacey nodded, saying, "Yes, Your Grace. Of course."

Unaccustomed to the role of chaperone, Tom strode off to walk the perimeter of the property. He kept his word and maintained eyes on the couple. Because, no matter how upstanding and honorable Lord Stacey might be, he was a young man, and most likely had a young man's appetites and urges.

As Tom strolled along the fence line of the farm, the sky overhead heavy and gray, his thoughts churned in time with the movement of his body.

He'd hoped to reverse the regressive stance of the dukedom. He'd wanted to wield his power to help others—but the Duke of Brookhurst had a metaphorical gun to his head. Either play the part of the supportive Tory, or Maeve couldn't marry the man she loved.

His own convictions—or the happiness of his sister.

Tom glanced at his sister and Lord Stacey as they sat on a stone bench in the front garden. Their heads were bent together, their hands intertwined. The air around them fairly vibrated with the intensity of their adoration. As Maeve's shoulders began to shake with sobs, Lord Stacey ran his fingers down her cheek before embracing her. Comforting her.

Another hot stab of envy pierced Tom.

Since his father's illness and passing, he'd consoled his mother and sister, holding them when they wept and listening as they poured out their grief. While he didn't begrudge them their need for succor, there was no one to give him the same consolation. No one to comfort him, or hear his broken confession that while his father had been a strict and uncompromising parent, Tom had loved him. Loved him and missed him.

He faced all of this alone.

Not only that, he saw that he was now the face of the Northfield dukedom. As the Duke of Brookhurst had said, Tom's conduct reflected on the Powell family. With the death of his father, he was supposed to become one of the pillars of English Society. The seventh Duke of Northfield. Not a title to be taken lightly. Nor were the responsibilities that came with that title easily shirked.

The life he'd known of gaming hells, opera dancers, and riotous pleasure—all of it had to stop. For his mother's sake, and for Maeve's.

His steps stopped. A galvanizing thought hit him.

"Fuck," he said softly.

The Orchid Club, and Amina, were now forbidden to him. The place—and the woman—were too scandalous. He had to close the door on that part of his life, though it had been part of the fabric of his existence for a year.

A new loss tore through him like a claw. Never to hear Amina's voice again, never to behold her as she walked with her queenly air and knowing gaze, nevermore to talk or flirt with her. All of it, gone.

It seemed impossible, insupportable. He wouldn't know how to exist without the club and without Amina. She was a constant in his life, a person of both gravity and spirit. He didn't want to walk away, but he'd no choice in the matter.

Today was Wednesday, which meant the club would be open tonight.

He firmed his jaw with resolve. This evening, he'd don his mask for the very last time, and see her just once more. When he did, he intended to make her a very bold, forbidden proposal that went against every rule.

One night together, before they parted forever.

Chapter 4

❦

*T*he newspaper fell from Lucia's hand, landing on the kitchen floor with a soft ruffling sound that she barely heard. She stared straight ahead, and everything she saw—from the fire burning in the hearth, to Kitty cradling baby Liam as she stirred up a pot of porridge, to the light in the windows shifting from morning to afternoon—appeared distant and far away, as if she was looking through the neck of a bottle.

"*Dio ci aiuti*," she whispered. "God help us."

"What is it?" Elspeth asked from her seat at the table. "You've gone white as whey."

Numb with shock, Lucia scooped up the newspaper and walked it to the fire. She threw the paper into the flames, watching it curl and turn black before finally breaking into ash.

She moved clumsily to the table and sat heavily in a chair. She ran her fingers back and forth over the grooves cut into the table's wooden surface, marks left by countless meals shared in this very kitchen with the people she cared about most in the world.

All of that might disappear. Far sooner than she could ever have feared.

"There were secrets Mrs. Chalke entrusted to me." Her words sounded stunned even to her own ears. "I didn't want to keep them from you, but I'd no choice. Holding those secrets was one of the conditions of taking the position as manager."

"Ours is a business built upon secrecy," Elspeth said. "We can't fault you for holding to it, if it meant our continued employment."

"*Grazie*." Lucia exhaled, hoping that this simple act might ground her when she felt utterly out of control. "The identity of the club's owner—that was one of the secrets. Exposing his identity compromised everything. So, I kept silent."

"Understandable." Kitty brought Liam over and gently lowered him into his high seat. "But we had our suppositions, didn't we, El? Thought he might be a banker or some rich cove who had a taste for fucking and an even bigger appetite for profits."

"That's so," Elspeth said. "But I was hoping he might be some bishop who liked to earn extra coin from sin while preaching against it from the pulpit."

"In a way, you're both right." Lucia looked back and forth between her two friends. "He was a man of the highest rank, the bluest blood, and moral. At least, he liked people to think he was moral, but it was he who came to Mrs. Chalke to propose the opening of the Orchid Club."

It felt strange to say even this much about the man who'd been their patron, when for over a year, she'd held firm to the knowledge of his identity. Holding tight to mysteries was her trade, and even with her dearest friends, it jarred to share them.

But it might not matter anymore.

She looked around the kitchen, taking in the rows of copper pans in their open cabinets, the soot-stained wooden beams in the ceiling, and the large table that dominated the center of the room, where later that afternoon, Jenny and her crew would prepare the sweetmeats and savories that fed their guests.

Tenuous, the lot of it. She might blink and it would disappear forever. Worse than losing her employment was the fact that the club employed a substantial staff, people whom she'd come to think of as a kind of found family in the absence of her own kinship by blood.

What if she couldn't save this? What if she couldn't save it for *them*?

"The owner of this club . . ." She swallowed. "He's dead."

A horrified silence reigned, broken only by the sounds of Liam slapping his hands on the tray in front of him.

"Does that mean that the establishment's finished?" Elspeth asked.

"I don't know." *Cristo,* how she hated saying those words, and hated that she didn't—couldn't—predict what might befall her and the staff of the Orchid Club. She was the mortar that fixed everything together, but there was nothing she could do to prevent the earthquake that threatened to shake the building into rubble.

Why hadn't she seen this coming? When she'd gone for her monthly meeting to deliver his share of the profits, he had been absent, with illness being given as the explanation. She hadn't known the severity of his poor health. Until now.

"If he was a highborn cove," Kitty mused, "it stands to reason that he's got an heir, and *that* cove is our new owner."

"True." Lucia hadn't considered that. "These English nobles love nothing so much as preserving pedigrees. Thinking on it, I recall our dead patron mentioning that he had a son."

"Then the club passes to that bloke," Kitty said. "Wouldn't it?" She looked at Elspeth as if searching for answers.

Elspeth held up her hands. "If you're looking for an expert in English aristocrats and their patrilineage, look elsewhere."

"So," Kitty continued, "he's got a son. And that gentry cove is our new patron. Then there's no harm for us in his sire's passing."

Unable to keep still, Lucia surged to her feet. "We don't know if his son knew his father's connection to this place. *Diavolo,* the son might not even know of the Orchid Club's existence."

"Be a hell of a shock when he finds out," Elspeth muttered.

"*Esattamente.* What if he's prudish, and the thought of owning a club for fucking horrifies him?" She paced, her thoughts tumbling over themselves, each scenario worse that the next. "He'd shutter us for certain."

They'd lose the club.

And without her income, she'd lose her dream. The home for girls could never come to pass.

She pictured them, the countless young females cast onto the streets of London without anyone to care for them, to protect them and ensure that they could have a life of anything but the meanest poverty and subsistence. But Lucia was going to help them. Not all of the girls, because that would be impossible, but surely it was better to improve the lot of a few rather than let all of them meet grim fates.

Lucia gasped, choked by desperation and fear. She couldn't fail them.

"Or maybe," Elspeth said in a placating tone, "he's one of those randy men who'll delight in possessing an establishment such as ours. He might like it and keep us operational."

"I hope so." Lucia braced her hands on the heavy worktable, trying to stay on her feet when she thought it very possible she might tumble headlong into darkness. "We'll know soon enough, when I deliver the owner's share of the profits."

"How long until delivery day?" Kitty asked as she tickled her son's foot. The baby giggled.

Lucia tried to take comfort from the infant's laughter. Happiness and joy had ways of persisting, even in the midst of chaos and potential disaster.

"Tomorrow." It was always the same. Every twenty-first of the month, she'd travel to Mayfair to bring their patron his portion of the take. With no guidance, there was nothing to do but hold to that plan.

"What do we do until then?" Elspeth asked.

She'd learned from an early age that anything and everything might vanish, and in the absence of security, she could only rely upon her own determination. Surely there had to be some way to keep the Orchid Club running and preserve her dream of the girls' home. She'd find some way to make that happen.

Right now, however, her mind and heart were both blank.

"We'll open the club a second night each week," she said. "Fridays. Until the new owner says we must close, we'll increase our profits as much as possible. Save them up in case we lose our employment and income."

Her friends nodded.

"In the meantime," she continued, "none of the guests tonight can know of our troubles. I'll tell the staff about our second night, I won't speak of the new owner to the rest of the staff till I know for certain what our fate might be."

"Is that wise?" Kitty wondered. "They might want to know."

"There's nothing any of them can do until we know what our new owner plans to do. And as for ourselves . . ." She let out a long breath. "We wait. And hope."

Chapter 5

Within his carriage, Tom stared out the window, watching the world shoot past him. Everything seemed to be going too fast. He hoped that tonight, he'd be able to gain his footing again, if only for a little while.

The vehicle sped down London's darkened streets, heading toward Bloomsbury. And release. But only for a brief while.

Absently, Tom touched the ducal signet ring on the smallest finger of his left hand. At the feel of the gold against his fingers, thoughts of his father flooded him, threatening to drag him down into the ever-present morass of grief.

Tom slipped off the ring and tucked it carefully in the inside pocket of his coat. Where he was going tonight, he couldn't have anyone recognize him.

It was for Maeve, and his mother, that Tom had made the choice that impelled him to Bloomsbury tonight. After this night, he would never again return to the Orchid Club.

A throb of loss pumped through him, but he put it aside. He meant to enjoy these last hours of freedom before donning the permanent disguise of staid, sober duke.

He adjusted the green silk mask covering half of his face. While wearing it, he could be anyone. A sailor or a tradesman or a vagabond. All cares could be set aside for a few hours in his final pursuit of selfish, wonderful pleasure.

The carriage pulled up outside a place Tom knew very well. He'd visited it weekly for almost a year, until recently, when he'd stayed at his father's bedside and failed to attend the Orchid Club's openings.

His footman jumped down and opened the carriage door for him.

"Wait for me in the mews," Tom directed the young man, though he needn't have bothered. The routine was well-known by his servants.

When the carriage drove off, Tom tugged down his dove-gray silk waistcoat and brushed at the shoulders of his gunmetal-gray coat. How strange to be out of mourning, even for a few hours, but he didn't want anyone inside knowing such intimate details.

After climbing the short flight of stairs to the door, Tom gave the customary secret knock. *Tap. Tap-tap. Tap.* Waiting, hoping, his heart rose in his throat in anticipation. They hadn't seen each other in too long.

Throughout these long weeks, he'd used the memory of her as a touchstone, a gleam of gold amidst the ashes. He needed that brightness now.

A moment later, the door opened a sliver and the black woman appeared.

After he'd exchanged the customary password with the doorkeeper, he entered. For good measure, he showed her a small coin, stamped with a mask. The token was given to whomever had attended the club more than three times, to demonstrate that they were familiar with the rules of the establishment.

The tangles of grief and responsibility loosened in his chest as he stepped into the foyer. A sense of ease and release crept through him. No one here called him *Your Grace*. Only the moniker for all guests: *friend*. *This* was where he was meant to be. Not the heavy-paneled study where all the matters of the estate were handled, nor the corridors haunted by England's men of power, where Tom was charged with both preserving England's traditions—regardless of Tom's own feelings on the matter—and preserving the Powell family's reputation.

He handed the doorkeeper money, which she tucked into the purse hanging at her waist.

"Most everyone is in the drawing room and the ballroom," she said, gesturing to the hallway behind her.

Familiar with the route, he made his way toward the sound of conversation, laughter, music, and sex. With each step, more and more weight fell from his shoulders. For the first time since his father's final illness, Tom felt genuinely buoyant. Yet that buoyancy was undercut by the fact that soon, he'd give this up, too.

He entered the parlor, and his gaze fell upon the

familiar sight of guests in various states of dress and undress. Bare flesh gleamed in the candlelight, laughter and sighs filled the air, and the scent of perfume and unbridled sexuality wafted like a tropic current.

Some weren't actively engaged in sensual pursuits. Two women drank champagne and chatted in low voices. A quartet played a game of cards—though it appeared the stakes were articles of clothing, as evidenced by the piles of gloves, stockings, and coats heaped in the center of the table. No one bid their masks.

The people in this room could have been anyone, from barristers to fishmongers, barons to abigails. That was part of the thrill. The man or woman someone was coupling with could have been their servant, or master. It was rumored that spouses had made love to each other without ever knowing their partner's true identity. But it was impossible to ever know the truth of this.

Tom took a glass of wine from a passing footman, then sipped as he surveyed the room. He took his usual place by the window. The moment a woman in a red dress began approaching him, he moved on. Over the course of the year, he'd fielded many offers of sex from interested parties, but he'd never accepted. That wasn't why he came to the Orchid Club.

He crossed the threshold of the ballroom. This was where he'd first met Amina, a night he'd never forgotten. As always, the notes of a waltz drifted from the musicians as the guests on the dance floor surrendered to the seductive air of unfiltered desire.

This was not sanctioned London. It was the secret, dark side. The place where people of all walks of life came for release, to cavort and be free.

He sensed a charge like unheard music, a subtle threading of awareness moving invisibly through his body. Despite being engaged in watching the unfolding action, Tom became conscious of a new presence in the room.

Amina had arrived.

She glided through the chamber, calm and assured, a small, unreadable smile playing about her lips as she stopped to chat with guests, making certain they had everything they needed. Tonight, her mask was emerald green, embroidered all over with gold thread and tiny pearls. The mask matched her richly hued gown, which hugged her curved body.

Tonight, her thick black hair was pinned up, though small brilliants seemed to twinkle in the dark waves. But it could have been his imagination. For surely whenever she was near, he had eyes for no one but her.

Riveted, Tom watched her glide through the ballroom, expertly weaving through the crowd. She kept that slightly removed smile on her face as she talked with the celebrants. Occasionally, she waved over a servant to provide more refreshments to the guests. She checked with the musicians and adjusted the position of a candelabra on a table.

This is my realm, she seemed to silently declare. The ruler of Bloomsbury. The empress of the Orchid Club. Regal and confident, her head held high, her shoulders back.

She caught sight of him, and he straightened to his fullest height. A thrum of excitement pulsed through him, all the way to his bones, as she approached. The lingering clouds of his unease lifted the nearer she came.

This close, he could see the deep brown of her eyes shining behind her disguise. Her pupils were large, fathomless.

"Rogue," Amina said when she stood before him.

"You chide me baselessly." His heart took up double time to have her so close and to hear her low, throaty voice again. Every now and again, he caught a hint of an unknown accent in her words, yet he could never ask after her origins.

She had to be from somewhere warm, a place where, beneath a gleaming sun, dark-eyed beauties felt temperate breezes caress their tawny skin. The thought of all Amina's flesh bared to the sunlight made his mouth water.

"I'm not a capricious creature," she said crisply. "I do nothing without reason."

"If you are my judge, I'm entitled to know the offense for which I am accused."

She clicked her tongue. "Even worse that you don't know." At his mystified silence, she explained, "Six weeks. It's been six weeks since I've last seen you within these chambers. I thought you'd enlisted or run off to Argentina."

He smiled to himself. "You think me an adventurer?"

"I think you dreadfully rude to have disappeared," she said coolly.

He bowed. "Family obligations, unfortunately, have kept me away."

A corner of her mouth lifted. "I forget, sometimes, that people have families."

Despite her wry smile, a note of melancholy tinged her voice, making him contemplate her kin. Did she have any, and did they know what she did to earn her bread?

Then, she said more lightly, "You're here now. That's all that matters."

"Thinking of this night has been a balm to me these past weeks," he said candidly. There was no need to dissemble or tell flattering half-truths. Not here. Not with her.

"If you've been troubled, I am sorry for it." Sincerity firmed her words. Perhaps he was, to her, more than another masked guest, something beyond a means to keep a roof over her head.

God knew she held greater significance to him than her role as manager of this establishment.

He bowed. "I'll find my way through my difficulties."

Or so he hoped. Every step put him deeper and deeper into unknown, perilous territory.

"Good," she said. "It would pain me to think of you in distress."

"Would it?"

She shot him a pointed look. "I've no reason to speak falsely."

"You are this club's proprietress. I would be inclined to believe that you'll say nearly anything to ensure a paying guest's return."

"It may be that I do not always give voice to my innermost heart," she said, inclining her head. "Yet I will not lie. Not often," she added wryly. "But, I won't dissemble with you."

Perhaps here, too, she wasn't telling the truth, but he chose to believe her. It filled him with dark pleasure.

"Appreciated, madam." Her presence beside him warmed him far more than any wine.

"We match." She glanced at his mask. He'd forgotten that his was green, nearly the same color as her own. She stroked a fingertip along her mask, and then his. Though it wasn't skin-to-skin touch, he nearly growled at the contact. "Coincidence?"

"Fate," he said.

She gave a half smile. "Fate doesn't exist. There are only choices."

"And what do you choose tonight, madam?"

"For now, I choose to spend my valuable time with an inveterate scoundrel. One who disappears like smoke." Her rich and husky laugh reached all the way down to his groin, making it tighten. Then she frowned. "In all this time, you've never joined in the activities in here. A displeased or bored guest is unacceptable in my establishment. I thought that when you stopped coming, maybe you'd grown tired of us."

"Nothing here has ever disappointed me." He was never returning after tonight, so it cost him naught to speak the truth.

Together, they observed the room and people within it. Half-nude guests danced together, while sighs and moans gently wafted above the music.

"You have never participated in the activity here," she said, "not once in the whole of a year."

After the too-brief conversation they'd had that first night, he'd returned again. And again. Each time, he'd been careful. Seeking her out, but trying not to appear too fervent. Yet every time, he made sure to engage her in banter, draw her out like a silken thread.

She was swathed in mystery, cloaked in secrets. Beautiful, aloof. How could he resist her? He wanted more.

But they played a sophisticated game, him and Amina. Always at a slight distance, like chess opponents strategizing the movement of their pieces on the board. A word here. A flirtation there. They both seemed to understand the way of the world, never revealing themselves entirely. All the while, desire was an invisible presence between them, gathering strength.

The last time he'd been at the Orchid Club, they'd spoken of their favorite secret places in London, little corners of the city that held unexpected joy. She hated the zoological gardens because of the caged animals, but loved to watch the birds take wing above a tiny square nestled in Chelsea. He'd confessed he would grab a cake from Catton's famed sweet shop and eat it while standing on the banks of the Thames, watching the ships drift along the water.

Then . . . he'd taken her hand. A brief touch. Their eyes had met, and the charge between them had crackled like summer lightning. He'd nearly gone to his knees from merely that contact.

She'd slipped away to see after other guests, but he'd felt her gaze on him the rest of the night. A promise of what could be. He'd excitedly planned what might happen the next time they met. But then he'd had to disappear. Leaving the potential unfulfilled.

Until now.

He stepped in front of her so that he commanded her full attention. She tilted her head back to look him in the eye. Always, she had that direct way of looking at him, and it shot awareness through him with a hard, quick intensity.

"I return to this place again and again for one reason," he said. "The same reason that brings me here tonight—*you*."

Her lips parted, yet she did not speak. Surprise flashed in the depths of her eyes.

He narrowed the distance between them, and this close, he caught her scent of night-blooming flowers.

"This will be my last visit to the Orchid Club." It pained to speak it, making it more real, more inevitable.

She frowned. "If I've said or done anything to drive you from here—"

"The world pulls me away, not you. I'd speak more on it, but the rules of the house . . ." He smiled regretfully.

"I . . ." She looked away, then back at him. "I'll miss you."

If she wasn't speaking the truth to him now, she was an excellent actress. She was the picture of regret. So he opted to believe her—it was a falsehood to which he'd gladly cling.

"And I'll miss you." For the rest of his life, no matter what befell him or what path his life took, he'd ache for her. "Before I take my final leave, I've one thing to ask you."

"And that is . . . ?"

He took her capable hand in his. She wore no gloves, and neither did he. The press of their palms together jolted through him, bright and hot. He'd anticipated her touch again with an unseemly eagerness—but now he saw that his eagerness had been entirely warranted. She felt . . . exquisite.

"Spend the night with me." To his own ears, his voice was all but a growl.

Her eyes widened. For a long moment, she said nothing. Hope rose and fell within him, like a bird riding currents of air.

"One night," he said in the silence. "In the morning, we'll part company forever, but until the sun rises, we'll give each other unimaginable pleasure. I promise," he went on, "you'll have nothing to regret, only memories of an extraordinary night. All you have to do is say yes."

She stared up at him. Her breath came quickly, mirroring the thundering of his own pulse. The heat between their bodies could start a conflagration that would raze the city.

God, how he wanted her.

One moment became another and another. He could see the thoughts racing behind her eyes, the calculation of risk against reward.

He prayed for her answer, craving it with a fierce intensity, yet fully prepared to walk away if she said no. The choice had to be hers.

Her gaze locked on his, and when she spoke, her words were firm and decisive.

"Yes."

Chapter 6

❧

Lucia's gaze moved over her buccaneer. He was tall, broad-shouldered, dark-haired and possessed spectacularly blue eyes, and his devastating handsomeness was like a weapon against which she could not defend herself. He had a clean, straight jaw and a very wicked, sensuous mouth.

"Yes?" he repeated.

"Yes," she said once more. Her pulse sped with each word from her lips. "I'll take you to my bed—for tonight alone."

Am I making a mistake?

Sleeping with a guest had always been forbidden, even when Mrs. Chalke had run the club. And yet, for a year, Lucia and the buccaneer had circled each other, drawn by an irresistible pull. All this time, she'd fantasized about him. What his touch would feel like, how it would be to caress his bare skin, or discover his taste.

She'd resigned herself to never knowing the answer

to these riddles. But after this night, she would never see him again. He'd said as much.

And tomorrow, she'd learn the fate of her club. Everything could come crashing down in less than twenty-four hours—the death of the establishment, the loss of employment for the twenty members of the staff, and the end of Lucia's funding for the girls' home.

The future was a morass of uncertainty. But tonight, just this once, she'd permit herself selfish pleasure.

No harm will come of this. There was no danger to her heart, no threat of a growing attachment. They would enjoy each other, and part company. She'd be safe.

His eyes darkened and his nostrils flared. The look of pure desire on his face stoked her own need.

"I've a carriage out back," he said.

"My rooms are just upstairs. No waiting." No time to reconsider or question herself.

"Guide us there."

With his fingers intertwined with hers, and her heart pounding, she led him to the foyer.

Elspeth rose from the low stool upon which she sat and stared at Lucia and the buccaneer's joined hands. Her wide gaze flew to Lucia's.

"I'm leaving everything in your hands for the rest of the night." Lucia looked levelly at her friend, but knew her gaze held a note of entreaty.

Only for tonight. For this single time, I'm taking something that's meant for me alone.

Perhaps Elspeth understood how much Lucia needed the solace and distraction of pleasure, because she nodded.

"Enjoy your evening," Elspeth said.

Silently, Lucia exhaled. She offered Elspeth a small, grateful smile before leading her buccaneer up the main staircase. As they climbed the stairs, she was acutely aware of his presence behind her, and the burn of his flesh against hers from merely the press of hands. The steps creaked with his mass, reminding her of his size, so much larger than her, giving her a foretaste of his weight on her. A thrill danced along her limbs and centered between her legs, where she was alive and sensitized.

The main corridor upstairs was lit by a single candle. Lucia stopped outside her door, fitting the key into the lock. She trusted her friends and the staff, but never knew when an inquisitive guest might manage to find their way into the private rooms where she, Kitty, and Elspeth lived.

As she slid the key into place, her buccaneer pressed close behind her, nuzzling her neck. For a moment, she simply held herself still, absorbing his touch. Her eyes struggled to remain open, and her hand trembled. She couldn't seem to unlock the door.

"You're up here early." Kitty's voice broke through Lucia's sensual haze. "I— Oh."

Lucia looked down the hallway to see Kitty standing outside her room, jogging little Liam on her hip.

Behind Lucia, her buccaneer stilled but didn't move away. His breath fanned warmly across her nape, making her breasts tighten.

A smile bloomed across Kitty's face. "As you were, soldiers." She saluted before disappearing into her room.

Alone, finally. Lucia opened the door to her chamber. Taking a breath, she stepped inside.

He followed at once, shutting the door behind him. She quickly locked it so no one would disturb them.

She leaned back, knowing full well that the movement pushed her breasts tightly against her gown's curved neckline. A shameless, proud display.

He stepped closer, and her breasts brushed his broad, solid chest. This was the closest they had ever been to each other, and her whole body felt acutely sensitized, aware of every point of contact. His thighs against hers, their hips cradling together.

"Am I to have you, then?" he rumbled.

She adored the hint of an Irish accent in his words, yet would never know more about where he came from, or anything at all about him.

Here she was, in her room, with an intimate stranger. A man she knew well, yet not at all.

More, a voice within her cried. *I need more than another meaningless fuck.*

She forcibly shoved the unwanted thought away. It was so much easier to reduce her need for him to the craving of one body for another. Delving deeper and learning him made him too real, turning him from a fantasy into a fully developed person.

No. She shouldn't crave that connection. It only led to pain and heartbreak.

"*We* are to have what we want," she said in a murmur, looping her arms around his neck and bringing him down, closer to her. He cupped her waist, heat from his body seeping into hers.

This is all I want, she told herself, trying to quiet her demand for affinity. *A good, hard fuck. Only that.*

For a moment, they merely gazed at each other, their mouths hovering closely. Then, as her eyes drifted shut, their lips came together. Softly at first. A brush back and forth as they learned each other's textures and the hints of their taste. His initial gentleness surprised her. She expected him to crash against her mouth and take, take, take. That was the way of most men. But not *this* man. He progressed slowly, learning her bit by bit.

Her heart thudded in alarm. This was too affectionate, too meaningful, reaching deep into her to find the place where she yearned for true intimacy.

She turned the kiss more demanding and ravenous. He responded at once, sweeping his tongue into her mouth with velvet strokes. She sank into the sensation. The man knew how to kiss a woman. He clearly took pleasure from the act itself, rather than rush it toward another destination. She took from him hungrily, as he gave her himself, deep and rich and lush.

I don't want to take another stranger to my bed, that voice within her interjected. *Who is he, truly?*

Stai zitta, she mentally hissed back. *Don't muddle things. They're complicated enough.*

She moved deeper into her room, needing to hurry toward the raw, purely physical needs of her body as if she could outpace her thoughts. He followed. After pausing briefly to light a candle, she let her hands roam over his body, and, *che bello,* he felt magnificent, solid and firm with tightly hewn muscle that shifted powerfully beneath her touch. This was all she needed to know—that he was beautifully made and could give her physical release.

If she wanted more, if she craved the comfort one soul could give another, she'd lock that craving away, where it couldn't hurt her.

His large hands caressed her everywhere, sweeping along the curves of her arse, cupping her hips, skimming up over her waist. Heat tore through her, turning her liquid and pliable.

The back of her dress dipped low, baring the skin between her shoulder blades, and she jolted with pleasure as he stroked her flesh there.

He cupped her breasts, and sparks tumbled through her entire body. She arched up into his touch. His growl resounded low within her, speaking directly to her need for the purely carnal.

Yes, just this. Only this.

His rumble grew deeper when he plucked her nipples into tight points, making her moan.

This was perfect. This was precisely what she needed. The fall into pleasure, heedless of everything but desire. Tomorrow didn't matter—nothing mattered but now.

It's not enough, that infuriating voice insisted. *What of your heart? What of the bond between two souls? I want that.*

There was no way to escape her own demands, much as she tried to silence them.

"Too many clothes," he muttered. He edged back slightly and moved to pull off his coat.

"Wait," she heard herself say.

He froze in midmotion. "You want me to stop?"

"Yes—but no." She drew a shuddering breath. *Don't say it.* "I need more."

Madonna santa!

His gaze sharpened. "Anything."

"I want . . ." She could not stop the words as they tumbled from her lips. "Give me one truth about you."

"A TRUTH," Tom said slowly as he struggled to make sense of what she'd asked. He lowered his hands.

Amina spoke in a rush, as if trying to get every syllable out before she thought better of it.

"Not your identity. That remains hidden. But tell me something about yourself."

"Why?" He pushed against the wall of his confusion. This was not what they had agreed upon.

"What does it matter?" Her words were almost sharp. "We'll not see each other again after tonight."

"Yet to speak of such things goes contrary to your established rules."

He tested his own response to her request and found . . . welcome acceptance. Finding a stranger to fuck was easy enough. He'd taken others to bed within minutes of meeting, with them knowing nothing about who he was or knowledge of what he feared or desired in the hidden recesses of his heart. Hell, there had been more than a few times his bed partners hadn't even known his name.

It hadn't mattered to him then. But the chance to have Amina discover more about himself felt as though he'd waded into a warm ocean, becoming more and more buoyant with each step.

For a moment, she was silent.

"I've had lovers before. Always, I made certain to keep them essentially strangers. You and I, we're destined to walk away from one another, but . . ."

He'd never heard her sound uncertain, not once, and yet she spoke as if testing out her thoughts that were unknown, even to herself.

"But . . . ?" he prompted.

She tilted up her chin as if in defiance. "I want this to be different. I want *you* to be different."

So—he wasn't the only one invested in their two-person planetary system.

What she suggested was a risk, yet secrecy was her stock-in-trade.

They'd part with the dawn, leaving him only with

memories of physical sensation. Yet to have her learn about him wasn't enough. He hungered for anything about her, small, gleaming pieces that he could hold tight to in decades to come.

"One condition."

She gazed at him warily. "Tell me your terms."

"In exchange for my truth, I want the same from you."

Behind her mask, her eyes went round.

His pulse throbbed. It was a gamble, demanding this from her. Much as he wanted her and the pleasures of her body, there was a chasm within him that demanded a deeper knowledge of this extraordinary woman. Perhaps he might not know the secrets of her mind and heart, but in the long years ahead when he was mired in cold, passionless duty, he could warm himself with embers of remembrance.

Her room gave some clues as to who she was. Though it was simply furnished, there were touches of vivid color everywhere. Vibrant green fabric draped across the foot of her bed, the table was painted a sunny yellow, and bright blue curtains hung in the window. A half-read book lay atop the table, though he couldn't see the title. Pictures from fashion journals were pinned to the walls, and a vase of purple Michaelmas daisies perched on a windowsill.

No pictures or miniatures of family.

Her silence stretched on, and each moment without her answer drew tautly along his flesh.

"An incentive," he said. "For every truth given, an article of clothing will be removed."

Her tongue darted out to moisten her lips. The quick, carnal action stoked the flames within him even higher.

Finally, she said quickly, "You go first."

Instead of giving in to the urge to pump his fist in victory, he inclined his head in agreement.

What to start with first? There were any number of things he could say. Simple likes and dislikes that didn't touch the core of him.

But he didn't want to hand her trifles. If they were to open to each other, and learn who they *truly* were, he had to begin with something of significance.

"There was a death in my family not long ago. One of my parents—thus, my absence from the club." With just a few words, an ache throbbed in his chest.

"I'm so very sorry." Sincerity was heavy in her voice.

"My thanks." Melancholy hovered close, eager to enfold him in its gray embrace. For all of his father's disapproval, the late duke's presence had been a constant. There were things that could be relied upon—the best sip of wine was always the second to last, the curve of a woman's neck never failed to delight, and the Duke of Northfield sat at the head of the dining table every Sunday supper, glowering at Tom with displeasure.

How could he miss a man who let him know at every turn that he was a disappointment? Yet he did, and the loss was an open wound, seeping blood.

He mentally bound the wound with a hasty field dressing. This night was not for sorrow. There would be time enough for that later.

"Now, I'll honor our agreement." He shrugged out of his jacket and draped it over a chair.

A smile touched her lips as her gaze turned avid. "When you do that, your shirt pulls across your muscles in a most agreeable manner."

It wasn't the first time a lover had complimented his physique. All that time at the pugilism and fencing academies apparently reaped physiological dividends. But it was *her* praise that made a little firework of gratification go off within him.

When she merely stared at the breadth of his shoulders, he prompted gently, "This bargain requires participation from both of us."

"Yes. Yes, of course." She cleared her throat, and then her brow furrowed as she seemed to decide what aspect of herself to reveal. "England is not my home. That is, I wasn't born here. I'll never return to the land of my birth." She said these last words with the finality of someone who had long ago resigned themselves to a hard truth.

A host of questions begged to be asked, swirling in his mouth, but he and Amina had made no provisions for queries, so he only nodded. He tucked away her revelation, setting it in his mental cabinet of wonders to be studied and admired later.

Blood shot into his groin as she bent down and

raised the hem of her skirts to reveal a pair of sleek ankles. Ribbons from her slippers crisscrossed up her stocking-clad calves.

Downstairs, he'd seen women in all states of dress, from fully clad to entirely nude. The sight had been arousing, but the modest display of Amina's lower legs made his whole body tight with a fiercer hunger.

She untied the ribbons before slipping off her shoes, which she set neatly aside, before letting go of her skirts. Then she straightened and looked at him with expectation.

He searched once more for something of himself to give to her.

"For the first twelve years of my life," he said, his fingers already working to undo his neckcloth, "I lived in Ireland. My mother's home."

He'd been teased mercilessly at Harrow for his accent, but instead of working to erase it, he'd held firm to his brogue. Like hell would he let anyone's ignorance shape his feelings about himself.

The neckcloth came loose, and he dropped it to the floor. The chill air of the room touched the flesh of his throat, and it was only then that he realized the fire wasn't lit. He'd been too focused on her to notice.

Amina stepped closer, and his breath caught as she ran her fingertips down the length of his bare neck, to linger at the hollow at the base of his throat. Sparks danced along his skin where she touched, all sense of coolness gone.

"The night we met," she said on a whisper, "was my first night as manager of the club. Being merely a server wasn't enough for me. I made certain that I became indispensable to our former proprietress, so that when the time came for her to step down, there'd be no doubt as to her choice of successor."

"Ambitious," he murmured.

"Always."

A rush of pleasure coursed warmly along his veins. *This* was what he craved, this knowledge of who she was beneath the layers of her persona. And it pleased him to know of her determination and drive, a person who took what she wanted.

He lowered his eyelids. "Garters and stockings next."

"Now you make my disrobing decisions?" she asked, her voice dry but her lips curving upward.

"Merely providing suggestions. And, if you'll permit me, I offer my services to assist you in undressing."

She laughed throatily. Her words dry, she said, "Never had an abigail."

He'd unclothed many women and was well versed in the intricacies of their garments—but none of that signified now. Amina was all that counted.

Smoothly, he lowered to one knee. She lifted her skirts once more and it was like the curtain going up on a play he'd been desperate to see. Excitement vibrated through him.

He settled his hands on her calves. Taut muscles moved sleekly beneath the openwork silk of her stockings. As he skimmed his fingers upward, her breath caught—and his did, as well. His pulse throbbed heavily in his groin as he stroked past her knees, reaching higher up her skirts, until he came to her garter. They were sapphire blue, dotted with embroidered pink flowers.

A little spike of gratification rose up. Here his knowledge of women's clothing was useful. He undid her garters quickly, and they fell in gentle curls onto the braided rag rug.

His mouth went dry.

He lightly stroked at the top of her stockings and couldn't stop the rumble that rose up within him when he brushed the silken skin of her thigh. Glancing up, he saw her chest rise and fall with quick breaths, and her lips had parted.

With patience he never knew he possessed, he rolled her stocking down her leg. He repeated the procedure with her other garter and stocking and, by the time he stood, her legs were bare and he was dizzy with lust.

He plucked at the buttons of his waistcoat.

She held up a hand. "First, a truth."

Words tumbled from him, as if waiting for this moment to be spoken. "Everyone expects me to continue my father's legacy. I'm to be another him—not my own man. The thought is like being hammered into a coffin while I still live. But if I don't . . . there's more at stake than merely my own happiness."

Hell. He hadn't expected to share so much, and

yet there was a rightness to speaking of these things with her, a purity that came not just from the fact that they would never see each other again, but that it was Amina to whom he confessed.

He threw aside his waistcoat, heedless of where it landed.

"My turn," she said in a voice as dark as wine. "My heart has been broken three times—and after that, I vowed never to let myself be hurt again."

"Let me hurt whoever hurt you," he said at once. His hands curled into fists and his muscles burned with the need to punish those that had dared cause her pain.

A bittersweet smile touched her lips. "Two of the people who broke my heart are dead. My mother, and the man who sired me. The third person was my grandfather, who was blood kin but no family of mine."

She spoke so simply, and yet each syllable spoke of immeasurable loss. They resounded within him as though she'd whispered in a cavern, the quiet words growing in strength with each echo.

"I'll take care of him," he said fiercely.

She shook her head, mingled sadness and anger in her gaze. "He cannot touch me now." She looked every inch the deposed queen, regal and wounded.

"Amina—"

She spun on her heel and presented him with her back. "The hooks, please. On my gown. I can't reach them."

Gazing at the bare column of her neck and the slope

of her shoulders, his fury on her behalf dissolved in a haze of desire. For all his experience taking off women's clothes, his fingers were suddenly thick as sausages, and equally clumsy. He fumbled with the tiny hooks until the back of her dress opened.

With movements supple and graceful as a cat, she slipped off her gown before facing him.

"God almighty," he rasped.

She didn't wear stays. Or drawers.

She stood in only a whisper-light chemise, and beneath the fabric he could plainly see the rosewood brown of her taut nipples and dark delta between her legs.

Without a hint of shyness, she let him look his fill.

If they didn't leap into bed soon, there was the distinct possibility that he'd lose his sanity.

"Here's my next truth," he said, his voice low and rasping with need. "I've never wanted anyone the way I want you."

Her dark eyes became almost black, and her cheeks reddened.

A conflagration blazed along his flesh to see her so aroused.

Impatient to feel her against his bare skin, he tugged off his shirt and cast it to the floor. His boots were next.

If she minded that he rushed his disrobing, she didn't give voice to it.

Instead, she murmured, "*Dio mio.*" Her gaze roved avidly over his torso. "You are . . ." She shook her head, her cheeks staining deeper with the flush of desire.

Reaching out, she placed her palm just above his heart, nestling her fingers in the dark hair that spread across his pectorals. "Where I am from, there are ancient statues of men like you. Statues of heroes and gods."

"I'm not carved from marble." His voice was deep, almost guttural. "I'm a man made of flesh."

"That is something about you that I know quite well." She looked downward, toward the hard column of his cock pressed against the front of his breeches, and her lips pursed with approval.

Holy hell, he might come from her gaze alone.

"Here is my final truth," she said, her words simple and unadorned. "I think I might die from my need for you."

And then, with a woman's timeless smile, she whisked off her chemise. Save for her mask, she was nude.

If a man could literally immolate himself, surely he would do so. She'd said he was formed in the likeness of a god, but he was merely mortal, while she had the ripe figure of a harvest goddess, abundantly curved.

"I'm the luckiest bastard in England," he muttered.

She reached up and unpinned her hair so that it fell in heavy black waves about her shoulders.

"No such thing as luck," she said confidently. "We make choices, for good or for bad, but they're ours to make."

Perhaps if rational thought hadn't evaporated when she'd stripped off her chemise, he could form a cogent and contemplative response. He might pick apart her words to consider what they meant, what they revealed. But that was beyond him at present.

She flicked her fingers toward his lower body.

"The breeches." Her words were crisp, commanding. "Remove them."

"I haven't given you a truth," he felt obliged to note.

"I want the truth of your body."

Never had he taken off his breeches so speedily. One moment he was in them, and in the next, they were on the floor. By habit, he didn't wear drawers, and, other than their masks, both he and Amina were naked.

Her sigh was long and appreciative. "*That* is a beautiful cock."

"And I want to fuck you with it." He lifted his hands. "But first—" He undid the ribbons of his mask and pulled his disguise away, letting her see his naked face. "My name is Tom."

She hesitated, and a cool trickle of fear ran down the back of his neck. He'd never been as exposed as he was at that moment. He was no stranger to nudity, but clothing only hid the body. With the removal of his mask, and the giving of his name, he opened himself to her. Yet she might not do the same. He would have reached out, only to have her withdraw, leaving him bared and undefended.

A moment later, she followed suit, removing her mask.

His breath caught. She had a face of arresting beauty,

with dark slashing eyebrows and sculpted cheekbones that should have been elegant but instead made her a creature of carnal, earthy splendor. He could write sonnets to her bold, assertive nose, and the lushness of her lips.

"My name," she said firmly, letting her mask fall from her fingers, "is Lucia. And I will not wait a moment longer. I want you *now*."

Chapter 7

$\mathcal{N}$ever had Lucia been this unprotected, so vulnerable—not with a lover.

Perhaps it had been a grave error to play this game with him, trading truths for clothing. He was fully human now, not just a fantasy. He hurt, and yearned, and possessed an entire history. Her buccaneer was a man named Tom.

And she wanted him. If anything with this exchange, her desire had grown, until she felt her pulse between her legs like a thudding drum, her breasts tight and sensitive.

This was not part of her plan. It should have been simple desire, with her taking refuge in uncomplicated lust. Yet with just a few words from him, she felt a piece of the scales around her heart fall away, welcoming him in.

Turning back was impossible. Her hunger for him had grown too large and couldn't be locked back in its cage. The beast was loose, and it demanded Tom.

All she could do now was follow in its wake and pray that, when it was time to bid him farewell, she might withstand the loss.

He looked at her now with fierce intensity, his gaze afire, his beautiful body taut, his cock thick and ready.

She still had some supremacy—because she knew that if she asked anything of him now, he'd obey her.

She moved away from him and walked on legs that felt sleek and powerful to the foot of the bed, where she turned and faced him. He took purposeful strides toward her, until their bodies were snug. Her sensitive flesh drank in the sensation of him, from the press of the hair on his chest against her breasts, to the length of his rigid thighs along her own. His hands cupped her arse while she looped her arms around his neck. His cock rose up in a hard, delicious curve that lay snug against her belly.

Without his mask, his face was even more handsome. She followed the angled line of his jaw to his expressive mouth, up higher to his hawkish nose. The vivid hue of his eyes was a jolt of clear color. His eyebrows were heavy and dark, eloquent, and they lowered into a look of almost stern severity as he gazed at her.

She shook to be the focus of so much singular need—not merely a desire for her body, but for *her.* All of her.

For a long moment, they only stared at each other, eager breaths mingling in the narrow space between them.

I won't think of tomorrow. Only this moment.

He lowered his lips to hers, but did not quite kiss her. "You're here with me. Now."

"We are together." She lifted up just enough to bring their mouths together.

Passion and desire pushed the kiss, and they devoured each other in fevered caresses that seared her.

She felt herself falling, until the mattress met her back. All the while, she and Tom kissed with a madness that verged on desperation. She was supple with need, her breasts aching and full, liquid warmth spreading between her legs where he wedged.

"Dreamed of you like this," he said in a rough, deep voice. He dragged his mouth along her neck, and then he bit her lightly. "Hungry for me. The way I've hungered for you."

Her head spun and she realized that he'd turned them, rolling onto his back so she lay atop him. His hands roamed over her body, stroking between her shoulder blades, down the curve of her back. Each kiss and caress stoked her higher and higher. He was both deft and reverent as he touched her hair, then he licked along her throat and over her collarbone, carnal and adoring.

"Sometimes, before I sleep, I think of this, of you," he said in a voice like whiskey. "I stroke myself as I fantasize how I'd touch you."

The image of him with his cock in his hand sent a rush of heat through her.

"Don't have to fantasize," she gasped. She sat up, straddling him fully, and looked down at him.

He stroked up over her waist, along her ribs, until he cupped her breasts. A deep sound of pleasure rolled up from him as he caressed her, and she tipped her head forward, hot and restless, as he teased her nipples and lightly pinched them. Between her legs, his cock surged, and she ground down onto him. They both moaned at the contact.

"Christ God," Tom said hoarsely, "you're beautiful."

She felt beautiful. Especially when he gazed at her as though she was both alluring sin and vital salvation. And she looked back, soaking in the sight of him in her bed.

He was made of tight muscle clinging firmly to bone, every plane sharply defined, his light skin smooth and taut. Dark hair curled temptingly over his pectorals and traced down in a thin line over the ridges of his abdomen. And there was that incredible cock of his, heavy and upright.

She was no stranger to the male body in all states of dress and undress. And she could say without reservation that he was the most exquisite creature she'd ever seen.

"You are unfair," she whispered. "All this time, you've hidden this away, denying me the pleasure of your form."

"Apologies." His voice was a rasp. "Ah, hell," he exhaled when she wrapped her hand around his cock and gave one slow, firm pump.

His fingers grazed down her belly to her mound, going lower until she moaned at the feel of him stroking between her lips. She couldn't recall ever being so wet and ready. They panted into each other's mouths with their caresses.

"There's a way I want to have you." He took her breath and gave it back to her. "Been dreaming of it for a year."

"Show me."

He slid out from beneath her then with fluid, muscular motion, rose up from the bed. His sure but careful hands positioned her so that she lay on the mattress, her hips at the edge and her feet on the floor.

With a firm, strong grip, he held her thighs as he stood between her legs. He released her long enough to grasp his cock and slide it along her folds, coating himself in her wetness. She moaned when he circled the head of his cock around her clit. *Santo cielo,* but she was already so close to her climax.

He notched himself at her opening. "Yes?"

"Yes."

His hips thrust, and he slid into her. She was filled utterly, delightfully stretched. She felt him everywhere within her, from her quim to her fingers and toes.

It was too much. Fucking a man she had revealed herself to was too close, too intimate. A wave of panic sizzled coldly through her.

But it felt too good to stop. She was subjugated by her need for him, and in small, incremental degrees, the panic receded.

Words in his unknown language streamed from him in rough, low tones. His body twitched, sweat slicking his muscles. Yet instead of pumping, he held himself still. She moved, driving him deeper into her.

"Hold, love," he growled. "Been aching for this moment for a long time. I mean to savor it."

"Savor later." Her voice was deeper than it had ever been, the voice of a sorceress caught in her own spell. "Fuck me now."

He snarled and plunged into her. She watched the movements play across his torso and arms. His mouth was open, his eyes heavy lidded. He varied his thrusts, some shallow, some deep, playing her body expertly.

What little control she clung to slipped away as he moved, and frenzy overtook her. She clutched at the blanket beneath her while he fucked her with fierce, beautiful intensity. Her back arched into the sensation.

She gasped when his fingers found her clit. He caressed her as he thrust, the head of his cock stroking against the spot deep within her.

Release came in a sudden, crashing wave. Sounds of abandon erupted from her in a deluge of pleasure. She was swept up in sensation, and only returned to herself when she felt him arranging her on the bed.

Sleek and sinewy, he climbed atop her to lie between her legs and stretched her arms over her head. When he pinned her wrists together with one hand, holding her firmly down, her breath caught.

They were eye to eye. She looked deep into the gaze of the man who was inside her as his free hand glided along her collarbone.

She wrapped her legs around his waist, crossing her ankles so that she clasped him.

In a voice hoarse in the aftermath of her cries, she said, "We're each other's prisoners." At least, for this night.

His gaze held hers as he sank into her, the intimacy striking her profoundly. A breath later, his hips drew back and then forward with his thrust. She closed her eyes as fiery pleasure shot into every part of her body.

He adjusted his position slightly, flattening his free hand on the mattress beside her head. Then he stroked into her, the base of his cock rubbing against her clit. Each thrust sent whirling sparks through her.

"*Dio,*" she moaned. "*Forte*—hard, like that."

His pace increased. Levels of shining, hot pleasure built and built within her. She ran toward it, seeking orgasm, and yet she wanted their sex to go on and on until she forgot what it meant to exist in any other moment.

Another climax enfolded her, shredding her into tatters of herself. She cried out until her throat went raspy.

"Yes," he rumbled. A moment later, he pulled free from her body, then stiffened and growled as he came. Still, he held her wrists.

Slowly, he lowered himself down to lie beside her and finally released his hold on her. Cool air traced along her lax, damp body, but she was too limp in the aftereffects of her release to move beneath the blanket.

"That was . . ." She didn't have words to describe

what had just happened. She didn't want words, fearful that they would reveal too much.

Deliberately, she focused on the feel of her supple body, the texture of the coverlet against her flesh and sheen of sweat cooling her skin. The air around her was heavy, replete with the musky scent that two creatures created with their lust.

"It was, indeed." His hand settled over the curve of her belly, and her heart contracted at how much comfort his touch gave her. "And it's only the beginning."

She turned her head to look at him.

"The beginning?" She winced at the mingled hope and fear in her voice.

His grin was wicked. "You couldn't possibly think that one time would be enough."

In her extensive experience, men got what they wanted and then promptly fled. She'd thought he would be no different.

"Glad to know I'm wrong," she said, trying to keep her words light.

"Quite, quite wrong." He leaned close and kissed her, long and thorough. He raised himself up on one elbow while his other hand stroked down her stomach, heading lower. "Let me show you just how delightfully incorrect you are."

THE first sooty light of dawn crept into her room, faintly illuminating him as he pulled on his clothing. From the bed, Lucia watched.

It was a wonder she had enough strength to remain conscious. Tom had been nearly inexhaustible, and creative, in his lovemaking. In a few hours, her muscles would be sore from strenuous use and stretching into new positions. But for now, she was as fluid as a melted candle, and her mind was equally liquid, too fluid in the afterglow to form cohesive thoughts.

Grazie a Dio. She didn't want to think too much, or examine the effect he'd had on her.

When he finished dressing, he approached the bed.

"I've never had a night like last night." His voice was tender, his gaze even more so. He smoothed a lock of hair off her face.

"For me, as well." She couldn't keep the sincerity out of her words. "It was remarkable."

Even in the dimness of the room in early morning light, his eyes gleamed. "I swear to you, I'll not forget you. Not for the length of my days."

But she wanted to forget him. Forget that two people could create such pleasure together. Forget that watching him prepare to leave made her heart feel like lead and sit heavily in her chest.

It had been a spectacularly bad idea to learn truths about him. No longer was he merely a construct of her imagination or an object she could use to find her own pleasure. He was real and human and subject to the same desires and vulnerabilities as she.

"I hope you have a good life," she said softly.

He cupped the back of her head and rested his forehead against hers. Her heart seized with the tenderness of the gesture. "I hope that you're given whatever your heart desires." He kissed her, gently, sweetly.

She swallowed around the mass in her throat. "Please." Her words were barely audible, even to herself. "Go now."

He straightened, then strode to the door.

Don't look back.

He looked back.

With all of her will, she forced herself to remain in bed rather than leap up and run to him. Her body ached with the effort. Instead, she stared at the ceiling. She heard the door open and shut, and then his steps in the hallway.

She could mark his progress all the way through the house, until he reached the foyer. Guests from the club were staggering out the front door. He joined their ranks, and then he was gone.

Forever.

Chapter 8

❦

$\mathcal{T}$om tried to make his step brisk as he strode into the parlor, despite the fact that his whole body felt ready to sink to the bottom of the Thames.

In the early-morning hours, he'd returned from Bloomsbury to Mayfair and barely had time to hastily wash, change his clothes, and throw back several cups of coffee before meeting with his men of business and reviewing mountains of paperwork.

The idyll of last night—of finally making love to Lucia—was truly over. He reminded himself of this as he entered the parlor. He'd put that part of his life behind him. His role as the duke, and protecting his family's reputation, superseded everything else.

"Ah, there you are, Tommy lad," his mother, Deirdre, said from the sofa. The sunlight caught in the strands of silver interwoven amongst her black hair, made all the more dramatic by her widow's black crêpe day gown. "Here we'd begun to believe you'd never join us."

She offered her cheek, which Tom dutifully kissed.

"Tommy's never missed taking tea with us." Maeve poured out a third cup of tea. Her eyes glinted when she threw him a cheeky smile. Clearly, her meeting with Lord Stacey had revived her spirits. "No matter what time he gets home."

He kissed his sister's forehead. "Never tell me you were awake at that hour."

After setting down a sheaf of documents, he lowered himself into a chair and prayed he wouldn't fall asleep.

"Well, no," Maeve said. "But my maid said she was on her way to the kitchen when she saw you creeping in, looking like you'd been wrestling with a bear all night."

Tom only offered his sister a mild look. No point in telling a girl of nineteen that her older brother had, in fact, been wrestling with a very lovely, sensual bear.

"Hush, *cailín*," Deirdre said as she plucked a small cake from the tray. "You're not to know the ways of men."

Maeve rolled her eyes. "If I'm to one day marry Hugh, *of course* I need to know the ways of men. I can't pretend he exists only when we're together, and then just disappears into a mist when we're apart."

"Oh, blast, you know our secret." Tom drank his tea, but wished for more coffee.

When Maeve moved to throw a candied nut at Tom's head, Deirdre said in a timeless mother's voice, "Children."

Maeve's hand lowered.

There was no point in reminding his mother that he was far from a child. The sheaf of documents beside him proved it.

Deirdre's gaze moved to the papers. "Oh, Tommy lad, don't tell me you plan on working whilst we have tea."

"No choice in the matter. God rest him, Father left me far more than this enchanting house."

He picked up the top sheet, which seemed heavier than a simple piece of paper.

Marrying an Irishwoman had been one of Edward Powell's sole acts of nonconformity—though Deirdre O'Connell had converted from Catholicism so they might wed. Other than his choice of bride, the sixth Duke of Northfield had been a man of unshakable belief that England's stability rested on the nation's traditional institutions.

Tom had thought that, when he finally inherited the title, he'd change all that. He'd quietly divested from the family holdings in the Caribbean and the American South, and all other investments that were entangled with the repulsive practice of slavery, but as yesterday's conversation with Lord Stacey—and the article in the *Times*—he discovered that extricating himself from the Duke of Northfield's political legacy here in England wasn't as easily achieved. It was, in fact, dangerous to his sister's happiness.

"What is that?" Maeve asked, nodding toward the paperwork.

"Notes on the Duke of Brookhurst's bill." Tom tried to focus on the words covering the page, but weariness—and dismay—made it difficult to read. He set it aside and made himself smile. "Care to join me for a game of pall-mall in the garden?"

"It's November." Maeve narrowed her eyes. "And you can't distract me from the Duke of Brookhurst's bill. He's Hugh's father, after all. I ought to be aware of my possible-future-father-in-law's actions in Parliament."

"I'm fit to curl up under the sofa and fall asleep," Tom said. "We can talk about it later."

Maeve looked disgruntled, but thankfully, she didn't press the issue.

How to discuss it with her? Many of those vagabonds were veterans, and it turned Tom's stomach to think that those men had given everything to their country but were given nothing in return.

Yet as Tom had discovered, voting against the bill meant alienating the Duke of Brookhurst and ending Maeve's chance of marrying the duke's son.

I can't let anything come between Maeve and Lord Stacey. At least one of the two Powell offspring would marry for love—precisely why he had to do everything he could to ensure their marriage happened.

Including his decision to never again visit the Orchid Club, or see Lucia.

His chest throbbed, and he rubbed it absently. It was as though the seeds of Lucia's true self had been planted in his heart and pushed out seeking roots, holding firmly to him.

He'd never know more about her, and that was for the best. What he'd learned of her—the courage she had to come to England from a faraway place, the expert way she managed the establishment, the pain she'd faced—made him ache with the need to know more, to understand her better. Which would never happen.

Despite his fatigue, restlessness pushed him to his feet, and he paced to the fireplace to watch the flames crackle.

"I'm glad one of my children recognizes the importance of marriage." His mother rose from the sofa.

"Mam," Tom said without turning around, "Father's hardly in the grave. Must we discuss this now?"

"If you're to fully embrace your responsibilities, yes. Tommy lad, look at me."

She had iron in her voice, as she always did whenever she commanded her offspring to obey.

As she approached, he faced her with his hands clasped behind his back, and schooled his features to look attentive.

"The getting of a legitimate heir cannot be done as a bachelor," she said. "A bride is a necessity, as is a son. You need both as the Duke of Northfield." She put a hand on his shoulder. "At the least, *consider* beginning your hunt for a bride. It would make me happy to know you have someone to care for you into your dotage."

He traded a look with Maeve. They both knew how expertly Mam troweled on guilt.

"I'll consider it."

"That's all I want."

A polite cough sounded from the doorway. He turned to see Norley, the butler, standing just inside the parlor.

"Yes?" Tom asked, grateful for the interruption.

"You have a visitor, Your Grace."

"We're not accepting visitors for weeks." Surprising that Norley, who knew quite well the rules for mourning, would suggest a caller during this time. "Is it a business matter?"

"In a manner of speaking, Your Grace. Forgive my importunity, Your Grace, but may I discuss this with you in the corridor?"

Maeve answered Tom's questioning look with a shrug. Baffled, Tom followed the butler from the room. He couldn't fathom what visitor was so pressing that Norley would break from custom and permit entrance to anyone. The mystery urged Tom into motion.

Norley moved down the corridor, until they were some distance from the parlor.

"If it is business," Tom said brusquely as he planted his hands on his hips, "have Mr. Ludlow take his particulars and make an appointment."

His secretary could make the necessary arrangements with his schedule.

"Forgive my insistence, Your Grace," the butler said, "but this visitor is quite important. And, might I add, your father always kept this appointment."

Tom frowned. "My father?"

"Yes, Your Grace. Today is the allotted day that

your father met this person. The twenty-first of each month."

"This is the only time I've heard of it."

During the final weeks of the old duke's illness, Tom had been thoroughly briefed in all the responsibilities he would soon shoulder. The attorneys and men of business had been quite exhaustive as they enumerated his future duties, down to the semiannual meetings with his private tobacconist.

No one had mentioned an important visitor who arrived on the twenty-first of every month.

"Fine. Show him up."

There was a brief pause before Norley spoke. "Your father always met this person in the larder."

The larder?

"And," the butler continued, "I strongly urge you to do the same. If I may be so bold, Your Grace."

Curiosity jabbed at him, urging him to investigate this mysterious appointment that his father kept every month in the larder.

"Very well."

"Do you need directions to the larder, Your Grace?"

"I should say not." A corner of his mouth hitched up. "No crock of jam or loaf of bread was safe from my midnight raids."

"Cook always baked extra bread just for you, Your Grace."

"Did he?" Gratified, Tom lifted his brows. "Be sure to increase his wages."

"Very good, Your Grace." The butler bowed and backed away, but Tom was already in motion.

Servants bowed and scurried out of his way as he strode belowstairs, his feet quick from curiosity. The lower part of the house was less known to him—it had always caused a stir whenever he'd been down here during regular hours. But Northfield House was still his home, and he found the larder quickly.

Wary and slightly annoyed at the visitor's intrusion, Tom used his knuckles to push the door to the larder open before stepping inside.

He started in astonishment when he found not a man, but a woman. She wore a crimson redingote and matching bonnet, and her slim back was turned to him.

In response to this unexpected surprise, his heart sped. Instinctively, Tom shut the door. If there was some kind of trouble, he needed to protect his family from it.

"Madam," he said sternly, "explain yourself."

The woman turned around, revealing a face of bold beauty. Her gaze met his, and they both jolted.

He rasped, "Lucia?"

Her eyes went wide as color leeched from her face. She stared at him for a long time, and then she lifted her hand as though she meant to touch him. But her fingers curled into a fist and she lowered it to her side. Yet she didn't unclench her hand.

They both went motionless with shock as the air vibrated with tension.

"Tom?" Her voice was barely a whisper. "You're . . . the Duke of Northfield's son? You are the duke now?"

"I am," he said warily. He felt himself treading on a path littered with snares. One false step could mean disaster.

She frowned, and then reached into her reticule and produced a substantial stack of cash.

Her voice turned businesslike. "This belongs to you, Your Grace."

Tom didn't move to take the money. "I don't understand."

"Your father didn't mention me?" Dismay edged her voice.

Cautiously, he said, "Nary a word."

Tom certainly would have remembered his father discussing a meeting in the larder with the woman who managed the Orchid Club. He eyed the large wad of pound notes.

She held it out to him.

"As I said, it was supposed to go to the late duke, but now it's yours."

"Ah," Tom said, finally understanding. "My father loaned you money, and now you've come to repay it."

"Your Grace, you misunderstand." She stepped closer. "What I give to you now represents your father's share in my establishment's profits. You see, your father created that establishment. And now *you*, Your Grace, are the club's owner."

Tom's heart seized in his chest as his brain furiously churned to make sense of what Lucia had just said.

"Your attempt at humor is not welcome." His words were cutting.

"I am not endeavoring to be comical," she said gravely.

A fiery tide of anger rose up within him.

"Slander's your game, then." The very idea that his father might have owned the Orchid Club was beyond preposterous. "My apologies," he added bitingly, "but your attempt at blackmail is a failure."

Lucia held up the stack of cash.

"Blackmail would be a new endeavor for me, but I do know that the perpetrator does not offer her intended victim money."

"There's no other reason for you to say something so utterly ludicrous."

He folded his arms across his chest as his body tightened with fury everywhere. What she suggested was outright defamatory. His father was newly dead, and here she was, spreading calumny about the late duke. There was only one reason why she would make such allegations.

Hard to believe that less than twelve hours before, he and Lucia had been exploring every inch of each other's bodies. Had he unknowingly bedded a blackmailer?

"I've spoken a few falsehoods in my life. This is not one of those times." She drew a breath. "Eighteen years ago, your father entered into a business arrangement with Mrs. Nancy Chalke, a known procuress. The intent was to operate a secret society that catered to the sexual desires of all classes and all inclinations. Through intermediaries, he purchased a home in Bloomsbury which would house the establishment. You know that as of one year ago, I replaced Mrs. Chalke as the operation's manager. Part of my responsibilities is delivering the owner's share of the monthly profits. And here I am," she said with a nod, "giving you—the new patron—your portion of the establishment's take."

He struggled to make sense of the tale she told him. Could he believe any of it? Could he trust her at all? He fought reconciling the woman before him with his lover from last night.

Tom had felt her lips against his and caressed her lavish curves. She'd stroked her hands all over his body, taken him into herself. He'd lapped at her like a starving man, drank her down with ravenous gulps.

Now heat washed through him, burning his face and collecting in his groin. Potent attraction blazed between them, even in the midst of this madness.

"I cannot believe you." The world shifted and spun around him. He pressed the heel of his hand to his forehead.

"What I've said is a surprise to you—"

"A goddamned earthquake," he spit out.

Despite his clipped words, her expression softened.

Gently, she said, "The death of a parent . . . it's no easy burden to bear. I understand. And you have my sympathy," she continued. "It cannot be comfortable knowing that your father kept secrets."

The world had turned to chaos. Nothing could be relied upon. If his father *was* the club's patron, could Tom trust that even the walls of Northfield House would remain standing? Or would one light touch of his fingers level the mansion?

"No mistress," he said in a harsh, grating voice. "No gambling debts, no bribes. No." He made another sound that approximated laughter. "Father owned a goddamned sex club. Made money from it. From people wearing masks and *fucking*."

Though the pursed set of her lips showed her sympathy for his situation, her eyes were clear and full of purpose.

"He did," she said in a placating tone, "and kept his reasons for doing so to himself. Neither you nor I can guess at his motivation, but there's something both of us cannot ignore." Gingerly, she took a half step toward him. "The club exists, and as manager, I must do my duty by it."

"Speak plainly," he said, unable to keep the edge from his voice.

"Keeping the establishment going is my responsibility, but that rests on whether or not *you* want to keep it open."

He reeled with the implication of her words, his

stomach clenched tightly as if he protected himself from punches.

"I—" He cupped his forehead with his hand. The world had devolved into a spinning whirligig of noise and light, and nothing made sense.

His father, a model of virtue and a faultless husband, had also owned the Orchid Club. The two notions were completely incompatible.

Frantically, he searched for the lie in Lucia's words, picking them apart. If she oversaw the establishment, she'd damage herself by going public with information about its owner. And, as she'd said, blackmailers didn't give money to their intended victims.

Nausea choked him. Should anyone ever find out about the late Duke of Northfield owning a club engineered so people could fuck anonymously, the family name would be ripped to tatters. The hell with his own reputation, but what about his mother? What about Maeve?

His sister's marriage to Hugh would never happen, not if the Duke of Brookhurst knew about the family connection to the Orchid Club. She'd be shamed into hiding, along with Tom's mother. Exile would be their sole option, seeking refuge in faraway places.

Jesus God, this was a fucking disaster.

"There's no need for anyone to learn that your father owned the club," she said reasonably. "That confidence has been kept. No one is truly harmed by the operation's existence. If anything, it brings pleasure and happiness to many. And," she added, coming a little closer, "you and I are the only two who know that you've succeeded your father as patron. Discretion has kept me housed and fed for many years. I'd never ruin my own livelihood by going public. So you see," she said gently, "the club can continue on as it has. Everyone profits."

She looked at him expectantly.

Fuck. She wanted him to make a decision *now*?

"I don't know," he finally ground out.

A frown creased her brow.

"Surely there's no debate," she said, as if it was perfectly reasonable for someone to decide the fate of his family in a matter of moments.

Anger bubbled up again, that he should be put in this position—by his father, by her.

"Goddamn it, I said I don't know!" Only when she stepped back cautiously did he realize he was shouting, and the sound reverberated off the walls of the larder. "I need time."

Her mouth opened and then closed, her expression smoothing out and becoming unreadable. After a moment, she set the thick bundle of money on a cabinet.

"This still belongs to you."

She took a step toward him and laid a hand on his forearm.

Instinctively, he leaned into her touch, craving the comfort that she had given him for a year, seeking the pleasure they'd made together. But she was a woman far more complicated than he'd ever imagined.

He pulled his arm away.

She watched him draw back, and an expression of grim determination settled on her face before she straightened.

"Before you make your decision," she said, "grant me one favor. Come to the club tomorrow night."

He frowned. "It's closed on Fridays."

"When your father died, I feared that the club's days might be limited." She spread her hands open. "So I've changed it to twice a week to ensure that the staff and I could glean the most profit from it with the time we had remaining."

He was torn between anger that she could be so mercenary in the midst of death and admiration for her drive.

"I'm to come to the club and do what exactly?"

"See what it's truly like, not as a place where people go to have sex, but as a business."

"The money there proves it's a business," he said coldly. He nodded toward the bundle of cash.

"Please," she entreated, "just come. And don't dress too finely." When he remained silent, she nodded, as if resigned. "That's all I will say on the matter. At present."

She moved past him and opened the larder door.

For a heartbeat, she hesitated. But he couldn't move, couldn't speak, pinned in place by disbelief, anger, and confusion.

Then she was gone, shutting the door behind her.

He staggered to the pound notes resting atop the

cabinet. His hand hovered over the money, yet his fingers refused to close around the stack of cash, no matter how much he commanded himself to take hold of it.

Because once he did, everything would become real.

Chapter 9

✦

$\mathcal{L}$ucia found Kitty and Elspeth in the kitchen, the scents of frying sausages filling the air with the aromas of domesticity. Elspeth sat at a small circular table and played with Liam as he sat on her lap, while Kitty stood over the hob, tending the food.

The moment Lucia stepped into the chamber, her friends both looked at her with expressions of expectancy.

"And?" Kitty asked anxiously.

"Was he very horrified?" Elspeth added.

Lucia drifted into the room. She set a pale blue box tied with brown satin ribbon on the long table in the center of the kitchen. It was her habit, on the day of the month that she delivered the owner's portion of the profits, to stop at Catton's on her way home.

"Cherry-and-plum tart for you," she said to Elspeth, then glanced at Kitty, "and ginger cake for you. I . . . was too distracted to get anything for myself."

"Much as I appreciate you bringing us sweets," Kitty said, taking the pan off the fire, "bugger the cakes.

What happened with the new owner? Did he scream? Laugh? Set slavering dogs on you?"

Lucia leaned against the table, both weary and humming with nervous energy. As briefly as she could, she explained what had happened in the larder of the duke's Mayfair home. When she was done, she looked back and forth between her friends' stunned faces.

"Damnation." Elspeth blew out a breath. "You'd no idea who he was when you rogered him senseless?"

"None," Lucia answered.

Her own mind spun with the knowledge of who Tom truly was. The world had turned completely on its head, leaving her dizzy and disoriented.

"What a damn muddle," Kitty said ruefully. She dished up the sausages and brought the plates over to the smaller table where Elspeth sat with Liam. She offered a plate to Lucia, but set it down when Lucia waved it away. "He didn't know about his father's ownership of this place, either?"

"If I'd shown up at his door and told him he was the next king of Napoli, he wouldn't have looked so surprised." Needing to move and release some of her uneasiness, Lucia pushed away from the table to pace. "Oh, but the horror on his face when I told him."

Elspeth transferred the bundle of Liam over to Kitty, who placed him in a tall chair.

"But he'd come here all the time," Elspeth said, "so why be horrified? It's not as though he walked a straight and moral path."

"Can't say." Baffled, Lucia lifted her shoulders in

a shrug, as if that one gesture could encapsulate the whole of her utter confusion. The man who'd adored her body with such skill wasn't merely a duke, he controlled the fate of her livelihood—and her dreams.

She'd broken her own rule of getting involved with a guest, and look what it had brought her. Nothing but turmoil.

"Whatever his reasons, I told him not to make up his mind about the fate of the club. Not until at least tomorrow night."

"Got something planned?" Kitty picked up a small piece of sliced pear and handed it to Liam, who promptly began to gum it.

Lucia's thoughts raced into catastrophic scenarios, yet preparing for these disasters had helped her stay nimble—and saved her hide—many times.

"I thought to give him a tour of the place," she said, like a general planning a battle. "Let him see that this isn't merely a place where people screw—it's a business that supports over a dozen people. That's got to make him decide in our favor." She said this as if she could convince herself of the outcome, as if speaking aloud her greatest hope made it more likely to come true.

"Let us hope so," Elspeth said grimly. "Thinking about finding another job makes me woozy. How do I tell a potential employer that my last work experience consisted of doing the accounting for a sex club?"

"On the positive side," Kitty said in a bright voice,

cutting a slice of sausage, "your future employer will know you aren't easy to distract." She popped a morsel into her mouth and smiled.

"You're the only thing that distracts me." Elspeth reached across the table and took Kitty's free hand. The two shared a tender look, fraught with intimacy.

Dio mio, Lucia thought as she looked back and forth between Kitty and Elspeth. *Never saw* that *coming. I've got my head buried in my own* culo, *and didn't notice my two closest friends falling in love.*

A throb of envy pulsed through her. She could never have that in her life, not without opening herself up to devastation and disaster. Just a single night with Tom had knocked her legs out from under her.

Elspeth squeezed Kitty's hand before letting go and starting in on her own meal.

"Think he'll show tomorrow?" Elspeth asked.

Glancing around the room, Lucia took in the kitchen that had seen not just the preparation of elegant delicacies, but simple, homey meals like the one her two friends enjoyed at that moment.

She'd always hoped that one day she could turn the running of the club over to a successor, and she, Kitty, and Elspeth could live next door to the girls' home. They'd all labor together to run the home—Elspeth in charge of the ledgers, Kitty overseeing the hiring and management of staff, and Lucia supervising everything while providing some teaching. There would be at least one orange tabby cat. Liam would grow up with two dozen adopted sisters, and the world would be, finally, secure.

"I can't say—I'm no astronomer," Lucia said wearily, and exhaled. "Even if I was, it's too smoky here in London to read the stars."

All she could do was hope, but hope seldom made for a sound foundation. Without warning, the whole structure could collapse, burying you alive underneath the rubble of your dreams.

Tom barely waited for the butler to announce him before striding into the Duke of Greyland's cavernous study. His friend stood at his approach and came forward with his hand extended. Tom inhaled, willing his body to stop vibrating with tension.

"Are all the chophouses and gaming hells closed?" Greyland asked as they shook. He frowned at their clasped hands, as though feeling the emotion that made Tom shake.

Tom pulled away.

"I went to the nearest den of ill repute and they advised me to come here," he said in a distracted voice. He glanced behind his friend and eyed the sheaves of documents stacked upon the desk. "That's become a familiar sight." He grimaced.

"Now you and I are both at the summit of mountains," Greyland acknowledged, "trying to keep from drowning in a sea of paper."

His legs needing to move, Tom strode to the carved stone fireplace and stared down into it. Behind their screen, the flames shifted and danced, as restless as he felt.

"Far be it from me to keep you from running the duchy." Tom fought to stop himself from pounding his fist into the stone. Words hovered at the tip of his tongue, but should he speak them? "I shouldn't have come. You're busy and—"

"Join me for a stroll in the garden," Greyland said with an air that was both genial and commanding.

Tom looked toward the windows, noting the film of frost collecting along the edges of the panes. "November gardens make for chilly strolls," he noted drily.

"You're equipped for it." His friend nodded at Tom's caped greatcoat. "All I need is to outfit myself similarly." Greyland went to the bellpull and tugged it. When the butler appeared, Greyland said, "My coat, and two folding knives."

"Yes, Your Grace." The butler bowed, then backed from the room.

Body still jangling, Tom walked the perimeter of the study. He held out his hand, touching the spines of countless shelved books as he passed. Now that he was here, uncertainty about his planned confession clung to him.

"How fares the duchess?" he asked.

"Marvelous well. She's the summer in the long winter that had been my existence."

Tom didn't have to look at Greyland to see the smile in his friend's voice.

A moment later, the butler appeared with his master's coat. "The knives, Your Grace," he added, pulling two folded blades from his pocket.

"One for me," Greyland directed his servant, "one for the Duke of Northfield."

Tom took an ebony-handled knife from the butler. "Plan on forcing me to fight you for my life?"

"All shall become comprehensible, if you can manage to endure a two-minute wait." Greyland waved off his servant's offer of assistance and slipped his arms into his coat. "There. We are fortified. Follow me."

Moments later, Tom and his friend ambled the gravel paths that wove through Greyland's substantial garden, the stones crunching beneath their boots. Tom struggled to keep his stride easy, though he wanted to run and run until his legs gave out beneath him. He made himself look around and study his surroundings. Trees planted alongside the paths reached bare arms up to the ash-colored sky, and the fountains were dry vessels holding crisp, brown leaves. The rose bushes had all been trimmed back, as well.

But not everything was asleep or dead in Greyland's garden. An ambitious gardener had planted late-flowering shrubs, and more silvery frost-glazed leaves and grasses. It held a spare, stern beauty.

"Going for a ride or taking a walk in the park means we risk being set upon by importunate MPs," Greyland said, his breath misting the air. "The garden gives us room to move without having to endure fulsome, ingratiating praise or heated jeremiads."

"Surprised anyone would subject dukes to a lecture," Tom said in disbelief. "And lecturing *you,* well, that takes bollocks of iron."

A corner of Greyland's mouth hitched. "A rare occurrence, but when one proposes levying higher taxes on this nation's most affluent, one should expect a certain amount of protestations." His friend bent down and picked up two slender branches which lay across the path. He handed one to Tom.

"We're to practice our ripostes and feints?" Tom swung the branch like a fencing sabre through the air.

"Observe." Greyland produced his knife and used the blade to scrape off bark. He leaned against a low wall. "Whittling isn't just for sailors and farmers."

Tom watched Greyland for several moments, learning the way of moving a knife over wood, and then his own hands quickly fell into the rhythm of whittling, and fragile calm settled over him. Which, he supposed, had been Greyland's intention all along.

They worked silently for several moments, the only sounds coming from the rasp of metal against wood. Within the confines of Tom's mind, however, all was noise and confusion as though a dozen carriages collided.

He careened off into the ether, nothing holding him down or keeping him steady. His father—the source of his gravity—had been proven to be full of duplicity and secrets, and with that gone, the world had no balance.

The blade of his knife skittered across the wood he

held, and he narrowly missed cutting the hell out of his finger. He cursed softly.

"I've something to tell you," he said abruptly. "Something that cannot be repeated. To anyone—that goes for the duchess, as well."

"I'd trust Cass with everything, including my life."

"I can take no chances." Tom tried to shove away his need to speak to someone, anyone. "Never mind—I'll not burden you with it."

He moved to stride away, but Greyland's hand on his arm stopped him. "I swear to you," his friend said, his tone low and sincere, "I'll tell no one of your confidence."

Tom drew in a breath. "Have you heard of the Orchid Club?" It seemed unlikely, given his friend's moral rectitude, and Tom never discussed his weekly visits to the establishment with anyone.

A stain of color appeared on Greyland's cheeks, surprising Tom. "I am aware of it."

Well . . . how unforeseen.

But he couldn't be distracted by his astonishment. "It . . ." He struggled to speak, even as the demand to confess pushed him from the inside out. Finally, he blurted, "My father owned it. And now I do."

To his credit, Greyland's expression barely changed, save for his brows edging up slightly. "That is unexpected."

"I only learned this afternoon. The manager delivered my share of the profits today."

Better to leave out the fact that Tom and the manager had just spent a torrid night together—it would only complicate an already thorny situation.

"My father," he growled. "*My father.* He'd deliberately positioned himself as a bastion of decency, while maintaining ownership of the Orchid Club."

Tom threw his branch away, and it careened in a spinning arc over the hedges. He felt himself in a similar trajectory, flung into the air as he twisted in confusion.

"If anyone learned of this," he said tightly, "the family name would be destroyed. My mother, Maeve— they'd have to retreat from Society entirely. How can Maeve marry with the disgrace poisoning her reputation? *Fuck.*" A crushing weight pressed down.

His father had willingly gambled with the welfare of his family, courted scandal. And Tom would never know why the late duke would take such a risk.

Greyland faced him. "The manager intends to blackmail you?"

"She'll maintain her silence," Tom said with certainty.

His friend began to walk again and Tom kept pace beside him. In a clipped voice, Greyland said, "You'll need to decide your next course of action."

"There's the hell of it," Tom snarled. "I don't know what to do."

"While Ellingsworth—I mean, Lord Blakemere— knows military strategy," Greyland said, "I'm an expert when it comes to navigating the treacherous waters of Society. Every step must be considered, weighed, analyzed."

"Not my usual modus operandi," Tom said wryly. "This entire world of respectability is not on my map. *Here be dragons.*"

"The dragons will swallow you and your family whole if you're not careful, and do it all with a haughty smirk." His friend shot him a measuring look. "The safest course would be to shutter the club immediately."

"The safest course," Tom said grimly, "isn't necessarily the kindest action."

"You have your family's reputation at stake." Greyland frowned. "What other factors need to be considered?"

Lucia's plea spun around Tom's head in dizzying circles. Her dark eyes haunted him—as did the feel of her skin.

Grant me one favor. Come to the club tomorrow night.

"For the first thirty-two years of my life," he said, stopping beside the dry fountain, "I'd done everything I could to ensure my life was as uncomplicated as possible. Now I'm trapped in a maze. In the dark."

"Whatever your choice," Greyland said with surprising kindness, "I know you'll act with the best of intentions."

"And pave the road to Hell with them." Bitterness coated Tom's words.

"You need not be perfect, Northfield," Greyland said. "What matters is here." He knocked the side of his fist into Tom's chest, and Tom rocked back slightly from his friend's strength.

"Mayhap you won't be the best," Greyland said sagely, "but you'll do your best."

Sudden emotion thickened in Tom's throat. "So it's true, then."

"What's true?" His friend looked puzzled.

"That Her Grace performed the same magic as Aphrodite did for Pygmalion. Turned cold ivory into flesh."

Greyland's frown deepened, yet amusement in his gaze softened its severity. "I wasn't made of ivory, goddamn it." His lips quirked. "I was granite." His expression sobered. "I don't know if I provided you any solace."

"An opportunity to vent is always welcome." In truth, though nothing had been resolved, Tom noted how the punishing weight of secrets felt a little lighter, his breath coming easier.

His friend's low, quick laugh turned to vapor in the chill air. "Let's repair inside for some excellent brandy before our nethers become frostbitten. You'll stay for supper, of course."

A night watching Greyland and his duchess trading secret, loving smiles? Tom would much rather be in bed with Amina—Lucia—disporting themselves until sunrise.

Good Christ, she was *in his employ.*

Yet for all the complications between them, he needed to decide what to do about the club. It would be so much easier to simply pretend there was only one risk associated with it—the threat to his family— but Lucia had been adamant that he consider the live-lihoods of the establishment's staff.

Though he'd seen the masked men and women who provided refreshments and kept the place orderly, he knew nothing about them. And he would never know, unless he took Lucia up on her offer and observed how the club truly functioned. To see it as a business.

He'd often accused his father of not seeing the other side of an argument, and willfully sticking to one ver-sion of the truth. If Tom didn't go to the Orchid Club to see it behind the scenes, he'd be guilty of the same determined ignorance—and *that,* he couldn't tolerate.

His resolve firmed. On the morrow, he'd return to the club, not as a guest, but as the owner.

"My thanks," he said, trailing after Greyland as they climbed the steps to the terrace. "We will have that sup-per together some other time. I'll make for poor com-pany tonight."

"As you wish." Greyland held the French door that opened into a rear-facing parlor. "It's probably for the best. Cassandra would challenge you to a game of cards, and I have it on excellent authority that she cheats."

Chapter 10

❦

"*A* profitable Friday night," Elspeth said as she and Lucia awaited guests in the foyer.

"It's not yet eleven," Lucia felt obliged to point out. Like bees buzzing in her belly, nerves made themselves known. "The crowd might thin."

"Or, there might be a rush at midnight and we'll have our best evening yet. The prince himself might come a-calling." Elspeth wrapped an arm around Lucia's shoulders. "Anything might happen."

"That's the beauty of chance," Lucia said. "It can't be predicted."

There were two risks tonight—adding a second night to the Orchid Club's hours of operation, and the possibility of Tom coming.

The evening's take might not be enough to compensate for the staff's extra hours of employment. She would feel the loss more keenly than anyone. She refused to deprive her workers, so she'd set aside her own money, just to be certain that her poor business decision didn't cost anyone but herself.

And if Tom didn't show . . . if he decided to simply close the club . . .

Risks were familiar territory. She knew them as well as others knew with certainty the rising of the tides. In Napoli, her mother played the *lotteria* every Saturday, and though Antonia couldn't read, she knew *La Smorfia* by heart. Whatever appeared to her in dreams found its corresponding number in the pages of that book, and both she and her daughter eagerly awaited the *lotteria*'s drawing, hoping against hope for a way out of poverty. They would dream of leaving the overcrowded, shabby Quartieri Spagnoli, retiring to a villa in Posillipo to live out the rest of their days in abundance and peace.

Every week, Lucia and her mother would be disappointed. But that never stopped Antonia from playing again the following Saturday.

When Lucia would ask her mother why she threw away good money on the slim chance that they might win, Antonia always said, *If you take no risks, nothing changes.*

Lucia would not be mired in a present where the world did not alter. There was always *more* and *better*—for herself, and the people she cared for.

But for once in her life, she wanted things to stay exactly as they were, with the club open and Kitty, Elspeth, and the staff all gainfully employed. It all rested on Tom.

"What will you do if he doesn't show?" Elspeth asked, as if reading Lucia's thoughts.

"We'll go on as we have," Lucia said with more conviction than she felt.

Elspeth dropped her arm. "Until he decides to shut us down."

"*If* he decides." She said this as much to remind herself as Elspeth. It was a foolish belief to think that if she spoke with enough conviction, it might make something come to pass. "Perhaps he'll permit us to keep our doors open."

The knock sounded, with a corresponding leap in Lucia's chest. Elspeth strode to the door and opened it. She walked slowly backward into the foyer as a man stepped inside.

His gaze went immediately to Lucia, and her breath caught in her chest.

"*These* are your lesser-quality clothes?" she demanded.

She eyed Tom from the black satin mask on his face to the tips of his barely scuffed boots. Everything in between—coat, waistcoat, breeches—would easily suffice as a banker's Sunday finest. As it was, every inch of Tom looked elegant, though slightly raffish from his incipient beard, and utterly delicious.

He held out his arms, and the fabric of his coat clung adoringly to the breadth of his shoulders.

"It was either this," he said drily, "or pay my groom for the loan of his clothing."

"Nothing to be done for it. You're here now." Lucia stepped closer, and his eyes flashed hotly as she neared, while her body hummed from his presence.

Oh, she hadn't forgotten their night together, either. She glanced at Elspeth. "No introductions tonight, but you're no strangers to each other."

Elspeth and Tom exchanged wary nods.

At that moment, Will lumbered into the foyer. "No problems up front, Amina?"

"None," Lucia answered. She waved to Tom. "Thinking about hiring this bloke, so I'm giving him a tour of the place."

"Best of luck, mate," Will said affably, giving Tom a wink. "Hope you don't got a maidenly disposition."

"Far from it," Tom said.

"Then you'll fit right in." With that, Will ambled back to his post.

"I've got the door," Elspeth said in the silence. "Go ahead with our, ah, prospective hire."

Fighting off a fresh wave of anxiety, Lucia straightened. She had precisely what she wanted—Tom was here, and willing to at the least hear her out—but now the true work of the night was to begin. Saints preserve her, hopefully she did right by her staff.

"Other than myself and the staff, you know this place best." She used her most efficient and competent tone as she led him from the entryway down the corridor to the drawing room. "Doubtless, you could draw a map if tasked to do so. But there's more to the club than its geography."

They entered the drawing room. People lost themselves in revelry and the pursuit of pleasure, the air was saturated with the thick scent of sex, and everywhere was bared flesh slick with sweat. But her gaze wasn't on the guests. Her attention rested solely on him.

Despite her worry, she lost herself for a moment in the impeccable lines of his profile, her attention fixing on the shape of his mouth.

She shook her head, struggling to regain focus. Crisply, she said, "Tell me what you see."

His alert, perceptive gaze scanned the room. "Servants circulating with trays. Some carry glasses and wine, others bear platters of sweetmeats and small plates."

"A guest should never have to ask for anything. Whatever they desire should just appear, as if by magic. But there's no enchantment here."

"Only tireless work," he said thoughtfully.

Her heart kicked with gratification that he noticed what she wanted him to see. "Two things are imperative when running an establishment such as this. You might be able to guess them."

"Service," he said after a pause.

"Precisely. And cleanliness." She nodded as two of the staff swept through the room, collecting empty glasses and plates and rearranging furniture as they went. "They ensure that guests can lose themselves for a few hours, the real world kept at bay."

Tom tilted his head toward Arthur standing discreetly in a shadowy corner of the room. "The hired muscle."

"You've met him. He and our other gent make frequent passes through the club's rooms to ensure everyone's safety. Staff go to them if they spot potentially troublesome behavior." She made a wry face. "They also keep the water closets clean."

Tom gave a soft snort. "Never considered the privy."

"We have to," she said with a nod. "We have to consider everything. The value of my staff cannot be calculated. They're as essential to the running of the club as blood is to the body."

Thinking of her dutiful, diligent workers, her chest swelled with mingled pleasure and care.

Tom observed the staff discreetly keeping the machine of the club running. His lips compressed and, even with the mask, his expressive face showed that he carefully considered each new piece of information.

"What I know of your life could fill a teacup," she said lowly. "Doubtless you own many properties, have shares in countless businesses. Hundreds of people depend on you for their livelihoods."

"Intermediaries manage a portion of my holdings," he said as if by habit.

"But the massive responsibility of . . . your position . . . that falls to you." She shot him a sidelong glance. "My responsibility is the Orchid Club. The scale's smaller, but the weight of responsibility is just as great."

A corner of his mouth turned up. "Funny."

"How so?" she pressed.

"We don't just share attraction." His gaze sizzled as he looked at her, and her body softened and heated in response. "We also share the burdens of duty."

"So we do." It was admirable, really, that she could keep her voice level when he spoke to her like this.

Stay on task.

With a nod for him to follow her, she strode from the drawing room into the ballroom. She noted with approval how he gazed not at the guests disporting themselves on the dance floor, but at the subtle, constant movement of the staff.

"They're never still," he said quietly. "And yet I barely noticed them until tonight."

"We learn how not to be seen."

His piercing gaze shifted to her. "I always saw you."

Her hand throbbed with the need to touch him, to slide her palm up his chest and feel the strength of his body. But yielding to attraction would only complicate matters—and imperil her heart.

"The workers here have always supported my innovations," she said as neutrally as she could manage. "They, like I, believe that we ought to give the guests exactly what they want, and we should also make changes so the guests are compelled to return again and again." Her gaze flicked to the empty stage at one end of the ballroom, and then to the musicians in the far corner. "After I presented the idea to the staff, they were in favor of adding both performances and music."

"Haven't seen a performance in some time," he noted.

"Admittedly, I haven't been attentive to maintaining them, but that should be remedied. Guests seemed to enjoy watching the spectacle."

"The addition of music was a clever one." He eyed her with admiration. "That's how the former proprietress came to choose you as her successor, by presenting her with good ideas."

Lucia permitted herself a little smile. She *had* worked damned hard to get to where she was, and she felt a glow of gratification that he saw her labors as commendable.

"I made sure she saw me as invaluable," she said primly.

She'd been one of Mrs. Chalke's girls at a brothel on St. Martin's Lane near Covent Garden, and when given the prospect to work one night a week away from the house, seized the chance. Opportunity was ripe, and she wouldn't let it rot on the vine.

"It was quick," she continued, "my movement from serving refreshments to overseeing the ordering of wine and supplies for the kitchen."

"I wager even that wasn't enough," he said approvingly.

"It wasn't," she said, which was a simple way of describing her measureless ambition.

Neapolitans all adored the *commedia* character Pulcinella. They cheered his antics, laughed at his ridiculous schemes, and empathized with his perpetually empty belly. But Lucia had always breathlessly awaited the appearance of Columbina on the stage. The wily, flirtatious character was always one step ahead of everyone else, and though she was a servant, she expertly manipulated situations to her mistress's advantage.

As a girl roaming the streets of Napoli, earning coin and favors by running errands and serving as an intermediary in the constant shift of things and services, Lucia had dreamt not of becoming an actress and performing the role of Columbina, but to *be* Columbina. To run the show, to be perpetually aware—to be, ultimately, the powerful force behind the scenes.

"One added duty wasn't enough to content me," she said with a tip of her head. "Maneuvered myself into hiring and training new staff, paying off local law enforcement, tallying the night's receipts."

Hardly had Mrs. Chalke a notion to undertake a task before Lucia completed it for her. *Shrewd gel*, Mrs. Chalke had said with a knowing smirk. *That's the way we get ourselves out of the gutter. Cunning and determination.*

"The Orchid Club belongs to you," she said in a matter-of-fact tone, "but it flourishes because it's *mine*. More than that, the staff wants for nothing because of my constant attention. I keep their wages high, protect them when they are threatened, and make allowances when they're unable to perform their duties."

She'd never acknowledged her own work—not at such length, and not aloud—but to speak of it now filled her with a surge of pride, as if liquid light flowed through her veins. It was too easy to dismiss accomplishments and dwell only on the negative.

But to do so meant robbing herself of purpose, of joy. She couldn't let that happen.

Confidently, he said, "They appreciate your efforts on their behalf."

She'd heard it from their mouths, but always fretted that it wasn't enough, that nothing she did would ever be enough. Why didn't she believe them? They wouldn't lie. At the very least, they wouldn't stay with her for this long. Yet they had. She drew strength from that.

"We're all living this dangerous, brutal world together," she said. "Merely surviving isn't enough. The least we can do is care for one another." A wave of emotion swept through her, but she didn't want to give him the impression that she was easily agitated. Trying to regain her equilibrium, she ran a hand down the front of her skirts. "Let's move on. There's more to see."

In short order, they visited the small pantry upstairs where Lottie cleaned glasses and plates as well as the chamber set aside for guests who had grown unruly or lethargic from too much drink. Drowsing people sprawled on mattresses piled on the floor, while George, a member of the staff, watched over them.

"Though the establishment provides only two glasses of wine," she explained softly so as not to wake anyone, "occasionally, they arrive having already imbibed. We try to turn them away, but they slip through from time to time. Our enforcers bring them here to rest until they've regained control of themselves, and then we have this good fellow minding them as tenderly as a shepherd with his flock."

"They're not a bad sort," George said affably. "Just a little disguised, is all."

"Seems as though you've a thankless task," Tom said. "Sitting here, watching this lot sleep off their drink."

"Ah, no," George answered with cheer. "I don't mind it. Gives me a chance to catch up on my reading." He held up a newspaper. "Amina buys a paper for the house, and us that know our letters get a chance to thumb through it. At our staff meal, she'll sometimes read aloud so that them that ain't got their letters know what's what in the world."

Tom nodded thoughtfully, his gaze flicking to her.

When she and Tom stepped back into the darkened hallway, Tom asked, "What of those guests who will not go quietly to their rest? Do they threaten you with exposure?"

"No one will speak of us, lest they tarnish their own reputations. And anyone who gets obstreperous here . . . well, one of our gents supplements his income with prizefighting, and the other grew up the middle of eight children."

"Ah." Tom's lips curved. "I was the elder, and the heir. It was my job to look out for my sister. She pestered me as little sisters do—always running after me and demanding I allow her to join in whatever I was about—but she was reluctant to smash her fist into my face. So I joined a pugilism academy to ensure I underwent the experience."

She donned a sorrowful expression. "You have endured a life of deprivation."

"Indeed, madam, I am much to be pitied." The corners of his eyes crinkled.

Intimacy wove between them. Part of her wanted to shrink back and remain protected, but he drew her ever forward, into his natural warmth.

"There must be more," he added.

Through her lashes, she gazed askance at him, her heart thumping. She couldn't stop herself from saying breathlessly, "There is always more."

Someone cleared their throat. Lucia spun around to see Kitty standing nearby, wearing a pained expression.

A flush rose to Lucia's cheeks. She needed to remain businesslike and detached with Tom, and here she was, flirting outrageously.

"Apologies for interrupting." Kitty edged closer. "There's a predicament in the kitchen that requires your attendance."

"I'll be there presently," she said briskly. Straightening, she followed Kitty down the corridor. To her surprise, Tom was close at her heels.

"I mean to see everything," he said when she threw him an inquisitive look.

In short order, they were belowstairs where the relative quiet above seemed a remote memory. Staff members rushed back and forth with trays, some empty, some bearing assortments of cakes and sweetmeats. The kitchen itself swarmed with activity as Jenny the cook and her assistants stirred pots, tended fires, and topped confections with candied nuts and flowers.

"Kitty spoke of a quandary," she said to Jenny.

The cook threw up her hands in exasperation. "I was counting on a second cone of sugar, but Sue went into the larder and came back with this." She held up a brownish lump the size of a child's fist. "Mice."

"Why did no one see this sooner?" Lucia heard the edge in her voice. "We could have provisioned accordingly."

Sue hung her head. "Begging your pardon, madam. It were my fault when Cook told me to check the sugar this morn, and I was stupid and told her without looking that we was fine." A tear rolled down the girl's cheek and dropped to the floor.

Some of Lucia's anger dropped away. "Go back into the larder and see how much honey we've got. Bring out whatever you can find."

Sue dashed off, then returned a moment later carrying a large crock.

"I brought it, madam." She approached Lucia, who directed her to the cook.

"Jenny, is there enough to serve as substitute for tonight?"

The cook lifted the crock's lid and inspected its contents. "Should be."

"Tomorrow, Sue," Lucia gravely said to the girl, "we shall have a discussion, you and I."

Sue blanched. "Going to sack me?"

"Your position's secure," Lucia said, her tone even, "but that doesn't mean you're forgiven."

"Aye, madam."

"Now back to work," Lucia reminded her.

The girl curtsied before hurrying to her station and picking up a knife to chop walnuts.

Seeing that there was nothing that required her further attention, Lucia motioned to Tom to follow her. Together, they climbed a back staircase.

As she held the railing, his hand stayed hers. Sparks shot up her arm and spread through her. She turned. She stood on a higher step and had the rare vantage of looking down on him. A shaft of light fell across his eyes, and the intensity of his gaze went all the way to her marrow.

"Most employers would've dismissed her," he said lowly.

"Sue's got three young brothers she's trying to keep from the workhouse, and her regular wages from the pastry shop barely feed them. I sack her, that's a week of rent she can't make."

"Not many would take that into consideration," he murmured.

"The club is my business," she said softly, "but the staff's my family."

"They are not your blood."

Her chest ached with a swell of affection. "They mean so much more to me—if they're loyal and work hard. But I don't tolerate anyone who won't give it their best. Likewise if they betray our guests' trust."

There had been a bloke last year who'd spoken to a vicar about one of the guests, and she'd sacked him without remorse.

She leveled her gaze with Tom's, and she didn't try to hide the emotion throbbing in her voice. "This establishment employs a staff of twenty, not including the musicians. They all have additional employment, but I pay generously for their discretion and industry. Perhaps they'd survive without their wages from the club, but London's costly, and a supplement from me means they can raise their families away from the filth and crime of Whitechapel."

She shuddered as she remembered the cold, artificial dusk that darkened Berner Street and Gravel Lane.

Escape had only come when Mrs. Chalke had brought her to the bawdy house near Covent Garden, where there was enough to eat and a warm bed free from vermin.

"Think on that," she said urgently, "before you decide whether or not to close the club."

His brow lowered, and his jaw firmed, but he didn't speak.

There was one final card to play in this game. Pray God it was the right one. "I've a final request to make of you before you make your decision." She held his gaze. "Tomorrow, at three in the afternoon, meet me in the rooms above The Green Oak gin house."

"No idea where that is," he admitted.

A wry smile curved her lips. "Why would you? It's in Bethnal Green."

"Not a part of town I know well. But is it safe for you to go there?"

She warmed from his concern, however misplaced. "I'll be fine. But," she went on in a warning tone, "I advise you to leave your ducal carriage at home and use a more unremarkable vehicle. And perhaps bribe your groom for his clothes."

"Noted." His voice was businesslike, but his eyes filled with heat. "Tomorrow, then."

Their gazes held. Desire rose up between them, crackling and alive. She could lose herself in it, let herself be burned alive by the passion that was never more than a moment away. It held a seductive allure, to forget everything and dwell only in the realm of the senses.

She had to deny herself this. She'd had her heart broken three times, as she'd said to him. Each time, she'd picked up the pieces and put it back together again.

Yet she knew that if he shattered her heart, the damage would be too great, and it would never be whole again.

Chapter 11

❦

"You sure you want to stop here, gov?"

From his seat atop the two-wheeled hackney cab, the driver eyed the exterior of The Green Oak gin house with distinct disfavor.

"This is my destination." Tom climbed down from the vehicle and gave the driver his fare.

The cabman quickly pocketed the coin, though his gaze was fixed on the cluster of threadbare men gathered outside the gin house. "I ain't waiting for you here."

"You needn't." Tom wasn't afraid, but he remained vigilant. Even in his groom's clothes, with the ducal signet ring left at home, he stood out here.

Some members of Tom's class enjoyed touring the city's rougher areas. From their perches of privilege, they observed the people living in direst need, as though gawking at animals in a zoological garden. Acquaintances confessed to Tom that it gave them a thrill to court danger, such as the possibility of robbery or assault committed by a desperate resident of

East London. Then, at the end of the night, the wealthy elite could return to Mayfair, secure in their comforts.

Tom never joined their number. He'd no interest in gleefully studying the impoverished for his own entertainment. Other thrills had appealed to him more—opera dancers, pugilism matches, knife-throwing competitions—and so the ramshackle street on which he now stood was largely unknown to him.

"If you're still breathing," the driver said, "you'll find me at the well near Fenchurch and Leadenhall Streets."

"My aim is to remain alive," Tom answered drily, "so I'll keep that in mind."

The cabman flicked the reins, and the vehicle drove away, leaving Tom standing on the curb outside The Green Oak.

He glanced up and down the street. A handful of shops faced the narrow lane, but dilapidated tenements made up the majority of buildings, their rough brick facades on the verge of toppling apart. The street itself wasn't paved, and mud spattered the shoes and bare feet of the people ambling down it. From a front step, a woman with a child on her hip stared at him cautiously. A handful of children in tattered scraps of fabric played with a wad of rags tied into a semblance of a football.

Heaviness pushed down on Tom's chest. The air here seemed thicker, grayer, choking with hopelessness.

Mayfair was very far away.

Why had Lucia brought him to this place? The Orchid Club was miles to the west, far from here, so she'd have no business in this part of the city.

A door stood just beside the entrance to the gin house. He approached and pushed it open, revealing a rickety set of stairs climbing upward. The humid, earthy scent of human habitation filled the staircase. The smell had the heavy ripeness of too many people in too small a space. Yet Lucia had said he was to meet her in the rooms upstairs, so he climbed the steps. They protested loudly beneath his boots.

At the top of the stairs stood a corridor, with several doors ajar. He walked gingerly down the hallway, peering behind each door. In one cramped room, a woman sat on the floor, surrounded by a mountain of shirts. She didn't look up from her needlework. Another narrow room held a man and a thin dog sitting close to a stove that emitted black smoke.

The dog didn't lift its head, while the man glanced up and looked at Tom with red-rimmed eyes. "What you want, nob?"

"I'm looking for someone," Tom answered neutrally.

"Ain't nobody here worth looking for," the man said wearily. "Unless you mean herself."

"Herself?" Tom raised an eyebrow.

"The dark-eyed mort. Always carrying a basket o' something when she visits, but it ain't holding food, on account of me asking for a bite and she said what she brung couldn't be eaten." A smile appeared on his weathered face. "Next time, she brung me an eel pie."

From what he was learning of her, that sounded precisely like Lucia. "Where can I find her?"

The man tilted his head to indicate the next room. "If you see her, tell her I wants a pork pie next. But I'll take another eel if she ain't got pork."

"I'll be certain to let her know." Tom touched the brim of his hat and moved down the corridor to the last open door.

He paused when he heard Lucia's voice.

"Try again, Letty. Don't worry if you can't get the loop just right."

"But I want it to look like yours," a young girl said, her East London accent prominent and her voice tight with frustration.

"It will, but be patient with yourself. It took me a month to get it right."

"Awright." The girl didn't sound convinced.

Curious, Tom rapped his knuckles on the door. When Lucia bid him enter, he nudged the door open, unsure what he'd find.

Ash-colored light from grimy windows surrounded Lucia as she bent over a girl sitting at a tiny desk, a sheet of paper spread in front of the child. The girl held a piece of charcoal, and it was clear that she'd been practicing how to cross her *t*'s. More girls, aged somewhere between seven and twelve, wore frayed, ill-fitting clothes and sat at small desks crammed into the room.

The gray walls were covered with plaster cracked into spiderwebs. One lamp burned, pushing back the gloom, and other girls within the chamber used it to illuminate the hornbooks they studied. The basket in the center of the room held a few slim volumes as well as more hornbooks.

"Who's this?" a girl with thick black hair demanded, staring at Tom.

"A friend." Lucia straightened, and while there was wariness in her posture, her gaze was warm. Answering warmth flared within him. "He's come to pay us a visit."

"Ladies." Tom bowed with the gravity he'd shown members of the royal family.

A handful of the children stared, but two others giggled. Tom's heart contracted at the sound.

"You here to learn your letters, too?" the black-haired girl asked. "It's hard, but Miss Lucia says that worthwhile things are hard."

Ah, hell. Surely Lucia meant to kill him by bringing him here. Like anyone who lived in London, he saw the faces of poverty everywhere, from crossing sweeps to girls selling flowers outside Covent Garden, to the children who'd hold your horse for a penny. It never failed to move him to pity, heaping coins into small outstretched hands. But to be in this small room with the city's unwanted girls, seeing their youth beneath the grime on their faces and seeing them at their studies—that was a dagger in his chest. For now there was no pretending that "someone else" would see to their welfare, or ameliorate their deprivation. He was face-to-face with his country's appalling treatment of the poor—of poor *women*—and helping these girls wasn't somebody else's task. It was his. It was everyone's.

"I'm sure," Lucia said, "that our friend would appreciate it if you read to him, Mary."

When the girl looked uncertain, Tom said, "If you don't want to—"

"No, I do." The child pushed up from her desk and, carrying a battered book, marched up to him. She eyed Tom as he towered over her.

Immediately, he crouched down so their gazes were level. God, but her eyes were serious, holding a wealth of experience that he could never possess.

Gravely, she opened her book and in a slow, faltering voice, read aloud. "The prin—, the prin—"

"Principle," Lucia said gently.

"The principle parts of a flower are the calyx, the corolla, the sta—, the sta—"

"The stamen," Tom said.

Doggedly, Mary continued. "The stamen, and the pistil." She shut the book with a decisive snap. "That's botany. I'm going to be a botanist and study plants."

"Noble work," Tom said with a nod, not knowing whether to despair of her chances of making this dream a reality, or applaud her for her determination and ambition.

Lucia approached, and Tom straightened. She set

her hand atop Mary's head. "Everyone's to continue their studies while I go out and talk with Mr. Tom," she announced.

"Yes, miss," the girls chorused. To his surprise, they appeared to do exactly that, dutifully bending over their hornbooks and primers.

When Lucia strode out of the room, Tom followed. They faced each other in the dim stairwell, the light so poor he could barely make out the details of her face. Yet he felt the intensity of her gaze on him, like a hand pressed against the base of his neck.

"They're like me," Lucia said. "No family, no home. No one to care about them."

Thinking on it now, he'd heard a touch of the streets in her voice. She'd lived a life he had never, and would never, comprehend, and the realization humbled him. The woman who stood before him now was regal and proud, having earned every jewel in her crown.

"You care." He folded his arms across his chest and looked around the stairwell. The floor was warped or missing pieces entirely. "How long?"

She glanced up at the stairs climbing to the next story, her gaze both sad and determined. "I started doing this two years ago. I walked through Bethnal Green, finding girls in the street, the ones that looked the most ragged and neglected. Most of them have one or no parents. They sleep in alleyways or broken-down boardinghouses where they have straw on the floor instead of mattresses, and eat infrequently."

Lucia rubbed a hand over her eyes. "I said that first day that I'd give them each a seedcake if they came for an hour. They showed up, and some left after that hour. But these other girls, they're the ones who stayed." Pride in her tenacious students was evident in her smile.

It was as though a hand gripped his heart. There was so much resolute hope in her smile, so much courage.

No one in Parliament ever wore such a smile.

Then she sobered. "There are always more girls. The hornbooks and primers, the charcoal and paper— those I pay for with my wages from the club." She exhaled. "It's not enough. It's never enough."

"You're but one person," he said gently.

"I'm trying to remedy that." At his questioning silence, she said, "Since I took over from Mrs. Chalke, the former proprietress, I've been saving. Bit by bit, but I'm nearly there."

He frowned. "Where?"

"To make a place for them," she said. "A permanent place. Not just a room in a tumbledown Bethnal Green tenement, but a home for them where they can be safe, there's always something to eat, and where they know that someone believes in them."

Her voice thickened, and she dashed her knuckles across her eyes. The sight of her tears squeezed him tightly as a vise.

He moved to reach for her, but she stepped slightly

away. He pushed back any sense of hurt, understanding that she didn't want comfort. She wanted to be heard.

"The club is paying for it," she said in a matter-of-fact voice. "I set aside most of my wages, saving up to pay for rent for wherever the home can find its location. Kitty and Elspeth add a bit when they can. But if the club dies . . ."

In the dimness, her gaze burned him, and he felt it all the way to his marrow.

"So dies the home." His breath heaved in and out as everything he'd seen, everything she'd said, leveled him with the force of a hundred cannons. He growled, "Goddamn it, Lucia. You play a dirty game."

"Life's a dirty game," she said without remorse. "The question is, how far is anyone willing to go to win?"

He rubbed at the space between his brows, where pressure built and built, threatening to rend him asunder. "What you're asking . . . to stake my family's reputation . . ."

"It's not without risk." She tipped her head in acknowledgment. "So many rely on me, on the club. And I rely on you." A note of pleading tinged her words. Taking a step closer, she held out her hand in supplication. "Keep it open. Give the girls in that room the chance to dream."

He looked toward the open door, and the children within the room, industriously learning. The city was full of girls like them, hawking nosegays and oranges, clambering along the banks of the Thames as they looked for anything that could be traded or exchanged for coin.

"Did you have the chance to dream?" he asked softly.

Her gaze turned melancholy. "It wasn't easy, finding something to wish for, something to reach toward. There were times when I had nothing—nothing but myself, and even that was a commodity."

He stilled as understanding hit him.

Oranges and nosegays weren't the only things girls sold.

"Yes, I did that. First on the street, then in Mrs. Chalke's bawdy house in Covent Garden, before she brought me on as a server at the establishment."

His heart thudded. He'd realized, in some distant corner of his mind, that she must have joined the ranks of thousands of females in London who sold sex for money. Yet it didn't seem fully true. Not until this moment.

"Did you . . ." He wasn't certain what question he wanted to ask, when so many flew through his mind like startled crows. ". . . Did you enjoy it?"

She lifted her shoulders in a shrug, and said wearily, "Some days, yes. Some days, no. Mostly, it was merely work." Her eyes narrowed. "And now you judge me."

He held up his hands. "Men of my class—hell, of any class—we all pay for women's bodies in one way or another. To sneer at you for providing the service I've paid for, that's hypocrisy. Only—" He felt his mouth curve in a rueful smile. "It might take me a moment to regain my sea legs."

"My past doesn't matter." She waved toward the roomful of children. "The present and the future do. What's your answer?"

He paced away from her, then back again, his thoughts and heart wrestling with each other. Should word get out about his ownership of the club, disaster for his mother and sister would follow. But if he shut it down, what would become of the staff, or Lucia's hope of opening a home for girls like Mary, who dreamt of becoming a botanist when all that grew in East London were weeds?

Protect his family, or give the girls of Bethnal Green something to help lift themselves out of the endless cycle of poverty? Could he do both? No one's life was more precious than another's, and their value had nothing to do with where they lived or who their parents were.

Caring for his mother and sister was his sacred responsibility. This wasn't a kind world for females, even ones of gentle birth, and so it fell to him to ensure Maeve and his mother's safety and happiness. Yet could he say that they were more significant and worthwhile than these girls in this shabby room? It smacked of more hypocrisy to pick one over the other.

He stopped abruptly and swung to face Lucia, who

watched him with a mixture of expectation and dread. He had to find a way to both safeguard his family's security and give the Bethnal Green girls some way to escape the grinding millstone of poverty.

"The club," he said after a long moment, "will remain open."

Her shoulders sagged and she let out a jagged breath. "*Grazie Dio.*"

"But no one can ever know," he said firmly. "If there is even a *hint* of scandal, the establishment is shut immediately. Do I make myself clear?"

She nodded. "Your father's secret was safe for over a decade. We'll keep your confidence with the same certainty." She took a cautious step toward him, her arms open. "Might I?"

He almost laughed. They'd done wonderfully carnal things with each other, learned every inch of their bodies, and created unfathomable pleasure. They'd known each other for over a year. In a way, they were strangers, yet they were so much more than that.

In answer, he closed the distance between them and wrapped his arms around her. The sensation of Lucia in his embrace shot through him like liquor, heady and hot. Her curved, soft form pressed into his tightness, and knowing that she'd forged herself into a creature of great strength and great heart made the feel of her all the sweeter.

Yet he realized something. "You're in my employ."

She stiffened. "I had forgotten." She stepped back,

breaking the embrace, and he felt the loss like a physical wound.

"We can't forget." He'd not take advantage of their unbalanced power.

"I wish I could." Her gaze skimmed across his mouth. "I want to kiss you."

He smothered a growl. "I want that, too. But it can't happen."

A fraught moment passed when he remembered her taste with perfect clarity.

Finally, she said, "The girls need me."

"So they do," he said evenly.

But neither of them moved, and he realized that he and Lucia were forever entwined, their lives tangled together in a complex series of knots that he wasn't certain he wanted to untie.

$\mathcal{D}$EEP bass voices echoed off the walls of the Long Gallery outside the House of Lords as several scores of soberly dressed men stood in assemblies of three and four, conversing gravely as they discussed the forging of political alliances and the fate of the realm.

Only Saturday, Tom had been in Bethnal Green with Lucia, and now he stood alone to one side of the lobby, his stomach churning and his mouth dry.

It was as though his life was a choppy sea, and he rode the waves as they crested and plunged. There was no sign of dry land, or the stability it offered.

Tom bit back a curse when he saw the Duke of

Greyland enter the Long Gallery. Greyland would demand answers, and Tom had none to give. None that
eased the sting of Tom's conscience.

As Greyland walked into the chamber, several
noblemen approached him, eager to have his ear, but
he held them back with an upraised hand. His gaze
fell on Tom, and his stern expression did not lift as he
neared.

"I cannot understand you, Northfield," Greyland
said. "Blakemere's a *veteran*. If he was here instead
of in Cornwall, he'd feel your blade in his back.
You voted 'content' on Brookhurst's accursed bill.
How—?"

"There's more at work than adhering to the principles of my conscience," Tom bit out.

In the top drawer of his desk in his study sat a letter.
A letter that had arrived early in the morning to ensure that Tom read it before coming in to Parliament
for the day's session.

The duke of Brookhurst had made his position very
clear.

> *Your sister and my son have formed a
> considerable attachment that honors both our
> families. But it is an attachment that will not
> survive should you turn from the course set
> by your father. I have made my position clear
> to Hugh. He shall not wed Lady Maeve—not
> if her brother takes it into his head to stand
> against me.*

I trust you will take my words to heart, and act accordingly.

Voting in favor of harsher punishment for transient veterans had caught in Tom's craw like a poison bone, but he'd had little choice.

The very thought caused nausea to churn through him.

When Greyland directed his frown at Tom's feet, his gaze was so honed that Tom felt obliged to look down.

"What the deuce are you staring at?" Tom demanded.

"I was determining whether or not you fit into your father's shoes."

Guilt and anger stabbed into Tom's stomach. "Damn it—"

Greyland lifted a brow. "None of that language here." He glanced around at the elegant Long Gallery, the atmosphere weighty with significance and tradition.

"Ah, Northfield!"

Hand outstretched, the Duke of Brookhurst strode toward him, accompanied by two other senior members of the Lords. The duke was a tall, trim man with a leonine mane of silver hair and a broad brow, his heritage evident in his aloof expression and the set of his shoulders.

He shook Tom's hand heartily, then sent Greyland a cool glance. "Your Grace."

"Brookhurst," Greyland said with barely contained incivility. "My . . . felicitations on the passage of your bill."

The duke gave Greyland a superior smile. "Yes, despite your efforts to defeat it." He sent a pleased look toward Tom. "I do hope that soon Lady Maeve will be able to accept callers again. Hugh's been moping around Brookhurst Hall like some knight errant pining for the damsel in the tower."

"When she can see callers once more," Tom said neutrally, "Lord Stacey will be the first one in our drawing room."

"Wonderful, wonderful." He patted Tom on the shoulder. "We ought to take supper together. Tomorrow night?"

Was that a command?

"Perhaps," Tom said. He'd rather dine with an adder, but there was no choice in the matter, and he'd have to swallow his share of venom.

'O, villain, villain, smiling, damned villain.'

"Very good." With a final nod, Brookhurst walked on, his silent companions trailing after him.

Tom felt Greyland's gaze on him. "Now you know. Keep Brookhurst happy, which keeps my sister happy."

"A thorny thicket," his friend said grimly. "Navigating it comes at a high price."

"Sometimes," Tom said in a dark tone. "there's little choice but to make a bargain with the Devil."

"I hope it's worth it."

It was as though the walls of Whitehall bore down on Tom, smashing the very life from him. Even Samson was crushed by the temple pillars, and Tom was no biblical man of strength. "As do I."

Chapter 12

❦

There had been a time, not so long ago, that walking through Mayfair's elegant streets set Lucia's pulse to hammering. The tall, imposing facades stretching up into the sky made her feel as small as a mouse, the expensive carriages jeered at her mud-stained hem and worn boots, and every face beneath a beaver hat or bespoke bonnet seemed to glare at her in a constant reminder that she was a poor foreigner, an outsider, and always would be.

Today, however, her heart thudded with anger, and her fist clenched around a crumpled newspaper as she stalked up South Audley Street. She passed the incomparable Chesterfield House without giving it a glance.

How could he?

She neared Grosvenor Square, and Northfield House loomed ahead of her. Despite her fury, the front door seemed as weighty as the entrance to a temple. Only once in her life had she ever tried calling on someone using the front door, and she'd been turned away.

More anger snarled within her gut. She'd thought that by now, she would have forgiven her grandparents for refusing to shelter their half-Neapolitan granddaughter years ago—her third heartbreak. But no. Fury and sadness continued to plague her.

Just once, she'd like to knock on a front door and be received like an honored guest.

She headed down the mews, dodging puddles and a pile of horse manure, passing grooms and housemaids and a footman. They gave her a wary nod of recognition, the way familiar strangers greeted each other.

After avoiding a maid furiously beating a rug, Lucia approached the back entrance. The servants' door stood open, and, after taking one final breath in a futile attempt to contain her rage, she went inside. A handful of maids and two men-of-all-work hurried down a corridor, barely paying her any attention. Sounds of chopping floated out from the kitchen, and distantly, a bell rang.

She knocked lightly on a door that stood ajar.

"Enter," a man's voice said.

She poked her head in. "Good afternoon, Mr. Norley."

The butler was seated at his desk with an open ledger spread before him, but when he saw her, he immediately stood. "Today isn't the twenty-first."

"I need to see him," she said tightly. "The matter is urgent."

He must have seen the anger in her face, and her determination, because he said with deliberate calm, "I will request his presence directly." Mr. Norley donned his jacket and gave it a tug. "Will you wait in the usual place?"

"Here I was hoping you'd see me up to the drawing room and ply me with cakes and wine." When the butler did not smile at her poor attempt at levity, she said, "Yes. I'll wait."

At his nod, she turned and headed back down the corridor. The larder stood between the kitchen and the scullery, and she pushed the door open and entered. Shelves lined the chamber—which was larger than her bedroom—and held wheels of cheese and jars containing spices and jams. Large crocks of milled flour also crowded the shelves. A cone of sugar stood ready atop a cabinet.

She'd been in this room over a dozen times, but it wasn't a comfortable place she looked forward to inhabiting.

Lucia shut the door behind her. Yet she could not remain still, and paced back and forth as she waited.

Finally, footsteps sounded on the flagstones in the corridor. The door opened, and Tom appeared before closing them in together.

His quizzical expression did little to stem the impact of seeing him again. He was lean and masculine and his dark mourning clothes only brought into sharp relief his handsomeness. But his magnetism only stoked her fury higher.

"Why?" she demanded hotly.

He frowned at her question. "You'll need to be a bit more specific."

"Why do you hurt the people I'm trying to help?"

His expression remained infuriatingly blank. "I still can't make sense of what you're saying."

She held up the paper like a warrior brandishing a sword. "I read about it," she spat, "the Duke of Brookhurst's bill for prosecuting transients, mostly veterans—and your vote in favor of it. The paper praised you specifically for continuing your father's voting legacy."

Briefly, he squeezed his eyes shut. "Ah, damn."

"After the other day," she said, taking a step toward him, "after you met the girls, I thought you understood. Foolishly, I believed you saw what I worked to do and that you supported it." Anger and sadness clogged her throat, and she forced her words out. "I was mistaken."

"Brookhurst's son is all but engaged to my sister," he said in a strained voice. "Opposing the duke means destroying Maeve's possibility to marry the lad. I have it in plain English from Brookhurst's own pen. He'll forbid the marriage if I don't do as he says, and vote as he desires."

The flame of Lucia's righteous fury guttered, but didn't extinguish. "A choice must be made. Do you continue on, acting like your father and maintaining old alliances, or do you do the much harder work of razing the castle to the foundations and building a new, modern structure?"

"It's not that simple," he said, his jaw firm.

"I never said it was simple." She held his gaze with her own. "There comes a time in everyone's life where we must look into the mirror and truly *see* ourselves. It's . . . a difficult task, and one I'm not above. But the work has to be done, or else"—she spread her hands—"nothing changes. Everything stays as it was, and rots."

"Goddamn it, you don't get to judge me." Agony was plain on his face.

She inclined her head as the last embers of her rage went cold. "You're right. That's God's work, and of a certain, I am not God."

He stalked past her to glare out the small, high-set window. "No one condemns me more harshly than I condemn myself."

Her heart contracted sharply at the self-recrimination in his voice and the tension of his posture. She moved to him and gently laid her hand on his shoulder. He went taut beneath her palm, but did not move away.

"I never had siblings," she said gently. "There was only Mamma and myself. But I used to wish for a little sister. Someone I could tell secrets to, and get into adventures with. Someone to love and protect." Bittersweet longing strummed through her in an old, familiar tune. "What you feel for your *sorella,* it's a beautiful thing—a rare thing."

"She was born a year after I came back to England

from Ireland." His tone was softer now, and warm. "A tiny thing with reddish-brown fuzz on her head and eyes so big you thought you'd fall into them. When she'd grip my finger with her hand, she'd hold me so tightly, I felt that grip all the way down to my heart." He exhaled. "I can't deny Maeve her chance to marry Hugh. One of us has to know love."

Lucia went still. "And you cannot?"

He gave a soft snort. "Duty is my obligation. My marriage—when it happens—must be shaped by political strategy, that's the way of being a duke. So I've been told since birth."

He turned to face her, yet she did not remove her hand from him, so that her palm rested against his chest.

Oh, but it felt good to touch him, and absorb the solid warmth of him beneath her. They had shared pleasure together a week ago, yet still her body hummed with it, with the sensations that he created.

But her need for him was only physical desire. Nothing more.

"Love is a weapon we use against ourselves," she said resolutely. "Better never to put the instrument of our destruction into our own hands."

He raised a brow. "How is it you've such a bleak view of love?"

"I watch, I learn." Mamma had been so alone, so mired in her illusion. It had fallen to her daughter to discover the devastating reality. That truth had been sneered at Lucia by her English grandparents, and revealed in a letter written long ago by her father.

Mamma had been merely a plaything to John Thompson, and her pregnancy was a burden he'd been eager to abandon. So he'd written to his father—the missive itself with its faded ink had been thrust into Lucia's hands as proof. Her grandparents then pushed her out into the street and locked the door behind her.

At thirteen years old, orphaned and utterly on her own in a foreign land, she'd realized that to believe in love was to invite disaster and pain.

"None of that is of consequence," she said with a shake of her head. "How will you move forward?"

"I've two choices. Follow the path of my conscience or follow the path of my heart." He exhaled and could not quite disguise the catch in his breath. "Either direction ensures someone suffers."

Never had she believed that people of wealth and privilege knew anguish, but in the sharp blue of his eyes she saw pain, like a wild creature caught in a snare.

She did not say, because she could not, but she pitied him.

$\mathcal{T}$OM did not want to be here tonight at The Golden Plough, and yet he found himself entering the chophouse, handing his hat, coat, and gloves to a waiting serving lad. All the while, his thoughts were back in the larder at Northfield House, when Lucia had looked at him with the fury of betrayal.

He couldn't blame her for her anger. It was a fierce thing, as devastating as a hurricane, and yet her wrath was no match for the recrimination he leveled at himself.

"The Duke of Brookhurst and his companions await you in the private dining room at the back, Your Grace," the serving lad informed him. Given that the young man had used the correct form of address, the Duke of Brookhurst must have informed the chophouse's staff that a duke would be dining with them this night.

Tom paused. "Companions?"

"Yes, Your Grace."

"Who are they?"

"Couple of gentlemen, Your Grace. I didn't get their names."

Tom managed a nod before heading off toward a supper he had no desire to eat.

He walked through the chophouse, and it came as no surprise that it was full of men he'd known almost his whole life. When he'd been home from school and allowed to join the adults at the dinner table, he'd sat silent and seething as his father and his friends had bleated their opinions on *preserving the nation*.

No one had ever asked him *his* opinion, which, in retrospect, was a good thing.

"Good to see you here, Your Grace," called the Earl of Clarington, his knife and fork poised above his beefsteak. He beamed at Tom with approval. "Capital, you know, having you continue your father's fine legacy."

Tom smiled thinly, but did not stop as he moved as quickly as possible through the main dining area. As he went, more men hailed him, their faces wreathed with approving grins.

The beginnings of a headache planted behind his eyes as he reached the back of the main dining area. It was easy enough to find the private dining room, as another servant stood beside the door.

Two more servants were positioned around the chamber, their chins high and their gazes professionally distant. Covered silver dishes lined up atop a sideboard. The chandelier blazed, adding its brilliance to the multitude of lit candelabras. A single round dining table stood in the middle of the room, topped with a white cloth, and seated around it was the Duke of Brookhurst and two silver-haired gentlemen Tom had never met.

"Ah, Your Grace," the duke said, rising. He extended his hand, and Tom had no choice but to shake it. "What a pleasure to have you join us."

"Say nothing of it," Tom said.

The duke smirked as he turned to the other men, who looked at Tom with eager expressions. "May I introduce you to two excellent chaps, Mr. Pratchett and Mr. Dillard, of the Midlands Canal Company?"

"Gentlemen." Tom gave them a clipped nod. A sinking feeling pooled in Tom's belly. Clearly, this was to be a supper with a purpose.

"It is *such* an honor, Your Grace," Pratchett—or

Dillard—said, clasping his hands together. "I was just saying to Mr. Pratchett that we have met some of Britain's most esteemed and distinguished men, but surely none of them compare to His Grace, the Duke of Northfield."

"Very true," Dillard said enthusiastically.

Tom suppressed a sigh. There was little less appealing than a sycophant. "I need a drink."

"Indeed, you do." The Duke of Brookhurst snapped his fingers and a servant bearing a decanter of wine stepped forward.

"Something stronger," Tom said to the servant. The lad bowed before retreating, and a moment later appeared with a glass filled with amber liquid.

"Whiskey?" Tom asked.

"Yes, Your Grace."

Tom took the glass. "Come back in twenty minutes with more."

"Yes, Your Grace." The footman faded back into his position against the wall.

After taking a healthy swallow of the burning liquor, Tom sank down into one of the chairs arranged around the dining table. The Duke of Brookhurst and the two canal men followed suit.

Tom regarded them warily. A time or two at White's, he had heard other members mention the Midlands Canal Company. The business venture was aggressive in purchasing rights to land, and though they generously compensated the owners of the land, it was clear that they would not permit anyone to decline their offers. Tom couldn't determine what the consequences of saying no entailed—none of the men at White's had articulated that clearly—but whatever the canal men wanted, they eventually got.

"Might I extend our sympathies over the loss of your father?" Pratchett said, his eyes brimming with an attempt at emotion.

Looking into the bottom of his glass, Tom made a noncommittal sound.

"A superior man," Dillard added. "Mr. Pratchett and I admired him greatly."

Servants uncovered the dishes of food and brought them forward. There was roast pheasant, a haunch of beef, collared mutton, and fricasseed chicken—and a lone dish of stewed parsnips, since, apparently, all the other animals in England had died in the making of this meal.

"As well you should," the Duke of Brookhurst said heartily. "The late duke never faltered in his support of traditional values. Which was why when I approached him to be an investor in the Midlands Canal Company, he eschewed the idea. Didn't think it quite seemly for a duke to pursue such modern methods for enriching his coffers."

Tom said nothing, only grimly helped himself to some of the chicken and parsnips. The other men also served themselves and began to eat.

"But you," the duke continued, "are a man of youth

and vitality. A man who both preserves ancient traditions whilst also looking forward to the future."

"Canals *are* the future," Pratchett added, leaning forward. "They ensure that Britain will retain economic supremacy over all other nations." He looked at Tom excitedly, but his expression fell when Tom only gazed at him with disinterest.

"After yesterday's vote," the Duke of Brookhurst said, "it became clear to me that not only are you a worthy successor to your father's admirable ambitions, but you can move our country toward even further global dominance. You know," he continued after taking a bite of pheasant, "many gentlemen of our acquaintance have begged for an introduction to Mr. Pratchett and Mr. Dillard, and *you* are the only man of our circle that I deemed worthy of the opportunity."

Lucky me. "Is that so?" Tom said warily.

The duke nodded. "Mr. Pratchett and Mr. Dillard are currently in an expansion phase, and are in search of men with exceptional initiative to invest in their enterprise."

Tom raised an eyebrow. "They want money."

"We don't speak of such impolite things," Dillard said quickly. "Not to gentlemen of your rank, of course. All such matters are to be handled by your men of business, and it is they who will negotiate terms."

"However," Pratchett continued, "you should be made aware of the fact that everyone who has lent their fiscal support to the Midlands Canal Company has seen their profits *quadrupled*."

Tom paused in the middle of raising his glass to his lips. "Quadrupled."

"Indeed, Your Grace." Pratchett beamed and Dillard did the same as Brookhurst looked on with a smug smile. "That is no exaggeration. In exchange for your faith in us—and your capital, naturally—you will see yourself amply rewarded."

"You see, Your Grace," the duke said with an indulgent look, "I would not extend such an opportunity to anyone but my closest allies, which you have clearly proven to be."

Slowly, Tom lowered his glass as his thoughts sped. The duchy's coffers were ample, but to increase an initial investment fourfold . . . that wasn't inconsiderable. It was damned tempting. He could funnel a portion of the profits into Maeve's marriage settlement. The rest could go into charitable organizations badly in need of funding, such as Blakemere's programs for veterans. Tom would direct a hefty chunk toward Lucia's home for girls—anonymously, of course. He could use the profits as a means to make amends for the choice he had been forced to make.

But the price—aligning himself even more tightly with the Duke of Brookhurst—and with a business that was most likely predatory in its practices . . . He felt the bulwark of his principles shudder from Brookhurst's cannonade. Could he do it?

He gazed at the watchful faces surrounding the dining table, all of them awaiting his answer.

"The matter needs further consideration," he finally said.

"Yes, Your Grace. Of course." But Dillard shot an uncertain glance in the duke's direction.

"This stage of our latest development requires a commitment within a week," Pratchett added.

"I wouldn't drag my heels on this, Your Grace," the Duke of Brookhurst said, a note of caution in his voice. "Such an opportunity is rarely made available, and it would be a pity if you were to lose out on this prospect due to inaction."

"I will think on it," Tom said through his teeth. He pushed his plate away, appetite gone. "I find myself overtired. Do excuse me." He rose, and the other men followed suit. He nodded at the canal men, who bowed deeply. "Gentlemen. Good night."

"I'll escort you out," the duke announced, and to Tom's dismay, strode with him toward the front door. As they walked, he clasped Tom's shoulder. "Appreciate you coming tonight, Your Grace. I spoke in earnest when I said you were worthy of this opportunity. I think it could do great good for your family. For *both* our families."

"Indeed," Tom said, fighting to keep weariness from his tone.

The Duke of Brookhurst nodded. "It will be a fine thing, won't it, when my Hugh and your Lady Maeve can make their betrothal official? The union will be an excellent one. Advantageous to everybody."

"They seem quite in love," Tom said. Gratitude surged in him when he espied the front door. So close to freedom—however illusory.

"Ah, yes. Love." The duke smiled indulgently. "The young must have their fantasies."

Tom stopped abruptly. "You don't believe they're in love?"

"I believe they believe themselves to be. However," he made a dismissive gesture, "we must have our eye on more practical matters. Namely, the union of your family with mine, and the consolidation of power in our hands. Yours and mine. It's precisely what your father would have desired."

And what of what I desire?

An image of Lucia rose up in his mind—not in bed, but in the room where she tutored the impoverished girls of London. Determination and pride lit her face, and resounded within him like a melody. She had such strength, such unwavering resolve. He needed both.

He needed her. But he couldn't have her.

Barring that, what he needed, more than anything, was time and space to consider and sort through the morass of his thoughts.

"Though your father had not invested in the canals," the duke continued, "I never doubted his loyalty to our cause. Should *you* back the company, however, I will take it as a sign of good faith—that I can rely on you. That Hugh and your sister can rely on you. If you don't . . . How do I know you are trustworthy?"

Fury stoked within Tom's chest, clouding his vision. He was chained like a goddamned bear, with the hounds of Brookhurst's threats tearing out chunks of his flesh.

Blackmail was the provenance of seedy garret dwellers—or so his youthful self had believed whenever he'd read salacious accounts in the papers. Never had he suspected that the nation's most powerful men resorted to such filthy tactics.

Clearly, he'd been wrong.

"We shall talk of this anon." The duke gave his back a hearty pat. "Get some rest, Your Grace."

"I shall try." But despite the weariness that pulled at his body and dragged down his mind, he knew that he'd find no respite in his bed tonight. Not when he felt himself stretched tightly like a man on the rack.

Sooner or later, he was going to break.

Two days passed with no communication from Tom. Lucia didn't expect him to write her, especially after the uncertain way in which they'd parted. Yet as she'd gone about the ordinary business of her life, she often found herself standing in readiness, her head tilted to one side as if to catch a sound of his approach.

In the interim, she'd finally begun her search for a location for the girls' home. Just to take that step filled her with excitement and hope. She'd visited two properties so far, but either they didn't meet her requirements or the terms were too dear.

Her enthusiasm for the project hadn't dimmed. If anything, her desire to finally have a site for the home blazed higher.

Today, she'd left off her search. It was Wednesday, and in less than eight hours, the Orchid Club would be open for business. She had no time for woolgathering or speculation or thoughts of tomorrow.

She, Elspeth, and Kitty—cradling Liam—stood in the kitchen and surveyed the baskets of ingredients Jenny would later transform into the guests' refreshments.

"Eggs?" Lucia consulted her list.

"Six dozen," Elspeth said with a quick look at the basket. Amongst her many valuable skills, she could count speedily and accurately from merely looking at a quantity of an item. Truly, her father had been a fool to deny her a position within the family accounting business.

"East India Sugar?"

"Two fourteen-pound loaves," Kitty said. She snatched Liam's hand away as he made a grab for one of the cones of sugar.

"Butter—"

A knock sounded at the service entrance.

"Expecting anyone?" Elspeth asked.

"All the deliveries were made this morning," Lucia said. "Must be a peddler or tinker." She checked the pocket of her apron and found a ha'penny. "I'll give them a coin and we'll resume our inventory."

Quickly, she headed to the back door before pulling it open.

"We don't need—" Her words abruptly halted as she beheld Tom standing on the back step, carrying a valise. Blankly, she said, "I thought you were a tinker or a rat-catcher."

A corner of his mouth hitched up. "Not especially adept at catching vermin. Though some of the hangers-on at White's might qualify." He looked at her warily. "The damned thing about trying to think is that there's always too much noise to put any thoughts together. So much clamoring for my attention—it was enough to make me consider Bedlam as a quiet alternative."

Her mind struggled to catch up to seeing him on her doorstep, hours before the club was set to open. "There's always Astley's Amphitheatre."

He smiled wryly. "I told my family and friends I was off for a few days of travel. Got in my carriage and had the driver pick a destination. But I didn't get far before I realized that the place I most wanted to be was here." He drew in a long breath. A note of uncertainty was in his voice as he said, "I'd like to stay here until Saturday, and put my thoughts in order."

"Here," she said slowly.

"If it's not an imposition." When she was silent, he said, "I've no designs on returning to your bed. If there isn't a spare room for me, I can sleep on the floor. With a few cushions, of course. I'm a duke, not a dog."

She looked at him for several moments, excitement and trepidation at war beneath the surface of her skin.

Having him close would prove a temptation, even if they didn't share a bed. The wise thing would be to refuse him.

Wise, perhaps, yet she heard herself say, "I'd have to check with Elspeth and Kitty. This is their home, too."

"Of course."

She left him standing on the back step as she hurried toward the kitchen. What he asked of her . . . she wasn't certain if it was a good idea, or a disastrous one.

I want him near me, her yearning soul murmured. *Just a few days. What could it hurt?*

Once in the kitchen, she quickly explained his request to her friends. "He needs a place to make sense of his thoughts. Only that."

"Surely there are fine hotels and inns where he can be alone," Elspeth said with a puzzled frown.

"It's not his own company he craves." Kitty sent Elspeth a knowing look.

"He's my employer," Lucia pointed out. With a good deal more assurance than she felt, she said, "There will be no encore of our night together."

Once again, Kitty and Elspeth shared a speaking glance.

"Stop doing that!" Lucia exclaimed.

"It's your well-being that concerns us," Elspeth said tenderly. She moved to Lucia and stroked her hand down her face. "The most pressing question is whether or not *you* are comfortable having him here."

Lucia's heart swelled with the pain/pleasure of her friends' concern. They knew her so well, and wanted what was best for her. Not many in this world could claim the support of two strong women.

"I can protect myself," she said, again hoping that the confidence in her words could serve to convince herself. "Moreover, it can't hurt to have the ear of a duke for three days. Powerful allies are always a worthwhile investment."

If she framed his stay as something that could work to her benefit, so much the better.

"Then our doors are open to him," Kitty said after a moment, and Elspeth nodded in agreement.

Excitement pulsed through Lucia's veins at this announcement. But, she reminded herself, she had to be wise and practical and approach his sojourn as a calculated decision rather than giving in to softer needs.

She found Tom leaning against the doorjamb, his arms folded across his chest. He straightened at her approach.

"It appears that the Orchid Club now accepts boarders," she said.

The flash of his smile struck her right in the center of her chest. "Grand." He picked up his valise and followed her to the kitchen.

Elspeth and Kitty broke apart, their whispers stopping abruptly at Lucia and Tom's entrance. Oddly, a measure of nervousness skittered through Lucia to have Tom finally meet her friends.

"I'm Elspeth, Your Grace," Elspeth murmured as she dropped into a curtsy.

"And I'm Kitty, Your Grace." Kitty also curtsied.

"None of that," he said warmly. "For the next three days, I'm merely Tom O'Connell, one of the staff."

Lucia frowned at him. "You cannot mean to *work* during your time here." A duke *working*? It was beyond fantastic.

"I can and I shall," he said, decisive. "I'll not be a sponger. While I'm under your roof, I'm yours to command."

Heat washed through her. Oh, if that didn't give her ideas . . . She willed her blood to calm as she said in an admirably businesslike tone, "If that's so, your timing can't be faulted. Tonight, we're hosting a night of performances of scenes from the Lady of Dubious Quality's books."

His expression brightened as he grinned. "I know them well. Very educational. Got a much-read copy of *The Highwayman's Seduction* beneath my bed."

"You and half of London," she said drily. "We've spread the rumor that the author herself might actually appear. She'll be masked, of course. But the excitement that she might be in attendance is sure to bring in more guests, which means there'll be more work for the staff." She arched a brow. "Are you prepared for a long night of exhausting labor? If not, now's your opportunity to withdraw your offer with no harm done."

He suddenly looked very imperious, and exceptionally ducal as he raised himself up to his full height. "Don't insult me."

Was it terribly wrong that a flush of arousal coursed through her to see him at his most aristocratic? "*Scusatemi.*"

"Your servant." He bowed.

It was such a gallant movement she couldn't stop the flutter of awareness in her stomach. "Let's find you a room," she said, trying to make her voice sound as detached and professional as possible. *As if that's likely at all. I'm an* idiota *where he's concerned.*

Gathering her composure, she strode from the kitchen, and heard him follow.

They wound their way up the servants' stairs.

"The bedchambers are occupied," she said over her shoulder. "Kitty and Elspeth used to have separate rooms. As of yesterday, they share one now, but Elspeth's chamber is still full of her things, so I'm afraid there's no choice but to put you in one of the empty servants' chambers on the top floor."

"If it has a mattress and is reasonably free of vermin, it will suit my purposes."

"If you had been a rat-catcher, I could state with assurance that this house hasn't any vermin, but you're only a duke, so . . ." She shrugged.

Behind her, he gave a soft laugh that stroked hotly along the nape of her neck as surely as if he'd touched her. "Fair enough."

At the very top of the stairs, she opened a narrow door and stepped into a cramped hallway. "Sometimes our staff sleeps here if they're too tired after work to go home. We have two girls come in during the day to help clean and cook, but they go home after supper, so you'll likely be alone up here."

"Excellent," he declared brightly. "I can indulge in my midnight vocal calisthenics without fear of disturbing anyone."

She pressed her lips together but couldn't stop herself from smiling. "This will be your chamber."

She waved to an open door, and stood back as he drifted inside.

Inside, the furniture arrangement was simple and serviceable, with a narrow bed, a washstand, and a battered clothespress. The pitch of the roof made him bend slightly to accommodate his height. Surely the valise he set down at the foot of the bed cost more than all of the furnishings together, but he merely looked around with an approving nod.

"Certain you wouldn't be more comfortable at an inn?" she asked.

He opened his luggage and removed several neatly folded shirts. "There's more tranquility in this small room than in any of the finest hotel suites." He set the shirts inside the clothespress, then turned to face her. "I'll be plain. When I'm near you I feel a sense of . . . peace."

Her stomach clenched, but she tried to ignore it.

"You didn't seem *peaceful* when we went to bed together."

Oh, *Dio,* why did she say that? Professional distance was what they needed.

"Well, no." A corner of his mouth curved upward. "I'd had a year of wanting you, and when you gave me the gift of your desire, I wasn't about to squander it."

The heat in his gaze proved that, if given that gift once more, he'd take full advantage.

The room became smaller, the air charged. Heat traced along her flesh. She had a vision of him laying her down on the slim bed and kissing his way down her body.

Yet he held himself still, making no move toward her, for which she was grateful.

She forced herself to step back, until she stood in the corridor. "Our work lasts until sunrise," she said with an attempt at composure, "so I advise you to get some rest. Be downstairs for the staff meal by five o'clock."

"Sounds as though you intend to run me ragged."

"Are you game for the challenge?" She planted her hands on her hips.

His gaze held hers and she felt like a girl again, experiencing the heady rush of attraction. "Whatever you throw at me, I'll be ready for. When I set my mind to something, I don't stop until I see it through."

"I remember your . . . stamina." *Madonna,* why did flirtation come so easily when she was with him?

Before she could say anything even more provocative, she turned and sped away. It was her custom to take a small nap before opening for the night, and she'd trained herself to fall asleep within moments.

Yet having him under her roof, knowing he was so close, any attempt at sleep would be fruitless.

Chapter 13

*L*ying on his bed, hands folded behind his head, Tom stared at the low ceiling pitched just a few feet from his face. He'd tried to open the small window, but had been unsuccessful in unjamming it, and so the air in the chamber was heavy and musty.

Certainly, he'd stayed at a few inns whose accommodations had been less than luxurious—that room on the road to Harrowgate, with the leaky roof and permeable walls that permitted every stray breeze to pass through the chamber—but sleeping in a room designated for servants was a first.

Yet he needed this. The room, the time to sort through the maelstrom of his thoughts. The nearness to Lucia. Even to think of her calmed the storm within him. She was fire, yes, and his desire for her hadn't cooled. She also possessed strength and certainty. All things seemed possible whenever she was close.

He sat up, carefully angling his body so he didn't slam his head into the ceiling, and checked his pocket watch.

Nearly five. Time to go to work.

He shook his head at himself as he stood. Dukes didn't work at establishments that catered to London's sexual needs. And yet, here he was, adjusting the folds of his neckcloth and tugging on his waistcoat like a footman preparing for his first day on the job. Nervousness danced along his limbs—foolishness to feel it, and yet he wanted more than anything to do a good job, to please her. After one last adjustment of his garments and smoothing his hair, he headed downstairs.

His heart kicked when he found Lucia in the ballroom. How was it that the sight of her never failed to hit him with a rush of exhilaration?

With her back to him, she spoke to a group of masked women and men standing atop the stage. Tonight, she wore a striking gown of sapphire with short, full sleeves, appearing regal as any crown princess.

Christ God, but he could stare at her for hours.

She did not appear to notice that he had entered the chamber. He had the rare pleasure of watching her without her awareness.

"The first performance will begin at eleven," she said in an efficient voice as she consulted a folio in her arms. "There are no clocks, so you're responsible for getting yourself to your places on time. I trust you've had adequate time to rehearse."

"Yes, madam," everyone chorused.

"And everyone knows the order of scenes, correct?" The performers nodded.

"One final note," she said, her tone warmer, "and

then I'll leave you to complete final preparations and rest. Two of our strongest men will be in this chamber during the enactments. Should the unlikely happen and any of our guests attempt to join you onstage or assault you, Will and Arthur will remove them immediately. Your safety is guaranteed."

"Thank you, madam," a brunette said sincerely.

Lucia nodded before turning away, and her gaze fell on Tom standing behind her. Their eyes met—and awareness tightened through his muscles.

She approached him with a wry smile, but he felt the thrum of gratification as her appreciative gaze moved along his body. "Are you certain you want to do this?"

"As certain as the sun."

"Then let us put you to work."

She led Tom into the corridor, and he tried to subdue his response to her nearness. "You may be this operation's owner," she said as they stood in the hallway, "yet beneath this roof, *I'm* in command. Everything that happens within these walls is my responsibility. I require everyone employed here to treat their duties with the same gravity."

He bowed. "Rely on me, madam."

She consulted a timepiece discretely tucked among the folds of her skirts. "As I said, at this hour, the staff usually takes a meal downstairs. There won't be much time to eat when the doors open, so my advice is to have your supper now."

"I hope you'll join them." *And me.*

"It's one of the best parts of my day," she said with a growing smile.

He gave a silent prayer of thanks to have her near him for a little while longer.

Together, they went downstairs and entered the servants' hall. It was a long room outfitted with an equally long table, with benches on all sides. Several loaves of thick-crusted bread were arranged on wooden boards. Most of the staff already sat, plates, cups, and cutlery arrayed before them. Chatter quieted as he and Lucia stepped into the chamber. The male members of the staff jumped to their feet.

"Who's this?" the cook asked as she stood holding a substantial pot.

"I'm the new hire," Tom said. "O'Connell. Tom O'Connell."

Everyone nodded and called out greetings. Thank God Tom had procured some clothes that didn't shout Bond Street.

"What's in the pot?" Tom asked.

"Mutton stew. With potatoes and parsnips."

He exhaled with relief that she hadn't added, *Your Grace,* and rubbed his hands together. "The smell is heavenly, and I fear I'll humiliate myself by devouring it with unseemly haste."

A blush stained Jenny's already pink cheeks. "We've quince tarts to follow."

Tom groaned. "Madam, you are diabolical. Quince tarts are my weakness."

"No one can best Jenny's quince tarts," Lucia said confidently. "She even makes me *pastiera* for Easter."

"Not as good as they do in Naples, I'd wager," Jenny said with a dismissive wave.

Lucia smiled. "Maybe even better." She glanced around the room. "But we'll sing your praises after we eat."

She sank down onto the bench. The male staff took their seats, and Tom lowered himself beside her. There wasn't ample space at the table, making his shoulder bump hers, and the length of his thigh fit snugly along her leg.

You're here to work and think. But his pulse wouldn't listen, and it rushed through him to have her so close.

Talk started back up again as the men and women who worked at the Orchid Club gossiped, teased, and told stories. Elspeth and Kitty sat beside each other, taking turns holding Liam as the cook and her assistants circulated around the table, ladling up stew and filling mugs with small beer.

Tom turned to the lad sitting next to him. "How came you to work here?"

"Most days I'm an apprentice to a stonemason," the bloke answered. "But a mate of mine, he said there was a place in Bloomsbury where the money was good and they treated you nice so long as you didn't shirk, and didn't mind an eyeful of folks joining giblets. That is," he said, reddening as he glanced at Lucia, "guests having amorous relations with each other."

Lucia gave a small laugh. "Gordon! I make my living watching people rut. No need to guard your tongue around me."

Tom chuckled. "And I like your way of saying it better. *Joining giblets*—that's a new one."

"I got another for you, sir," another man said from the other end of the table. "Dancing the blanket hornpipe."

"Or a buttock ball," Jenny threw in.

Within moments, everyone at the table shouted their favorite expressions for sex and roared with laughter.

"*Inzuppare il biscotto*," Lucia said. "'Dunking the biscuit.'"

Saints and sinners, but Tom liked hearing her say filthy things. It aroused him, heating his blood, but more than that, he loved to hear her so light and playful when so often she was made serious by the burdens of responsibility.

But hell if he'd be left out of the fun. "Board a long boat," he added.

Pleasure coursed through him when the room erupted into more hoots, including Lucia's laugh. Kitty clapped her hands over Liam's ears, but her mirth was the loudest.

When everyone calmed down, Tom took a bite of stew. The cook watched him apprehensively.

The flavors of long-simmered meat combined with herbs and wine sang like a chorus. He shut his eyes and made a sound of deep animal pleasure. "Run away with me."

"Ah, lad," Jenny said breathlessly, "'tis but a plain

stew." She batted her eyelashes as she spoke. When she caught her assistants looking at her in disbelief, she snapped, "Go on, then! Have your supper, then come right quick to the kitchen. Can't expect the guests to feed themselves."

With that, she dashed off.

For several moments, the table was quiet save for the sounds of forks on plates and the draining of cups. It was informal and cozy, and a damned sight more agreeable than any of the elegant Mayfair dinners he'd attended.

Yet he couldn't quite feel fully relaxed with Lucia beside him. Every time she moved, she brushed against his body, and it was bloody sensual to watch her eat with an unrestrained appetite. She would make small noises of appreciation, rocketing him back to their night together, and recalling the sounds she made when lost in her passion.

"You've got a brogue, sir," Rose, one of the maids said, her words also marked by an Irish lilt. "County Galway?"

He snapped his thoughts back to less erotic subjects.

"Kerry," he said. "Close to Tralee. Born here in London, but they took me to Ireland as a babe. My ma wanted me raised as she'd been." As he spoke, he could hear his accent thicken. "It was a grand childhood— I ran wild in the Slieve Mish Mountains—but they brought me back to England when I turned twelve for schooling. I miss it there, I do."

"The longing for home never quite goes away," Lucia murmured. Her gaze was down-turned and faraway.

"That, it doesn't." The need to take her hand in his and offer her comfort burned strongly, but he couldn't be so forward in front of the other staff.

"And you?" he asked Rose.

"Ardcath," she said. "But the farming life wasn't for me, and I wanted far away, so I came to London."

"I heard that you Irish make the best storytellers," one of the men said. "Can't trust a word out of your mouths."

Tom stilled, and he heard Lucia's quick intake of breath.

"Arthur," she said in a warning tone.

As anger pushed along his limbs, Tom's hands curled into fists beneath the table.

Though it had been spoken in jest, Arthur had just called Tom a liar. Jibes about his Irish blood rose up from time to time, like sores, and he'd brawled often at Harrow and Oxford for lesser slights.

But this was Lucia's place of employment. He could swallow his anger—for her.

After a moment, he exhaled slowly. "Might I say that you are indeed extraordinarily handsome."

There was a long pause, and then everyone at the table laughed at the joke. Lucia chuckled, too, but Tom could hear the relief in her laughter.

He kept himself from starting in surprise when he felt her hand curve around his beneath the table. At her touch, tension eased from him.

The rest of the meal passed quickly as talk flowed

with the ease of colleagues who had seen just about everything. He found his food going undisturbed as he watched Lucia laugh and gossip, color high in her cheeks and her dark eyes bright. She was called upon to mediate a friendly dispute between two of the serving women, and her opinion was solicited when one of the male staff asked about the best gift to give a sweetheart. She even loaned the chap a few coins so he might buy a proper bouquet of flowers rather than pluck a lone blossom from someone's yard.

Lucia had spoken of being far from home, and yet *this* was her home, amidst the boisterous camaraderie and controlled pandemonium beneath the Orchid Club. Whatever her grim thoughts on romantic love, what she felt for her staff and friends was pure and generous.

Conversation quieted as she checked her timepiece. "We've thirty minutes until the doors open. Time for a quince tart, and then it's off to work."

Everyone quickly downed the final bites of their meal before rising and hurrying to see to final remaining duties.

"Come with me," she said to Tom as he stood.

Another kick of nervousness hit him as he wordlessly followed her back upstairs and into the foyer.

"The front door's our responsibility for the next hour," she said. She held up a purse. "You know our knock and the watchwords, but remember that the admittance fee is variable."

"Guests pay what they can afford. A good policy. Ensures everyone has access to pleasure."

She smiled at him and brightness spread through him at the sight. "Glad you see what makes the Orchid Club so special." Her expression grew serious, and she picked up a dark blue mask from a nearby table. "Let us don our armor."

With the look of a knight riding into battle, she tied the ribbons behind her head and adjusted the fit. Lucia was Amina once more.

His body reacted at once, growing tight. This was how he'd first seen her, how she'd carved a place within him. A lifetime would pass before the image of her in her mask could fail to move him.

"Do you have a mask?" she asked, clearly unaware of his thoughts. "We have spares for whoever forgets one."

"Brought one from home." Shouldering aside his instinctive response to her, he pulled a black mask from his coat and affixed it in place.

Her eyes darkened as she beheld him, filling him with pleasure that he wasn't alone in this desire. They stared at each other for long moments, poised on the brink of doing something very, very foolish.

The special knock sounded at the door. He and Lucia broke the bond of their gazes as they went to admit the night's first guest.

The next hour passed in a whirl. Tom and Lucia met guests at the door, took their money, and explained the rules of the house to any newcomers who did not show them the token. All the while, he felt Lucia's attention on him, carefully observing as he interacted with the scores of people that passed across the establishment's threshold.

When a hesitant series of taps heralded another guest, Lucia stepped back to let Tom admit them. A woman with graying hair timorously stepped inside, her slender fingers fidgeting with her mask. She exchanged the watchwords with him, all the while, her gaze darted around the foyer like a frightened mouse.

"This is your first time here, aye?" Tom asked.

The woman nodded and audibly swallowed. "I promised myself I would come after my year of mourning was over."

He offered her a gentle smile. "A lovely indulgence, and one you surely deserve. Remember, everything that transpires within is voluntary. There's naught you have to do if you aren't inclined to. If, at any time, you feel at all uneasy, find me or someone else on staff. We're here to ensure your comfort, security, and enjoyment."

The widow nodded, her shoulders straightening. "Thank you."

Tom took her hand in his and bowed over it. "Entirely my pleasure."

As the woman headed back toward the drawing room, Lucia drew close. "Beautifully done," she said admiringly. "We've had newcomers turn and flee after taking two steps past the door."

"A bit of reassurance was all she needed. She'll find her way."

They looked at each other, her approval warming him. Their breath aligned, and he fought to keep from tracing his finger along the sleek line of her neck so he might feel the soft heat of her skin.

Her pupils widened and she wet her lips.

"I'm here to relieve you." Elspeth's voice broke the spell.

Lucia put several steps between herself and him, and it was like taking air from his lungs. In the voice he'd come to think of as the Manager, she said, "Please go down to the kitchen and make certain there are no problems. Ask Jenny if she needs anything."

He nodded before striding off to fulfill her request, eager for a task to clear his head. Belowstairs, he found the cook bent over a tray of cakes, carefully piping little icing flowers onto each one.

"You're an artist," he said in amazement.

She blew a lock of hair off her forehead. "Wasted effort, if you ask me. People come here to fuck, not to marvel over sweetmeats."

"True. But I'd wager they wouldn't have much interest in fucking if you gave them substandard food." He nodded sagely. "Can't swive anyone properly on an empty stomach."

One of the assistants giggled. "If I was the sort who had time for embroidery, I'd put that on a pillow." The girl immediately got back to work when the cook shot her an irate scowl.

"Are you well provisioned?" Tom asked Jenny. "I'm at your service, should you require anything."

"We've everything we need for tonight. Lucia makes certain of that." She adjusted the placement of cake slices on a platter. Quick as an adder, she slapped Tom's hand as he reached for a piece. "Lemon cake's for guests, not thieving lads."

"Such cruelty," he said with a smile.

"Get on with that rogue's grin of yours." She waved him toward the door.

He edged around two servers bearing empty platters, and headed back upstairs.

The evening was in full swing, with guests abandoning themselves to the pursuit of pleasure. Several of them milled around the stage, awaiting the performances. Tom exchanged nods with the two burly men who served as muscle, including the one who'd called him a liar. He breathed around the flare of anger that wanted to grow into resentment. Instead, he winked at the serving woman from Ireland. She gave him a saucy wink in return.

They were all working together, laboring to keep the establishment running smoothly. This sense of fellowship was entirely absent from the House of Lords, and even at White's, the members concerned themselves only with their own needs and gratification.

It was . . . strange. Oddly wonderful.

This was no cure for worries over alliances and the fate not only of his family but of the nation itself. Nothing went away. He never forgot who he was or what responsibilities weighed on him. And yet he could lose himself in the movement of straightforward work, and the camaraderie that came from truly putting one's back into a shared enterprise.

He had no answers for the questions and doubts that plagued him. They might come . . . or they might not. For now, he was here, with the staff of the Orchid Club, laboring to make the night a success.

He found Lucia keeping an eye on the ballroom, and went to her as though drawn by unseen threads that tied them together. She always pulled him toward her.

"Happy to report that the kitchen is a smooth-sailing ship," he said brightly. "Though your cook chased me away from a piece of lemon cake."

Lucia patted his arm. "Should you discharge your duties well, I'll make certain you get cake."

"Bloody right, I will." He affected a brooding glower, a contrast to the pleasure he found in being lighthearted with her. "My sweet tooth is a fearsome thing, and it will not be denied."

Lucia opened her mouth, but before she could speak, a middle-aged male guest bore down on her.

"I was promised scenes from them naughty books," he said with irritation. "Been here an hour, and there's no one on that stage."

Tom scowled at the man's rudeness—and to see the guest direct that insolence to Lucia set his blood to boiling.

Yet her smile was placid. "Patience, sir. The performances will begin shortly."

"When?" the man demanded. "I didn't pay half a crown to watch amateurs fuck."

Tension radiated up Tom's arms and he realized he'd turned his hands into fists.

Lucia, however, showed no fear. Her expression remained placid. "My friend—"

The guest moved to grab her arm. Tom found himself standing between her and the guest, gripping his wrist. There was a roaring in his ears and he choked on the rage that clogged his throat.

"Either calm yourself, *sir*," he said through bared teeth, "or you will be shown the door and barred entrance. Understand?"

Grimacing in pain, the guest wilted. "Yes. I . . . I understand."

Tom released him. Barely able to manage words, he growled, "Go."

As soon as he could, the man scurried away, losing himself in the throng.

It took a moment before Tom felt he could speak, fury making anything but inarticulate snarls impossible.

"My apologies," he finally rumbled as he faced her. "I know full well that you are capable of seeing to your own welfare. But when he went to grab you, I . . ." He shook his head as if that could dispel the anger that wanted to drive his body into motion. "If you want me to leave, I'll abide by your will."

"I . . ."

They stood face-to-face, a handbreadth between them. Her eyes wide and dark, she looked at him. Seeing that vulnerability in her gaze stirred dark, primal instincts in him, instincts that demanded he protect her and hurt whoever tried to harm her.

"Girls on the street and in the bawdy houses," she finally said in a low voice, "we looked after each other. But we were comrades in arms. It's been years since . . ."

"Since . . . ?"

She looked up at him, raw candor in her eyes. "Since anyone—especially a man—has come to my defense."

Her spare confession shook him, down to the depths where the hulking, rough part of himself dwelt. He wanted to rip the city apart in search of anyone who'd hurt her, and tear those bastards into shreds. "You're worth protecting."

Protectiveness was not new to him—when it came to Maeve, he would literally kill anyone who hurt his sister. When it came to safeguarding others, he tried to stand up for them, and then, when the threat had passed, his anger would dissipate quickly. He'd once come to Blakemere's aid when three toughs had attacked in a country pub—and thirty minutes later, bought them a round of ale as they nursed blackened eyes and bloodied noses.

Yet to bear witness to someone threatening and bullying Lucia . . . He could not let go of his fury. It clenched him tightly, needing release. But it wouldn't matter if he had the opportunity to thrash that son of a bitch, his rage would continue. Because she had been hurt, because there had been times where no one had protected her. That was unacceptable, unendurable.

He'd been living a life of ease and privilege, not knowing that at the same time she'd been fighting for survival. Yet he knew that now. And from this moment forward, he swore she'd never again know suffering or injury.

He was a fucking *duke*. He could make anything happen.

She pressed her lips together, and a gloss of what suspiciously looked like tears shone in her eyes, until she blinked them gone before he could reach up to brush them away. "No need to depart. Your consideration is appreciated."

"I'm happy to pummel him into a smear on the carpet," he added darkly.

"Not necessary." She edged back slightly, donning that invisible mask of the Manager again, yet he could see the vulnerability beneath in the dusk of her gaze. "But I would like you to take a turn through the rooms and ask the staff if they need anything. On your way, let our muscle know about that guest and that they ought to keep a close watch on him. If he acts out again, put him on the curb."

Much as he wanted to stay, he had to yield to her authority. He took a step, then turned back to her.

"Having you in command . . ." The hell with being

professional with her—he'd lost that ability long ago. He felt his gaze heat. "I like it."

Before she could answer, he strode off, once again grateful for something to do. The stage of being smitten with her was long past. Hell, if he was being honest with himself, he was already beguiled by Lucia, and it wouldn't take much for that to tip into infatuation.

Doesn't matter what you feel. You want to protect her, then keep away from her. The line between you can't be crossed.

He kept himself busy by talking with the two burly men keeping guard, and then he looked in on the young woman washing glasses. They glittered like a wall of crystal as they were stacked beside her.

Suds climbed up her forearms and she shot him a wry look. "I'll never give up my life of glamor."

"Anything I can do to help?"

"You're a darling, but there's nothing to be done but make my way through this."

Logically, he knew servants kept Northfield House operational. Without them, there would be no meals, no baths, no clean clothes and beds. Yet to truly see how much arduous labor was involved was humbling.

He thought suddenly of Brookhurst, and his insistence that he and Tom and other men of authority ensure that nothing changed or altered the systems that gave them power. To them, people like the scullery maid were not fully human, only means to achieve a goal—such as clean glasses. But how could Tom pretend that the staff of the Orchid Club were merely living cogs in a machine, and nothing more? How could he plow onward, convinced of the supremacy of his opinion, discounting the experiences and lives of everyone around him?

He couldn't.

Seeing the disparity in power wasn't new to him, but never before had he been given the means to make profound change in that disparity. Once he left the Orchid Club, he could enact real transformation.

But the price . . . Maeve . . .

Goddamn it, he wasn't certain what his next step would be. And if once he thrived on living life in the margins, now he needed more certainty—especially with Maeve, his mother, and Lucia's safety at stake.

With a nod, he left the girl to her mountain of glasses.

He returned to the ballroom, where Lucia observed the guests as they danced and caroused. The movements of the guests were growing wilder, their touches more bold. Instead of the usual couples or trios, groups of four, five, and more were forming, as though the need for more and more sensation built. It took him a moment to understand why this might be, until he noticed that the largest groups were forming around the stage in anticipation of the forthcoming performances—like pagan worshippers around an altar.

"Your ploy of hiring someone to be the Lady of Dubious Quality is working," he murmured to her. "The guests can barely contain themselves."

"I didn't hire anyone," she said.

They exchanged baffled looks.

Seconds later, a woman in a golden mask and matching cloak drifted through the room, a secretive smile playing about her lips. A lanky blond man in black trailed behind her, and his gaze was full of warning for anyone who so much as glanced in her direction. She seemed strangely familiar.

Lucia gripped Tom's hand. "My God . . ."

"She's here to be anonymous," he said lowly, "but I want to thank her for many a night's pleasurable reading."

When the woman in gold stationed herself close to the wall, her male companion keeping close, Lucia checked her timepiece. "Her appearance is opportune. Excuse me."

She walked to the stage and climbed the small steps. Positioning herself in the middle of the dais, she raised her hands. The musicians lowered their instruments and Lucia said in a clear, projecting voice, "Friends, if I may beg for your attention."

Guests streamed into the ballroom, many of them wearing only their masks. The groups that had formed around the stage broke apart. Everyone turned expectant faces to Lucia.

"On behalf of the Orchid Club," she said, "I thank you for honoring us with your presence on this most exciting night. I shall not make myself tedious. You all came to watch enactments of the Lady of Dubious Quality's work, and it is my great privilege to yield the stage to our performers. The first scene is from *The Highwayman's Seduction.*"

A man dressed in a greatcoat and mask climbed onto the stage, two pantomime pistols in his hands, followed by a pretty woman wearing a low-necked gown. Dazzling gems that had to be paste adorned her neck and dangled from her ears. The performers bowed at the audience, who applauded.

Lucia descended from the stage and went to join Tom.

"My thanks in your choice of material," he said appreciatively.

"It was happenstance that we'd arranged to perform this piece before I knew of your preference for it, but I'm glad now that we selected this one."

They beamed at each other, and something radiant poured through him. Something free and light that buoyed him upward.

He nearly staggered under the realization—this was happiness. He hadn't realized it had been missing from his life until it returned, created and given to him by her.

It was a hell of a gift. He'd never felt bigger, more expansive, and he'd never felt more reverential.

"Much as I would enjoy watching the performance," she whispered, "we're here to ensure the establishment functions properly. To that end, let us move on."

The rest of the night passed with unusual rapidity.

Lucia directed Tom in certain tasks, but once he knew his responsibility, he did not need to be told again. He was in constant motion, little time to think or reflect—which suited him fine. A small break from too much contemplation was welcome.

Now and again, he'd pass through the ballroom and catch a glimpse of the performances. Many of the guests watched with rapt attention, and others found so much inspiration, they fucked within twenty feet of the stage. The lady in the golden cloak and her black-clad companion took their leave of the club midway through the third act—with guests whispering excitedly in her wake.

"I find myself almost superfluous," Lucia wryly said to him as they passed each other. "I've only to think about righting a piece of overturned furniture before it's restored to its original position. The flow of food and drink is moving effortlessly, and hardly any guests need to make use of the room set aside for unruly revelers."

"Perhaps you ought to delegate more."

"Perhaps I should."

They broke apart as duties required attending. He brought up wine, set furniture to rights, and took a turn watching the door. As the hours wore on, the novelty of physical labor turned to deep weariness, though it wasn't unwelcome. When he'd find his bed later, he knew he would sleep more profoundly than he had in a long time.

He seized a moment to lean against a wall in the

dark corridor, tipping his head back. Sensed a nearing presence, he didn't have to open his eyes to know that it was Lucia. The tiredness pulling at him lessened until he nearly forgot how his body ached.

"How do you fare?" she asked gently as she laid a hand on his chest.

His heart thudded beneath her touch. "Splendidly well," he said, though he continued to prop himself up against the wall. "Admittedly, the day has been a long one. I awoke at six which was . . ." He consulted his watch tucked into the pocket of his waistcoat. "Twenty-two hours ago."

"Did you not nap when I suggested it?"

"Too excited to sleep," he confessed with a self-effacing smile.

"Go upstairs," she said in a soft voice, pressing her hand more firmly to his chest, "and get you some rest."

He straightened, but she did not remove her hand. "When business is done for the night," he said firmly. "That's when I will go to bed. I gave you my word that I was here to help, and like hell will I go back on my promise."

Her exhalation was warm against his face. "I wish I knew what to do with you."

"Trouble is," he said with grim humor, "I know exactly what to do with you, but I'm a goddamned gentleman, and so I won't do any of it." He pushed back from the wall, and, thankfully, she dropped her hand and stepped away. "Fortunately, I'm going to be so exhausted when I finally get to bed, I won't be able to torment myself with thoughts of you mere steps away."

Even in the darkness of the corridor, he sensed the heat in her gaze.

"Now, excuse me," he said, "but I've a job to do."

With that, he left her.

Chapter 14

Sleeping after a night's work always came easily to Lucia. All she had to do was strip, fall into bed, and within moments, she was in blissful unconsciousness.

Not last night. After shutting down the establishment and finishing the accounting, she'd lain beneath the covers, wide awake and intensely aware that she had only to climb a few steps before she could slide into Tom's bed. She'd feel the long length of his body against hers, be enveloped in his heat and scent. They could fall asleep together—or not.

She must have dozed because when she woke, late-afternoon sunlight filtered into her room. After taking care of her needs and quickly washing, she threw on a simple day dress and apron before heading downstairs.

As she walked down the belowstairs corridor, the sound of laughter in the kitchen drew her close. She heard Kitty's high, bell-like giggle, and Elspeth's throatier chuckle, and beneath all that, a man's deep laugh. Tom. Her pulse quickened, and she hurried forward.

She poked her head into the kitchen, eager to observe without being seen.

Effie, one of their girls-of-all-work, stood at the hob as she tended a panful of sausages, and even she threw a cheerful smile over her shoulder. Kitty sat at the small table where they took their meals, Liam in her lap and Elspeth hovering close.

Tom stood nearby, and though he was dressed, something was missing. His neckcloth was currently in Liam's grip as the baby gnawed on the length of fabric. As adorable as that sight was, Lucia was more transfixed by the fact that the neckcloth's absence revealed the column of Tom's neck and the hollow of his throat.

"I hope you don't mind drool in place of starch," Lucia said, coming into the kitchen. *Bene.* Her voice was level and didn't betray any of her arousal.

Smiling, Tom turned toward her. It was a brilliant smile, full of humor and energy, and it was more potent than any whispered words of seduction.

"I'll set the newest fashion," he said cheerfully. "We've been rudderless since Brummell fled to the Continent. Now I can seize my chance." He held a mug out to her. "I'd a feeling you'd prefer coffee over tea."

The simple domesticity of the gesture warmed her. She'd only shared such homey moments with Kitty and Elspeth, but never before with a man. Yet it didn't seem strange or unwelcome. It felt, in fact, as though she'd created a small fortress for herself out of pillows and blankets—cozy, snug, and comforting.

"*Mille grazie.*" She took the mug and inhaled the roasted scent of coffee before taking a sip. "*Perfetto.*"

"Before young master Liam decided he wanted my neckcloth for his tea, Elspeth and Kitty regaled me with stories of your early time here at the Orchid Club." He leaned down to prop his elbow on the table, putting his chin on his fist. "Did you really punch a guest in the nose and then threaten to cut off his cock?"

"This was before Will and Arthur had come on board," Elspeth added. "So we weren't prepared for rowdy guests."

"To be fair," Lucia said, her blood rising to think of that moment again, "that *cretino* insisted that one of our servers was on the bill of fare. When he became unruly, I had to educate him. Told him if he wasn't careful, his *cazzo* would be thrown onto the sidewalk beside his unconscious body."

She smiled blandly.

Tom shuddered. "Remind me never to cross you."

"Do you need reminding?" She raised an eyebrow.

"If I did before, I certainly don't now."

"Hot food. Watch your backs." Effie came forward, carrying the pan of sausages. "Take a seat or you won't get your supper—or breakfast, or whatever you odd folk want to call this meal."

Everyone gathered around the table, and within moments they were absorbed in their food. Lucia had watched Tom at the staff meal the day before, but she still found the sight of him eating to be fascinating. His table manners were exquisite, elegant and fluid, yet she was drawn by the sight of the tendons in his wrists as he used his knife. He had rather large hands, yet they were still beautiful.

I'm sighing over a man's hands. What has become of me?

"Me, Elspeth, and the baby are off to the shops after this, then a trip to Catton's," Kitty said between bites. "Join us?" She angled a look at both Lucia and Tom.

Regret in his eyes, he shook his head. "Can't risk the possibility that someone I know might see me. I'm supposed to be rusticating, and being one with my thoughts. Unless someone is willing to fall on their bayonet and keep me company . . ." He cast a comically hopeful gaze at Lucia.

Normally, she adored visiting the shops. She'd spent so many years in Napoli with her face pressed against the windows of *pasticcerie* selling delicious sweets. She recalled well the feel of the pavement beneath her feet as she was chased away from the *bancarelle*, "stalls," and their abundant goods—pots and pans, toys, soap, and all the things she could never afford.

Now, whatever she didn't set aside for the girls' home, she loved to spend on pretty ribbons and presents for her friends. A weekly trip to the shops always held some wonderful surprise.

But . . . Tom would be alone, like a panther in a cage.

"If it's company you're after," she said in an off-hand tone, "I'm happy to oblige. Mind," she added, raising a finger, "it won't be a day of idleness. There's always a dozen tasks that need tending to. You might be rusticating, and a nobleman, but I intend to put you to work. Such is your fate after showing me how well you took to it last night."

"Alas," he said without any hint of sorrow.

Chatting about the day's tasks, they finished their meal quickly, and brought their empty plates and cups to Effie.

"And Cook set this aside for you." The girl handed Tom a slim paper-wrapped bundle.

He eagerly opened it. His face brightened in a way that was both adorable and delicious. "Ah, but she's a goddess!"

Lucia peered at the parcel and, smiling, shook her head. It was a slice of lemon cake. "Aren't you going to eat it?" she asked when he tucked it atop a high shelf.

"There are times for devouring, and times for savoring. I prefer to savor my pleasures." His gaze held hers, and with a hot rush, she recalled vividly their night together and her shameless plea. *Savor later. Fuck me now.* "Anon, I'll take my time with it, and lick up. Every. Crumb."

Santo cielo, but she should have reconsidered spending a whole day locked up with him in the house.

"We're off," Elspeth announced, tucking a scarf around Kitty's neck, who kissed her for the service.

Lucia snapped out of her haze. "Do you need money? I can fetch some from my room."

Kitty rolled her eyes. "No, Mama, we have more than enough of our own blunt." Yet she smiled as she said this.

When Elspeth pushed a pram into the kitchen, Kitty bundled Liam into it. Soon the trio had gone, promising a treat for Lucia and Tom—if they were good.

"Effie," Lucia said to the girl, "I'll need water boiled for laundry."

"Yes, madam." Effie quickly walked out back to where the pump was, leaving Lucia alone with Tom.

"If you have no objections," he said lightly as he leaned against the large table, "I might henceforth take all my meals here."

She felt her eyebrows rise in surprise. "Surely they feed you properly in Mayfair."

"But the company here is excellent," he countered evenly. "No ceremony, no dull tedium."

She hadn't considered that anyone of rank and privilege might find any part of their lives dull or tedious. But it made sense that, if habituated to all privilege, things like never-ending beefsteak on expensive china became dreary.

Ah, to have such problems . . .

"And what of your mother, your sister?" she asked, planting her hands on her hips.

"I'll bring them, too," he said magnanimously. "They'll enjoy themselves. Mam never could resist a bit of *craic,* and Maeve would find life belowstairs fascinating. And, I *do* own this house."

The irony struck Lucia, and she couldn't stop herself from letting out one caustic laugh. "Yes, I can hear it now, 'Mama, dearest sister, please dine with me with the staff of the Orchid Club. What's the Orchid Club? Merely a jolly place where the people of London wear masks and fuck. Won't that be a fun family outing?'"

There was such disparity between her and the duke's family, a gulf that could never be bridged. A shard of resentment buried itself in her heart.

"Perhaps inviting my mother and sister might be a trifle ill-advised," he said, his expression grim. He looked, at that moment, very alone.

She exhaled, releasing her grip on her bitterness. Neither of them could help being born into their lives.

"They still don't know about this place?" she asked gently.

"No, and I'll go to my grave with the secret. At all costs, they must be protected." His expression turned even more somber.

"Your father kept this place hidden from them for years," she said quietly. "You'll keep the confidence for decades to come."

Hopefully, he drew strength from her assurances.

He lifted his brows. "You truly see this place in business for decades?"

"In truth? I can't say." She rubbed at her forehead as she thought of the years to come. "When I worked at Mrs. Chalke's in Covent Garden, I knew all girls of our profession had a short time before we aged out—and it wasn't work I planned on pursuing forever. Even mistresses lose their bloom after a while."

His expression turned contemplative. "Never gave much thought to the business of sex."

"It *is* a business. Becoming part of the Orchid Club held much better prospects for me. Someday," she said, hearing wistfulness in her voice, "I would love to leave it behind, too. Just run the home for girls . . . but we'll need steady income, and in London it's easier to get a lungful of coal smoke than an extra tuppence."

She let out a long breath. "That's a discussion for another day. For now, you and I have an appointment with a closet."

"WE keep lost and forgotten garments here," Lucia said, pulling open the door to a narrow closet. Piled high were shirts, chemises, shoes, and dozens more pieces of clothing.

"Anyone ever claim these?" Tom asked.

"Never. But I hold on to them for a few months. Today, I'll sort through them, wash the ones that are in good condition, and donate the lot to a few charitable organizations in Whitechapel and Bethnal Green."

He held up a waistcoat to his torso, but the garment was much shorter and wider than his body.

"Doesn't stop for you," he said softly, "does it?"

"What doesn't?" She plucked a few chemises from

the pile and looked for fabric that was too thin from use, and tears that couldn't be easily repaired. "Set the usable garments at your feet."

"Thinking of others." He set the waistcoat down before picking up a single shoe.

"We've no use for lone shoes. Put what can't be used over here." She pointed to a spot on the floor, allowing the task to take over so she couldn't lose herself in the significance of his words. "*Ovviamente,* I'm not constantly worrying about other people. Need to feed myself, and remember to take a bath now and again."

"You said you'd been born in Naples, your father was English. That's what brought you to England." He studied her. "Yet you wound up in Covent Garden—so I'm guessing your English family didn't welcome you with open arms."

Old hurts flared back to life, sharp and cutting like dozens of knives. It didn't matter that fifteen years had passed since then, she still bled from their wounds. Tersely, she said, "There's no point in this line of questioning."

"I mean to decipher you," he said pensively.

Anger was easier to feel than sadness, and she welcomed its icy simplicity. "I'm not a puzzle, Your Grace." She wadded up a torn pair of stockings and cast them into the discard pile. "Not something to be solved to help you while away the time."

"You misunderstand me." He leaned against the

wall. "I crave knowing everything about you, not because I'm bored or in search of a plaything."

"Then why?" she snapped.

"Because you fascinate me." He spoke plainly, and his gaze held hers.

Heat stole through her and made a task as simple as breathing into a challenge. Her irritation shifted quickly into something much more dangerous—desire.

To distract herself, she picked through a mound of discarded fans, shawls, and ribbons. Lightly, she said, "My tale isn't so unique."

"Indulge me, then."

Very well. She could talk about this without falling into the trap of feeling. *Just speak of it as though it happened to someone else.* "You know Thompson Ironworks?"

He straightened. "Can't find a bridge built within the past thirty years that hasn't made use of their iron. Stephen Thompson's richer than half the nobility."

"My father was Thompson's son," she said flatly. "He wanted a Grand Tour just like the aristos. After Paris and Berlin and Zurich, he settled for a time in Napoli, the way all fine gentlemen did to hear our opera and visit the ruins in Pompeii. My mother, she was his housekeeper."

"Ah."

"Yes—ah." She swallowed down the choking that always rose up when she thought of the scoundrel that was her sire. "When she told him she was pregnant, he swore he'd marry her and take her back to England."

"She believed him?"

Lucia's mouth twisted as her hands knotted around an Indian shawl. "She'd come to Napoli from her poor village," she said defensively. "Her heart was open and trusting. To her, there was no reason not to have faith in him."

There was never any sorrow when she spoke of her father's death, only the painful absence of feeling, if it was possible to hurt from a lack of emotion rather than a surplus.

"Before any arrangements were made for a return to England," she said, her words cutting, "he died in an accident. Fell to his death when scaling Vesuvius. My mother mourned him like a widow. She never took another man to her bed after his death. But she couldn't go back home to her village, not with a bastard in her belly, and an existence even more meager than the one she knew in Napoli. So she remained, and took in washing, or mended, just to make sure I didn't go hungry."

She blinked hard, but tears always came whenever Mamma haunted her.

Tom regarded her steadily. But there was no condemnation in his gaze. Instead, she saw him piecing together the fragments of her existence—and what he discovered pained him. "What of you, while your mother worked?"

"Did my share." She pushed on, determined for

him to know everything. If he learned who she truly was, in every way, he might turn from her. Such a repudiation would hurt, but she had to face it, just as she'd faced it before. It hurt less when one jammed the knife in oneself rather than suffer a wound at someone else's hand.

"The streets of Napoli are full of children," she continued in a hard voice. "Urchins, you might call them. I was one of them, running errands, making exchanges, always staying a step ahead." She smiled wryly. "Bartered my way into literacy. My mother kept a few of my father's English books—sentimentality, you know. There was a poor English painter who lived near us, and I'd steal bread for him in exchange for him teaching me to read."

"Ingenious," Tom said, and there was no mistaking the admiration in his voice.

She hadn't expected that. "Just the will to survive."

It wasn't an easy or quiet existence, and too well she recalled the panic and confusion when political factions fought in the street. She shuddered, remembering the twitching bodies at the end of the hangman's noose when the Parthenopean martyrs were executed in the Largo del Castello.

She'd gone to the execution in hopes of earning some coin from the spectators as she fetched them cooling ices or something to eat. Yet she'd been frozen in terror as men and women met their deaths before a roaring crowd.

All life is precarious. A hero one day, an enemy the next.

"You left that behind to come to England," he said, bringing her back to the present.

Despite her desire to speak without sentiment, more tears threatened to spill. "My mother died—malaria. I was thirteen." The *dottore* had been muzzy with wine, and no help at all, as Mamma sweated and gasped and shuddered. Lucia had laid her body atop her mother's, trying to hold her still, and feeling the fever burning her flesh. "Before she breathed her last, she urged me to go to England, to find my father's people. They'd take me in. He was an important man's son, surely they'd raise his daughter in luxury. So—" She forced her shoulders into an attempt at a shrug, feigning nonchalance, then gathered up the pile of clothing that was salvageable and easily washed. "I went."

"You were aught but a child." Tom frowned, following her as she headed downstairs to the laundry. "Naples to England isn't an easy voyage. Or inexpensive."

"A few items of my father's were sold, and I convinced a fisherman to give me passage to Capri, where the English ships docked. I found a British captain willing to take my money for the voyage. The voyage was . . . long."

She'd been sick and terrified, praying to her mother for relief and courage.

"Turned out," she said in as offhand a voice as she

could manage, "my important grandfather was unimpressed with his *bastarda* granddaughter. He showed me a letter written to him by my father—making plain the plan to abandon my mother rather than bring her to England."

"Christ."

"Again, I learned how to survive, this time in the cold and gray streets of London."

It had shocked her, the frigid English climate, and the leaden skies, and the fact that life in the big English city was no better than it had been in Napoli. The difference was that here, she was considered a foreigner.

She pushed open the door to the laundry room. Inside, the large copper pot in the hearth steamed. Lucia tossed the shifts, chemises, and shirts into the boiling water, then added wood ash to the mixture. Tom watched with fascination.

She eyed him. "Seen laundry done before?"

"I've seen it, surely. Have I *washed* laundry?" He shook his head. "But I'm keen to try my hand at it."

"Truly?" she asked, surprised. "It's messy, hot, and tiring." She picked up the heavy wooden bat.

"In that case . . ." He shucked his jacket, setting it aside, and then his fingers flew over the buttons of his waistcoat before pulling it off. A moment later, he'd tugged off his shirt and put that on the ground, as well.

He stood before her, bare from the waist up.

Dio aiutami.

Her recollections of their night together hadn't been embroidered by the passage of time. He truly did possess a body that made her mouth water and her hands itch to feel all that taut muscle, and rediscover ridges and planes and the texture of the dark hair that swirled across his chest.

Desire for him was far easier, and much more pleasant, than dwelling on the past.

"How . . ." She wet her dry lips. "How is it a duke has the form of a Roman statue? I thought men of your class did nothing but eat and drink and fuck. You should be soft as pudding, not . . ." Her hand made a vague gesture toward his torso. ". . . Not like this."

His smirk proved that her words pleased him. "Pugilism thrice weekly, riding, fencing, as well. And never underestimate the health benefits of all that fucking."

Her body went supple. She'd firsthand experience of the benefit of his sexual experience. "Let's see if your brawn isn't merely for display." She handed him the wooden bat. "Use this to pound the clothes in the tub."

"As my lady wishes."

This day was proving to be an unending torment as she watched the shift and play of his muscles as he worked the garments in the tub. Truly, she could earn a goodly amount of coin by charging admission to this display.

"You found yourself without family in a foreign land," he said between thumps of the bat. "Tell me what happened next."

The hot glow of her arousal cooled. "Are you not weary of the subject?"

"As I said, you are a source of endless fascination." A droplet of sweat traced along his pectoral muscles, then dipped over the ridges of his abdomen.

Come tu sei per me. "As you are to me."

"My story's not so unusual." Once more, she reached for a tone of bored indifference, as if she could convince herself to feel nothing. "A girl finds herself alone in a strange place and there's only so many ways for her to earn her bread—and it's worse if the girl has no trade or skill."

"Thus the desire for the girls' home." He stopped his labor, his gaze distant and thoughtful. "God, I'd honestly no idea."

"Didn't you?" she asked pointedly.

He dragged his forearm across his brow before resuming his work. "Truth is," he said darkly, "I've seen poverty. Seen it, but never known it. Some tenant farmers in Ireland barely scratch a living out of the earth, and when I could, I tucked bits of my supper into my pockets and took them to the barefoot children outside cottages."

His forehead furrowed. "Forgotten about that," he said to himself. "Or how I'd get a thrashing from my tutor whenever he caught me sneaking food out of the house. 'It gives them false hope.' That's what he'd say to me between strikes of the cane. 'A mouthful today, and not a bite tomorrow is crueler than nothing at all.'" He exhaled through his nose. "Damn me, but I ought to do more for Ireland."

"Perhaps you ought."

For several minutes, the only sounds in the laundry room came from the pounding of the bat in the tub.

"I still cannot figure it," he said abruptly. "Why my father would risk the reputation of his family, his name."

This was simpler to speak of than her past. "He used to interrogate me when I'd come to deliver his portion of the profits. 'How many guests came to the club with a companion? Were they slow to start rogering each other or did they get to rutting at once? Did more women than men attend, or was it evenly matched?'" She shrugged. "I never questioned what compelled him. So long as he kept the doors open, I knew I had a chance to make my dream of the girls' home a reality."

Tom grunted. "Mayhap he liked it, being a respected figure in public, and having this salacious secret."

"I suspect," she said drily, "that many men of principle live such double lives. They enjoy the contradiction, the duplicity."

He continued battering the garments with strokes that grew more and more violent. "What if they're forced to do things against their will? What if they have to weigh the costs and benefits to every action, and can't ever honor the wishes of their own heart? Is that deceit, or is it what responsibility demands?"

With each word, he pounded harder and harder.

Her heart squeezed—she hadn't thought of what he faced or the burdens he carried. She'd been focused on her own needs and fears. Yet she saw that he, too, struggled. That was why he was here, to briefly escape the heavy weight of a responsibility that made him do things he didn't want to do.

For all his wealth and power, he wasn't free.

"Tom." But he didn't seem to hear her, and she placed her hand on his bicep.

He paused, his chest heaving, and sweat slick over his body. "My sister's happiness depends on me acting contrary to my beliefs. And if I do the wrong thing—if I invest in a business that hurts some, but will net me a profit I can use to help many others—how do I choose? Which is more important." His jaw tightened. "I don't know. I don't fucking know."

"You'll find your own way," she said gently.

Brimming with uncertainty, his gaze held hers. "I'm glad one of us believes that."

Chapter 15

It was nearly impossible to see stars in the night sky above London. Lampposts and smoke choked the atmosphere, and even the half-moon was merely a white smear. Yet as Tom reclined on the roof, his hair still damp from his recent bath, he kept his head tilted back, watching the sky.

Great God, but he was exhausted. Even at a distance, the process of cleaning clothes had always appeared laborious. Yet nothing could have fully prepared him for the grueling work that was doing laundry.

After the garments had been thoroughly pounded with the heavy bat, he and Lucia had rinsed everything in a second tub of cool water. Then had come the wringing. Hells above, the wringing. She couldn't afford a clothes mangler, so getting the water out of the clothing had been done by human labor. Hours later, his hands were only barely uncramping.

All that to get a bundle of garments ready to be given away.

For all her steely-eyed will to survive, Lucia had a heart that was bigger than London. Perhaps she considered it a liability—but he surely did not.

But could he afford to have a heart where his dealings with Brookhurst were concerned? The question of investing in the Midlands Canal Company continued to gnaw at him, taking bites from his spirit. He'd come to the Orchid Club for a place to hide himself away, but this could not be ignored.

God above, he still did not know what to do.

"Ah, here you are."

He turned his head to see Lucia peering at him from the attic door.

"Supper's on the table," she said, "if you want it."

His stomach rumbled—it had been many long and taxing hours since he'd last eaten—but he wasn't yet ready to abandon his contemplation of the sky.

"I'll be down in a quarter of an hour," he said. "Begin without me."

There was a pause. And then, "Care for some company?"

He patted the shingles beside him. "Room for one more."

After shutting the door behind her, she eased down beside him. Together, they contemplated the city.

"That's St. George's tower." She pointed to the southwest, and the sharp peak and its statue of King George I. "When it's very still, I can hear the bells toll the hour, and on Sundays, if I'm not at St. Patrick's in Soho."

"A Catholic church, yes?"

He felt her tensing. "What of it?"

"My mother, she was Catholic and converted to marry my father. I've asked her if she regretted her conversion, but she said a Huguenot, Henry IV of France, became a Catholic to rule Paris, and she'd do the same—in reverse—if it meant becoming my father's wife."

"And a duchess," Lucia said drily.

"That, too." He angled a look at her. "Is your faith very important to you?"

She exhaled. "In Napoli, our lives are intertwined with the church. Like this." She wove her fingers together. "Like everyone in the city, I always looked forward to the celebrations for the miracle of San Gennaro. There are garlands of flowers, and a procession to the Piazza del Duomo. We all wait to see the miracle of the liquefaction. His blood," she explained at his questioning gaze. "It turns from dry to liquid, and if it doesn't, we fear disaster."

At his silence, she said tartly, "You think, like your countrymen, that we're backward, and superstitious."

"Faith is a mysterious thing," he said slowly. "I wish, sometimes, that I had more of it."

"My mother would have converted, for my father's sake."

He knew now the reason for the sorrow in her voice when she spoke of her mother, and he ached for her.

"Given that choice, between love and faith, which

would you pick?" Tom tried to speak lightly, but did not quite succeed.

Her laugh was wry. "As you said, faith is mysterious. Yet it doesn't ruin a person the way love can."

The bitterness in her words struck him all the way to the center of his being. The injury to her had been so great, she'd developed thick scar tissue all around her, nearly impenetrable. He hated that she'd been hurt so badly, that no one had been there to protect and care for her. Everyone deserved a champion.

"You sound like a cynical rake," he said.

"I speak from experience," she replied flatly.

He mulled this over. "When it comes time for me to marry, I'll do so dutifully, selecting a suitable woman who finds me tolerable enough to endure my touch and bear me an heir."

She angled a glance at him. "Sounds calculating and cold."

"That's the way of things when you've the weight of centuries on your back." Since his earliest days, he'd known that at some point he'd assume the title and have to put aside his needs, his desires, all for the perpetuation of the title and the forging of alliances. No wonder, then, that he'd done everything he could to indulge his most primal, elemental instincts in the time he'd been given. The marital state was for duty, not the heart.

Passion, desire, and love itself—he'd learn to live without them.

He cast a surreptitious look at Lucia. What would it be like to be forever joined with a woman like her? A woman of fire, who challenged him and demanded a place for herself at the world's table?

The thought made his heart pound.

No point in indulging such fantasies. Even if she could somehow allow herself to love and be loved, they were divided forever by the structures of society, ridiculous as they were.

"An exalted view," she said, waving toward the skyline as it stretched up toward the dark sky.

Lights burned on the street and in windows, creating a luminous hillscape.

"From up here," Tom said thoughtfully, "I've noticed things that I have never noticed before. The way the secondhand clothing peddlers' voices rise and fall as they walk the streets. The clatter of the tinkers' tools. Footmen stopping in their errands to flirt with maids. In Mayfair, I'm too ensnared in my own concerns to notice the pulse of life, but I can feel it here."

He lay back fully, his gaze cast skyward.

"I came to this place," he said quietly, "to the club, because there's a man of great power pushing me into a partnership I don't want. It violates my principles—such as they are. I've already compromised myself once for him, and the more I do it, the more he'll demand of me."

"Then refuse him. You're a duke. Surely you have more power than he does."

The scrape of a laugh escaped Tom to hear such a complex relationship reduced to a simple yes or no. "He's a duke, too, with a greater sphere of influence than I. And if I cross him, or turn away from whatever he offers . . . he will hurt people I care about."

"The debate, then, is between what your heart wants and what is best for those you love." She rested her chin on her knees. "A tangle."

"It is," he said wryly, "and a damned one at that."

For a moment, they were silent. Then she murmured, "In the deepest part of yourself, what do you want? Not for anyone else. Just you."

"I want . . ." He searched within himself, finding those dusty unused corners of his heart that ached for something beyond his own gratification. *Oh, nothing significant. Only the minor conundrum of the meaning of life and existence.* When had he given that any thought? When had he lived beyond one moment, and the next, and the next?

"I want to be a good man," he said at last. The simplicity of his words and the need they expressed startled him. And yet it felt right that beneath all the complications and alliances and navigations, underneath all that, was the core desire to do good. To be the best man he could, hurting as few as he could, helping as many as he could.

His time here at the Orchid Club had shown him what it meant to join with others for the greater good. He'd toiled and sweat and laughed and cared, wearing down the veneer of polish that a lifetime of privilege had slathered on him. Everyone had a story, everyone lived their lives and—for the most part—did their best given the limitations of their circumstances.

He'd been bloody lucky to be born a duke's heir. The least he could do was use his accidental power to raise others up.

A thought seared him hotly and permanently as if he'd been branded. He could almost smell his own burned flesh.

He had to stand against Brookhurst and everything the man stood for. He'd reject the offer to invest in the Midlands Canal Company. Vote according to his conscience, not the demands of others—especially not the duke. Their fraternity must end and, with it, the generations of collaboration.

And what of Maeve? What of her and Lord Stacey?

God help him—he had to tell her that his days as the Duke of Brookhurst's eager collaborator were over. Either she would understand and forgive him . . . or she wouldn't. Life without his beloved little bird stretched before him, barren and bleak. Her wit and laughter and kindness would be gone from his life forever. How would he endure it?

Because, if he was half the man Maeve believed him to be, he had to make this decision.

Surges of energy filled him, at the same time a yawning fear opened in his belly. He was both invigorated and terrified, and it was only then that he realized one could feel these two emotions at the same time.

He realized that he'd fallen silent for a long while, and finally spoke. "I can feel myself changing—the way I used to lie in bed and ache because my body was growing. And it hurts now as it did then. I . . . want to do the right thing, but it's not so simple. Nothing is simple."

She was silent for some time, and then his pulse raced as she leaned close, her spiced floral scent surrounding him. Her face hovered inches from his, and her eyes were profound and searching.

He held himself very still. Waiting. Hoping.

She kissed him. It was soft, verging on tentative, as if she did not quite trust herself or this thing between them that could not be suppressed or stopped, no matter what they wished.

When he did not move, she pulled back. "You don't want me anymore."

"Love," he said on a growl, "I want you so much I'm drowning in it. But, I'm your employer. The power here is all mine, and that's not right."

"What about what *I* want?" she demanded hotly. "What if *I* want *you*."

He groaned. "How you tempt me."

"Whatever happens between us," she said, "it has nothing to do with the club—it's about me as a woman and you as a man." She cupped a hand around his jaw and he instinctively stroked his skin against hers. Her breathing hitched, but she did not look away. "Understand this. I don't want or need saving. My life is not perfect, but it's *mine,* and I'll find my way. On my own."

"I understand." He threaded his hands into her hair, and at the slightest urging, she brought her mouth to his.

The kiss was long and fevered and shot liquid fire through his body. Only now he realized that each moment without her had been a torment. But he wouldn't waste this chance with her. He stroked his tongue into her mouth and rumbled when her own tongue lapped against his.

"Christ above," he said on a rasp, "but I want you. Need you. Can I come to you tonight, when the house is asleep? Can I show you just how much I hunger for you?"

"Let me come to you," she whispered. "I don't want to keep Kitty and Elspeth awake, and I've a feeling we're going to be quite noisy."

With that, she slipped away. The door to the roof opened and closed. She was gone so suddenly, he half believed the whole encounter had been a dream. Yet the taste of her on his lips proved that it had been real, as real as the desire between them.

He was alone again, splayed atop the roof as though he'd fallen there from a passing cloud. He was stunned, too, as if he'd dropped from the sky.

But through force of will, he collected himself and brought his senses back into full awareness. Because, for as long as he could, he was determined to devour each moment with her.

SUPPER was a delightful torment.

Tom sat in the kitchen with Lucia, Elspeth, Kitty—and her baby—dining on pigeon pie and trading stories about the most outrageous things they'd ever seen within London's city limits—not including acts performed within the club's walls.

"Once," Elspeth said, "I saw a cat sitting atop a dog, who rode on a horse's back."

"Ah, you've lived the life of an innocent," Kitty replied, "but I love you, regardless."

Elspeth batted her lashes in response.

"In Cheapside," Kitty said, "I saw a cup-shot bloke attempting to suck his own cock."

"Was he successful?" Tom asked, intrigued. "To know that a man can do that to himself opens up many possibilities."

Kitty snickered. "He was successful enough."

"As they say," he said sagely, "even bad fellatio is time well spent."

Kitty rolled her eyes before turning to Lucia. "Now you."

Lucia tapped her finger on her chin in thought before her expression brightened. "I saw a fellow, nude below the waist, his *uccello* flopping everywhere as he ran through Shoreditch. And a woman, her bare *zizze* bouncing as she chased after him."

"He must have had something she wanted," Elspeth said with a chuckle.

"That item is inexpensive and quite easy to obtain," Lucia answered.

Tom pressed a hand to his heart. "You wound my sex, madam!"

"An injury which will heal quickly," she said with a saucy wink. "And what of you? What outrageous display have you seen?"

"I cannot name names, of course," he said in a low voice, as if someone might be listening, "but at a rout I witnessed a gent of very esteemed, aristocratic lineage pissing out a window and directly into an elderly lad's tricorne."

Though he'd been witness to and participant in many, many sexual acts, he had a feeling that these women wouldn't find any of them particularly outrageous.

Lucia shook her head. "A fashion critic." She reached over to take hold of Liam's chubby foot as he sat on Kitty's lap. "What about you, *piccolo*? Tell us about the wonders you've seen."

Being a baby, Liam had nothing to contribute to the discussion but gurgling.

Tom's cheeks ached from smiling, and yet, for as much as he enjoyed the conversation, his whole body burned in anticipation of what was to come. His gaze returned to Lucia as she sat opposite him.

Her face was alight as she continued to jest with

her friends, and her hands danced through the air as she talked, and she was so lovely he could barely keep from lunging for her.

Her gaze caught his and held for just a moment too long . . . It was a wonder that the food on the table wasn't charred from the heat that rose up between them. The minx knew it, too.

After using her fingers to pop a morsel of piecrust into her mouth, she very slowly and with deliberation licked her fingers. One at a time. Her tongue darted out to run along each finger. She didn't even look at him as she did so, but it didn't matter.

Tom's cockstand felt as though it could have knocked the table over. Thank God he was sitting, a napkin spread across his lap. He liked Elspeth and Kitty, and it seemed somewhat impolite to sport a massive erection in front of newly made friends and an infant.

"Oh, for God's sake." Elspeth threw her hands into the air. "If you two are going to carry on in this fashion, just go upstairs already."

"We'll do the washing up," Kitty added with a smirk.

Lucia was already on her feet. Never before had Tom wanted to drop to his knees and give thanks. After taking a deep breath, willing his body's response to calm, he stood.

"Much appreciated," he said gratefully. He reached for Lucia's hand and she clasped his. Heat from her flesh seared into his as they moved quickly out of the kitchen.

Wordlessly, they ascended up and up into the very top of the house. Anticipation was a hard beat in his veins, and he struggled not to take the stairs two at a time, as he had when he was young and bounding around with the unbridled enthusiasm of youth. But he was a man now, his needs a man's needs. And he needed her.

Judging by the way her breath sped and the thrum of her pulse in her neck, she needed him with the same intensity.

They reached the door to his room. They still had not kissed, but if his mouth touched hers, he'd have to have her right there and then, wherever they stood. So he didn't kiss her, and instead he reached past her to open the door and wave her inside.

She entered, stepping into the darkness, and he followed, closing the door behind him.

The moment he came into the room, he was thrust back against the door by Lucia's lush form. She kissed him fiercely, and electric sensation hurtled through him when her fingers wove into his hair and angled his head down.

Desire shot its bright blaze through him. Growling, he kissed her back, devouring her with all his pent-up hunger. Her tongue stroked against his. Flames licked up his groin, and his cock was hard and demanding as it strained against the front of his breeches. He cupped his hands around her arse, fitting her against him. Even through the layers of clothing, her heat saturated his flesh. As their hips curved into each other, she moaned into his mouth and he reveled in the sound of her wild, ungovernable need.

She writhed against him, sleek and aflame. He brought one of his hands up, tracing over the curve of her hip, the dip in her waist, and higher, skimming along her torso until he cupped her breast. The weight of it in his hand was the answer to questions he hadn't realized he had asked. Through the cotton of her gown, he caressed the tip of her breast until it formed a tight point. Gently, he pinched, and a throaty sound escaped her.

"Want you," she said, her words taut with hunger.

"Can't be as much as I want you."

He felt her smile against his mouth.

"Didn't know we were in competition."

"We'll make it a friendly competition," he said between kisses. "Who can give the other more pleasure?"

He rubbed her nipple and was rewarded with her gasp.

"What does the victor get?" she asked breathlessly.

"In this contest," he said as he trailed his lips along her neck, "everyone wins."

She pulled back just enough to say huskily, "I take my competitions very seriously."

"As do I." He licked her collarbone, adoring the musk of her skin. "I will be a gentleman and let the opening salvo be yours."

Her eyes gleamed. "Prepare yourself." She reached

for the fall of his breeches. "For days, I've wanted to feel your cock in my hand."

If he hadn't been achingly stiff before, now he was hard and burning as an iron. He released his grip on her, and growled when she made short work of the buttons. He nearly shouted when her warm fingers curled around his cock.

"I remembered that you didn't wear drawers," she said with a smile in her voice. And then she exhaled with appreciation as she stroked him.

He lost his ability to think. He lost everything but the feel of her pumping her hand up and down his shaft. Heat gathered low on his spine as his hips moved to meet her touch.

Tom barely noticed that her other hand was undoing the folds of his neckcloth, but he jolted with pleasure when she lightly bit the side of his bared throat.

"Fuck, yes," he said on a groan. She was everything he needed. All that he wanted. She gave and took with fierce abandon. Though he prided himself on his stamina, when it came to her, arousal launched him toward a speedy climax. "I'm about to spend."

She pulled back slightly but did not release his cock. "Not yet."

His sight glazed with lust, he watched as she slid down his body. With her free hand, she undid the buttons of his waistcoat and stroked him through his lawn shirt. Little daggers of sensation pierced him wherever she touched. His breath caught when she sank onto her knees before him.

Her gaze fixed on his. He couldn't look away to save his life. A knowing smile curved her lips as she licked around the crown of his cock.

Sparks cascaded down his spine. He thought he would explode when she lowered her head to take him into her mouth.

"Ah, love," he growled. "That's perfect."

She made a little hum of acknowledgment, and it reverberated through him. He took huge, gulping breaths as she pumped him between her lips, her hand stroking the base of his cock. Her mouth was hot and wet and faultless as she sucked and licked. Faint light from outside filtered through the curtained window, allowing him to see the low back of her dress and how it exposed the muscles shifting between her shoulder blades.

He was pinioned in place by pleasure, unable to do more than watch her. One of his hands pressed against the door, and he brought the other up to lightly curve along the back of her head. She reached up and curled her fingers around his, tightening his grasp on her.

"You want me to fuck your mouth?" His voice was a deep bass, hardly human.

She nodded, never taking her lips from him or her gaze from his.

He needed no further encouragement. Holding her head in place, his hips moved faster. He watched with dazed fascination as his cock slid in and out of her mouth, his skin gleaming in the half-light. When her eyes went heavy-lidded with pleasure, he knew he was lost.

"Going to come," he managed to gasp.

She didn't pull away. The suction of her lips increased and she took him even deeper.

His climax leveled him, streaking through his entire body with the force of cannon fire. More sensation bloomed as she swallowed him down.

Only after the very last pulse tore through him did she move back. She did so with a smile, licking her lips and making sounds of gratification.

Though his bones felt made of India rubber, he managed to help her stand.

"I win tonight's round," she said huskily.

He pulled off his clothing, scattering it everywhere. "The night's not over."

She raised an eyebrow, but didn't protest as he led her to the bed and lowered her to sit on the edge. When she made room for him to sit beside her, he shook his head and knelt before her. Gently, he placed his hands on her knees and urged them apart.

The stunned expression on her face turned wicked.

"Shall I keep going?" he asked.

"I'd perish if you didn't."

A satisfied smile curved his mouth. "We don't want anyone perishing."

He collected handfuls of her skirts, uncovering her legs. As inch by inch of her was revealed, he kissed her. Ankle, calf, knee. The heat of her skin burned through her stockings. He continued to go higher.

To his delight, her smooth bare thighs appeared

over the tops of her garters. Again, she hadn't worn drawers. He wasn't the only one who'd anticipated this night.

Tom licked the skin of her inner thigh, then inhaled deeply as he scented her arousal. When he bared her quim, he made a sound he'd never heard himself make before, more suited to a wild creature than a civilized man.

But he wasn't civilized now. He was primal and hungry and burning to devour her. To give her ecstasy.

"Fucking Christ almighty." He could barely form words as he caressed her.

She was wet. So wet. His fingers were glossy with the evidence of her arousal. She mewled as he stroked her, and more sounds climbed up her throat as he traced her pussy and circled the tight knot of her clit. He'd always loved this part of a woman, and touched Lucia with rough reverence. She panted with need when he stroked two fingers up into her passage and thrust.

He hadn't spoken Gaelic in years, and yet he turned to it now to tell her how perfect she was, how he worshipped her and hungered to possess her fully. How she was the sole source of his happiness and if he could spend the rest of his life giving her pleasure, he'd gladly do so. All the while, he caressed her quim and fucked her with his fingers. He pressed against the swollen spot deep within her passage, and she cried out in ecstasy.

Her body arched back as she came. Slickness coated his hand. She crumpled onto the mattress as her orgasm receded.

She breathed out. "Ah, God."

"That was merely the prelude," he said with the solemnity of a knight making a vow. He lowered his head and licked her.

Her hips lifted up from the bed. He held her in place as he stroked his tongue over her and into her, dipping into her entrance. Her taste filled him, smoky and sweet, and he adored her with his mouth. Lightly, he took her clit between his lips and sucked. As he did so, he pumped his finger into her. She threw back her head and let out a long, keening cry of rapture.

He continued to worship her as he fucked her with his tongue and finger.

"Yes," she wailed. "Yes. That's—yes—"

She broke apart with a cry. Her climax rolled from her body into his, and he soaked up her pleasure. When she thrashed against the mattress, he didn't relent. He continued to thrust and lick until she came once more, longer this time. Only then, he gently slid his finger out and pulled his mouth away.

As he lowered her skirts over her legs, he looked up at her. Her eyes glittered through lowered lashes.

"You're right," she said, her words faintly slurred. "We both won."

"The night's barely begun," he murmured. "Let us continue our winning streak."

Chapter 16

❧

$\mathcal{L}$ucia couldn't possibly want more, not after the mind-dissolving orgasms Tom had given her.

Yet his words made her whole body catch fire.

He leaned up to kiss her, and she tasted herself on him. With his clever fingers, he worked the fastenings down the back of her gown until the neckline hung loosely. He stroked down her neck, over her collarbone, lower, and he made a thrilling sound of animal hunger when he found that she'd purposefully not worn a shift. She gasped, her lips against the shadow of his beard, when he caressed her breasts. When he stroked her nipples, she writhed with pleasure.

She peeled off her dress, flinging it aside, before sliding from the bed to kneel as well, pressing her body to his. His cock surged against her belly, and he snarled when she clutched at the curves of his buttocks to bring him closer still.

"Need you now," he rasped.

"Yes."

He turned her with a firm, guiding hand so she faced the bed, her upper body pressing into the mattress. He caressed one hand down the cheek of her arse. She purred in response.

His hand came down with a decisive, stinging slap.

She stiffened in surprise, then moaned as hot sensation flooded her.

He repeated the spank on her other cheek. Shamelessly, she wiggled, and her mouth formed a sly smile when he growled in response. Her smile fell away when he stroked down her arse and dipped between the lips of her slick quim. She sucked in a breath as she pushed herself back into his touch. His fingers found her aching clit and circled it until she was lost in a fever.

He stilled for a moment. Looking back, she saw him tightly gripping his beautiful, thick cock. When he positioned himself at her entrance, she dug her nails into the mattress, eagerly bracing herself.

Still on his knees, he thrust into her. She jolted exquisitely with the force of his stroke.

He plunged in and out, one hand clutching tightly on her hip. The other hand lavished attention on her clit, caressing her in time with his thrusts. She jolted from the ferocity as he drove into her. Her taut nipples rubbed against the bedclothes, adding to sensation.

She managed to reach behind her to cover his hand on her hip, then brought him up to the crown of her head, urging him to tug at the roots of her hair. When he did, lush fire poured through her. Only to him could she permit herself this ceding of control, this tumble into surrender when in every other moment of her life, she had to be in command. There had to be trust between lovers for one to yield to the other, and with dawning awareness, she discovered she had faith in him—with him, she could let everything fall away, secure in the knowledge that he would never willingly hurt her.

It was startling, terrifying, and wonderful. She lost herself in the expansive openness that was trust. Her back arched and she pushed back against him in wordless demand.

He rumbled his approval and his thrusts grew deeper, even stronger.

Her orgasm erupted, cascading along her body. She cried out. And still, he fucked her, never relenting until she came again, and once more.

"Ah, damn," he growled, then went rigid as he pulled out and groaned his release. His seed shot across her flesh. He draped over her back, and they fitted against each other, his front to her back, panting.

They climbed into his bed, the span so narrow she lay half-atop him. She let herself drift in and out of sleep, soothed by the beat of his heart and the rise and fall of his chest as his large hand splayed against her back.

She never *slept* with her lovers, preferring to have her pleasure and then leave. Yet she couldn't make herself move away from Tom.

Stay, her body whispered. *Stay with him.*

She roused from a doze, her face pressed against his chest. He made gentle sounds of sleep, and it engulfed her in a warm cocoon. But as she splayed over his body, desire licked through her. She stroked her hand up his chest, the hair crisp against her palm, before lightly scratching her nails down his torso.

"Insatiable," he rumbled.

"No shame in that." But she was insatiable for *him,* and if she wasn't caught in a frenzy of need, such unending hunger for one particular man would have frightened her. She couldn't care now, not with his hot skin against hers and his scent coating her.

"None at all," he murmured.

They kissed, and then he rolled so that she was under him. Her legs opened. In one single, potent thrust, he was inside her.

"Want you so much." He punctuated each word with a stroke. "I'm lost in you."

"I have the same madness," she said on a gasp.

Despite her revelation of trust, she told herself that this thing between them was only lust—a feeling she knew well.

He hitched her leg higher onto his hip, his thrusts hitting her at precisely the right spot.

She came hard, her back arching up. A moment later, he pulled out and snarled as he climaxed.

As they collapsed onto the bed, she felt herself spiraling beyond the limits of lust into something much more dangerous. There it was again—her faith in him, that frightened her even as she turned toward it. She could not stop herself, gladly throwing herself into the fire that would surely reduce her to ashes.

Checking her timepiece, Lucia saw the time to be three o'clock in the morning. It was Friday night—or, more specifically, early Saturday—and activity at the club showed few signs of slowing down. New guests continually arrived. The establishment's entire staff never had a moment of rest as they went about their duties in a frenzy.

She'd lost count of the number of times she had run up and down the stairs and the loops she'd made through the club. Dimly, she felt her feet throb, but the ache belonged to someone else. Weariness didn't touch her. Instead, energy zigzagged through her body, always pushing her forward.

By all rights, Lucia should have been dragging herself through her workday. She and Tom had barely slept the night before, and instead of napping as she always did in preparation for the evening ahead, she'd been exploring his body with the zeal of a woman who'd long been denied the pleasures of her lover rather than someone who had fucked herself raw only hours before.

As she stepped into the drawing room, she handed a server several bottles of wine she'd just brought up from belowstairs. She caught sight of Tom flipping a chair back onto its feet, and her stomach tumbled as if *she* had been the piece of furniture.

"There's that smile again," Elspeth said, coming to stand beside her.

"What smile?"

"The one that I've never seen you wear for longer than five seconds. Until . . ." Elspeth looked at Tom, who now conversed with Arthur in a corner of the room. "I keep turning around and finding you beaming at him like he personally invented cake. And I should know, because I look at Kitty the same way."

Lucia busied herself collecting glasses. "He and I, we're enjoying ourselves. It needn't mean anything." But her skin was flushed and her heart beat at an unseemly speed.

"I never said a word about anything meaning something. That was your inference."

Caught.

Lucia's hand hovered for a moment over an empty wineglass before she shook her head and picked up the vessel.

"What will you do," Elspeth asked softly, "when it's time for him to go back to his world?"

Lightly, Lucia said, "We haven't discussed it."

But at the thought of his departure, something huge and empty opened up within Lucia, so suddenly and powerfully she pressed her lips together to keep from gasping.

Lovers she'd had, and yet none of them made her

truly *feel* as he did. His insight, his heart, his joy in the pleasure of being—they were rare qualities to find in anyone.

"Perhaps you ought to." Elspeth stroked a finger down her cheek. "Through all the years we've known each other, I've never seen you this happy."

A hard knot formed in Lucia's throat. "*Cara.*"

"I'd hate for you to lose that because of fear." With that, Elspeth plucked the glasses from Lucia's fingers and strode away.

The trouble with friends, Lucia thought as she plunged back into her work, is that they saw beyond all masks, both literal and figurative, all the way down to the needy, love-starved soul beneath.

L UCIA stood in the foyer as the very last guest walked out the door on unsteady legs. The guest in question, a black man with the clothing of a prosperous man of business, had drunk only one glass of wine the whole of the night. His wobbly gait was the result of being the object of two women's attentions for hours, clearly evident in his lopsided grin.

"Next Wednesday?" he asked as he stood on the threshold.

She inclined her head. "We shall await your presence."

"Rely on it." Despite his weakened physical condition, he whistled as he strolled off into the dawn.

A smile curved Lucia's mouth as she shut the door

behind him. *This* was why she truly enjoyed her work. When that guest had arrived earlier in the evening, he'd been tense as a cocked pistol, deep lines of strain framing his mouth. Clearly, the Orchid Club had worked its magic on him.

Her smile faded when she turned around and found Tom standing beside his valise.

"Oh," she managed to say. It felt as though she'd been running at full speed down a hill, joyous and free in her movement, and then slammed into a stone wall.

"Much as I hate not contributing to cleaning up," he said regretfully, "I'm due home before breakfast."

"Yes. Of course." Her feet were bolted to the floor, and she could only stare at him across the expanse of the entryway.

"I . . ." He balled his hands into fists. "I need to go. Don't want to, but I must. I promised my family that I would be gone for three days only. And Parliament won't wait for me."

"I understand." The urge to fling herself at him, to wrap her arms around him and beg him not to leave, was an insistent demand she forced herself to ignore.

"Three days ago," he said, his gaze searching, "I sought shelter, and you gave it to me. You gave me . . . so much. A roof over my head, labor for my hands, pleasure for my body. And my heart . . ." He swallowed hard. "Goodbye, Lucia."

"Goodbye, Tom." There, she spoke with admirable

restraint, as if parting with him once more didn't rend her apart. She wouldn't ask when she could see him again. She would be sophisticated, affable but not clinging. Whatever happened in the future couldn't touch her. She was as she'd always been—aloof and in command of herself.

Who are you trying to convince?

She refused to answer her own question, even as he turned and walked out the door.

Chapter 17

"*T*he house hasn't descended into chaos in my absence, I see."

Tom strode into the dining room and pressed kisses to the cheeks of his mother and sister as they sat at breakfast.

"Maeve has threatened to disguise herself as a lad and sneak out," his mother said as he took his seat at the head of the table.

"Only to see Hugh," Maeve replied. "We both love *As You Like It,* so I should think the prospect of his soon-to-be fiancée wearing breeches for a clandestine assignation wouldn't be too off putting."

"Discussions of furtive rendezvous are generally done out of earshot of one's parent," Tom said drily.

He nodded as a footman stepped forward to offer him coffee, then inhaled the scent deeply as the beverage filled his cup. God, but he was weary. He'd arrived home, and there had been just enough time to quickly bathe, change, and gather up a stack of waiting correspondence before joining his family for the morning meal.

Hopefully, Lucia would get a few hours of sleep before heading to Bethnal Green and her waiting students.

God, if only I could be back with her.

The day stretched before him, a daunting mountain of hours he had to climb. Monday would see him back in the Lords. He had only today and tomorrow to acclimatize himself before he'd meet Brookhurst not as a future relative and fellow investor but possible disinterested party where the canals were concerned and opponent on future votes. The decision he'd made on the roof of the Orchid Club, in the depths of night, now confronted him in the light of day, in this breakfast room.

He'd have to face it now. And tell Maeve.

He took a bracing sip of coffee before moving to the sideboard and assembling a breakfast plate, loading it up with rolls, eggs, and grilled sausages.

"Someone awoke hungry." His mother eyed his plate as he sat.

"Travel stirs the appetite," he said. "Besides, I've been up for hours and this is the first meal I've taken in a long while." And it gave him something to do other than stew about Maeve's reaction to his choice.

The last thing he'd eaten had been stewed beef with the staff of the Orchid Club—over twelve hours ago. Now he was back home, back amongst the world he'd known his whole life, where little changed except, on occasion, the decor.

He glanced around the dining room of Northfield House. His mother had refurbished it three years ago, changing the dark-paneled walls to sophisticated and modern pale yellow plaster, and selecting two massive silver chandeliers to light the chamber.

The staff's dining hall at the Orchid Club wasn't nearly as elegant, with its rough stone walls and long, battered table, and he wished more than anything to be there now. Laughing and telling tales with the staff as Lucia sat beside him, adding her voice to the harmonious bedlam.

The notion of time was clearly a construct, if three days in Bloomsbury could feel like three minutes.

And now I've become a philosopher, speculating on the nature of time itself.

He hadn't taken more than a few bites of his breakfast before he felt his mother's assessing gaze fixed on him.

Quickly, he ran a hand along his jaw. He'd shaved, so the state of his beard couldn't be the source of her interest. Glancing down, he checked to be certain all the buttons of his waistcoat were fastened in the proper order, and that the knots of his neckcloth were respectable.

"What?" he asked warily.

"The country air must have agreed with you," she said. "You're . . . different, somehow."

What could he tell her? *I worked at a secret sex club and there's a woman there who makes my blood sing and I've reached a crossroads that will affect the course of our family for generations to come and who am I, anyway?*

"Despite the fairy stories you told us as children," he said with an attempt at whimsy, "I'm not a change-ling. Same Tom who's been giving you a headache for thirty-two years."

"Let him eat in peace, Mam," Maeve said with a shake of her head.

"It's a mother's labor to harass her children." Deirdre dabbed her lips with a napkin and stood. As Tom got to his feet, she waved him back down. "Saturday's my letter-writing day, so I'm off to give my children some much-needed peace."

A moment later, she was gone, and Tom and his sister were alone.

He eased back down to his seat before resuming his breakfast.

"It's true, though." Maeve propped her chin in her hand. "You *do* seem altered."

Rather than acknowledge the truth of that statement, he rolled his eyes. "Saints protect me from the meddlesome women in my family."

"You may be older by thirteen years," Maeve said primly, "but I've considerable experience running after you and knowing your moods. Something's troubling you."

Though he did need to speak with her, he'd no great eagerness to tell his sister that he might very well cost Maeve her beloved Lord Stacey.

"There's nothing—"

"Tommy." Her gaze was serious. "Please. You can unburden yourself to me. I promise that whatever you say, I won't fall to the ground with the fits."

He set his knife and fork down. Damn it. This had to be done, and he both abhorred and welcomed it.

There's nothing to be done but face this. You owe it to Maeve, and to yourself.

After a long moment, he said, "There are many forces—Lord Stacey's father included—that want me to fall into line and do what's expected of me."

She looked at him with her piercing, astute gaze. "And what do *you* want?"

"To create change in the world." He thought back to the revelations he'd made on the club's roof, and again he felt that dual sense of excitement and dread. "I've a tremendous amount of influence now. I want to use that influence to shape England into a better country, one that doesn't cling to outdated prejudice to ensure that a few people hold the reins of power."

He sat back, slightly stunned. Speaking all this aloud made it even more real, more necessary.

"I'm glad, Tommy," Maeve said, her eyes shining. "I want you to act from your heart, not a sense of duty. Something's holding you back, though. What is it?"

Unable to meet her gaze, he glanced away. Now that the moment was here, getting the words out of his mouth seemed an impossible task. This could end his relationship with his sister, and to lose her would be like cutting out his heart and expecting him to go on living.

Softly, she said, "It's me, is it not? You're protecting me."

Stiffly, he nodded. "Acting from my heart . . ." His words sounded gruff, almost severe. "It means opposing the Duke of Brookhurst. And if I do, the duke will forbid Lord Stacey from marrying you."

A long silence followed, and when Tom looked back at his baby sister, her brow was furrowed in thought.

"Oh, Tommy . . ." She rested her head in her cupped hand.

"I'm sorry, Maeve." He reached for her, and while she didn't take his hand, she didn't pull away, either.

"The price of your conscience is considerable," she said after several moments. Her voice was low, barely audible.

"I wish it came with some other cost." Regret tightened his throat. "Brookhurst's powerful, and of a certain my crossing him will close doors to me, but that's nothing, truly nothing, by comparison to what it will cost you. It's . . . a damned conundrum."

Maeve got to her feet and paced to the window. Tom stood, but when he moved to follow her, she held out her hand in a silent demand for silence and space. He could only watch, and wait.

When he'd been eighteen, and home on holiday from school, one day he'd gone off on his own to meet a girl in the village. The whole way there, as he'd hurried down the bridle path, he'd thought only of the pleasure he was soon to have. Halfway to the village, though, he'd become aware that someone followed him.

He'd spun around, only to find Maeve in her grass-stained pinafore, trying to keep up on her short, little girl legs. But instead of looking guilty for being caught away from home and away from her nurse, she'd smiled at him.

"Go home, Maeve," he'd said, trying to sound stern like their father.

"I'm coming with you, Tommy," she'd announced firmly. "We'll go to the village and I'm going to buy you a boiled sweet. I saved for it. See?" She'd rooted around in the pocket of her pinafore and produced a tiny handful of coins.

"Where did you get that?"

"I told Cook that I'd peel potatoes and collect eggs." She had said this proudly.

"You forced him to give you his own money?" He had shaken his head. "Maeve, he *works* for us." Tom would have to compensate Cook for the loss of his hard-earned coin.

Maeve's eyes had filled with tears. "I'm sorry,

Tommy." She'd dropped the coins to the path. "You're not here mostly and I wanted to get you a boiled sweet because I love them."

All Tom's annoyance had scattered like so many scraps of paper cast onto the wind. Jesus, God, but he loved her.

"Come on, then." Tom had crouched down and collected her coins, putting them into his own pocket to return to Cook later. "Let's get ourselves some boiled sweets and maybe even a berry cake, if they have them." He'd stood and held out his hand to her.

She'd run to him immediately, sliding her slightly sticky little hand into his. Together, they'd walked into the village and he'd gotten her the promised sweets and cake. When the girl he was supposed to meet marched by the shop window, fire in her eyes because he'd forsaken her, he'd had not a single regret.

He could lose that. Lose Maeve.

Anguish spilled acidly through his veins, burning him from the inside out. For thirty-two years, he'd been physically a man, but in his heart, he'd been a boy, free from making decisions that cost him anything more than a few hours' pleasure. But this choice . . . this would surely kill him.

No, it wouldn't kill him. He'd survive, and have to find a way to live without Maeve's bright flame illuminating his life.

"Maeve," he said on a rasp.

"If the Duke of Brookhurst's disapproval keeps

Hugh away," she said at last, turning back to face him, "I don't want him in my life."

He started. He couldn't have heard right, not when her choice meant losing the man she loved. "Are you . . . certain?"

"Quite." Her smile was brave, though he could see the effort it cost her. "We're people of principle, us Powell siblings."

Relief crashed through him, nearly making him stagger on his feet. Yet he ached for her, too, because certainly she would soon face her own heartbreak when Lord Stacey disappeared.

Sometimes, life was a goddamned bastard.

"That we are." He took her hand in his, and was plunged back into the past, on that bridle path, grasping her little hand that was so small yet held so much power. "Thank you, little bird. To be sure, there's trouble ahead. Da's old friends won't like my new course."

Her lips curved slightly. "Remember how I climbed that tree, the big oak, and I got so scared I couldn't climb down?"

"I do. You screamed fit to dig furrows in the earth."

He'd stood at the foot of the oak, praying whatever deity was listening would keep tiny Maeve safe and whole.

"You just charged up after me, never worrying about breaking your own neck." Her gaze softened. "My big brother's afraid of nothing."

His lips quirked into a wry smile. "God help me be the man my little sister believes I am."

Somehow, he managed to drag himself through the remainder of the day. Though it was technically Saturday, enough work had piled up in his absence that he could not ignore it until Monday. He sequestered himself in his study to catch up.

All the while, Monday hung over his head like a sword. A prison bill was coming up, and he knew how he had to vote—but it felt like pulling the trigger and waiting two days for the bullet to slam into his chest.

For all this, for the magnitude of what his decision meant, his mind refused to stay where he needed it. The damned thing kept rocketing back to Lucia— where was she at that very moment and what was she thinking, hopefully of him?—and he found himself staring off into nothingness.

When he discovered that for fifteen minutes he'd been reading the same line in a document detailing Monday's parliamentary schedule, he cast the paper aside before raking his hands through his hair.

It was useless. He knew his mind on the matter, and to try to attempt anything remotely productive was futile. He stalked from his study and spent the rest of the day playing lawn bowls in the garden with Maeve. After supper, they included their mother in a game of spillikins.

It was all very normal and calm, and if he was quietly going mad because he wanted to saddle his fastest horse and ride back to Lucia, he kept that madness carefully contained. No one noticed.

Except he returned to the parlor after using the water closet to find his mother and sister on the sofa whispering to each other. They abruptly broke apart at his entrance, and while Maeve fixed a bright smile on her face, his mother quickly walked to the fire and poked it with an iron as if she was Hestia, tending the hearth of Olympus.

"You looked like a pair of conspirators."

"Oh," his mother said in an offhand voice, "we were merely talking of the weather. It should be fine and clear tomorrow, for all that it's heading into winter."

"It's not like you, Mam." He flung himself down in a nearby upholstered chair.

"To discuss the weather?"

"To avoid saying what you think of me directly to my face. You've always been very free with your opinions about my life."

"About everyone's lives," Maeve added, then blinked innocently when her mother shot her a fierce look.

"Can't a mother care for the well-being of her children?"

"Perhaps we should have this conversation when you aren't brandishing a fire iron," Tom suggested.

His mother set the metal rod down before setting her hands on her hips. "You *do* seem distracted lately and not quite yourself, and there's one remedy that will surely calm you. A wife."

The very *last* thing he needed or wanted in his very complicated life.

"Mam, no."

"Maeve agrees with me."

Tom glared at his sister. "Judas."

"Think on what Mam says," Maeve said, her gaze starry. "It's such a wondrous thing, to have someone to confide in, someone you can't stop thinking about. Someone with whom you can be your truest self. It's a marvel."

His already frayed forbearance nearly snapped. This was not a conversation he wanted to have—not now, at any rate. Not when he was filled with thoughts of Lucia, remembering the lush silken feel of her body against his, the taste of her. How her touch calmed the tempest within him, yet her gaze set him aflame.

He could never bring her to Northfield House— not through the front door. He couldn't introduce her to Maeve or his mother. They'd never dine together or play spillikins or sit in quiet comfort near the fire, safely nestled within the walls of his ancestral home. Lucia could never be a part of his world.

"I'm going to bed," he said, turning away.

"But, Tommy lad—" his mother protested.

"Good night." He kissed Maeve's cheek and then his mother's and hurried out of the parlor as fast as he could without breaking into a full run.

He reached his chamber and disrobed before slipping on a dressing gown. After pouring himself a glass of whiskey, he sat beside the fire in his chamber, turning Maeve's words over and over. *It's a marvel.*

But she was fortunate. Though it was better for her to make an advantageous match, she could select a husband of her choosing, letting her heart guide her decision. And her heart had made its choice.

Tom could not afford to be so lucky.

*B*Y noon on Sunday, he paced his study, gut churning in anxious anticipation of the following day—and taking a public stance against Brookhurst. God, if only he could get it over with, rather than this . . . inaction.

More than anything, he needed Lucia. Her sagacity. Her bravery. She inspired him to be something better than he was. He believed in himself when he was with her.

The hell with it.

He ordered his carriage, and in short order was on his way to Bloomsbury. The journey took far too long.

Elspeth answered the door when he knocked. She held a piece of toast and took a meditative bite as she regarded him on the front step, shifting restlessly from foot to foot.

"She's in her room." Elspeth stepped back to permit him entrance.

"My thanks," he managed to say before bounding up the stairs.

Energy crackled through him as he took the steps with long strides. He felt certain he looked like a display in a lecture on the wonders of electricity, bright arcs tracing from his body in all directions.

The door to Lucia's room stood open. She sat on her bed cross-legged, her brow furrowed as she read a book.

The agitation within him calmed, even as his heart thudded to see her again.

He rapped gently on the door.

She looked up. Her frown eased and transformed into a smile as she unfolded herself and rose to standing. "An unexpected pleasure."

"I don't intend to disturb you." He moved into the room, pulled by her nearness.

"If you arrived banging pots and pans, followed by a parade of trumpets, you wouldn't disturb me." She tapped her fingers across his chest, and tiny flares of heat flashed over his skin. "Is there a reason for your visit?"

One of her brows lifted and she glanced at the bed.

Arousal surged, but he tamped it down. He captured her hand in his and kissed her fingertips, then startled a laugh from her when he gently bit one finger.

"What I require is you fetching your coat and hat, and accompanying me on an outing."

"Dare I ask what this outing might be, or do you prefer a surprise?"

"Sometimes surprises are welcome, but they can also wreak havoc." He thought of the letter that had reached him in Cornwall, summoning him back to London, and his father's deathbed. A spur of unexpected grief rose up. It could strike at any moment, without warning, speeding him back to the moment when the physician had announced that his father had breathed his last.

Rather than shove his sorrow aside, as he might have done even a week ago, he now breathed through it, giving it space to simply be. Gradually, it receded—but it would always be a part of him, his father's absence as much a fact of life as the sun overhead, casting shadows.

"Are you well?" Lucia asked gently, her voice breaking into his thoughts.

He inhaled, nodding. "You and I are going to a fair on the outskirts of the city."

She tilted her head, her brow furrowed in thought. "The last one I went to was Bartholomew Fair four years ago with Kitty. Still have this." She walked to a cabinet and produced a souvenir silver spoon with an engraving on its handle.

"That spoon shall be alone no longer," he declared, "when we purchase it a companion today."

She set the spoon aside and regarded him with curiosity. "You're a man of significance and consequence.

Surely your responsibilities demand your company and leave little time for country outings."

"Madam," he said gravely, "between you and them, there's no choice to make."

A smile spread across her face, dispelling grief's shadow. "They can go to the Devil?"

"There's a lass. Now get your coat."

Chapter 18

❧

The fair sprawled in a field to the west of London, a motley collection of booths, tents, and outdoor amusements that resembled a patchwork quilt of humanity. Noises of every variety tumbled over one another—drums and fiddles vied with barkers shouting for visitors bundled into heavy coats to visit their attractions—while the scents of roast meat and penned animals were thick in Lucia's nostrils. It was chaotic and cacophonous and she adored it.

"This is so much like the *fiere* in Napoli," she said to Tom as they ambled from booth to booth, her hand tucked in the crook of his elbow. "I wish you could see it. So much life and color."

Bittersweet memories made her throat ache, and she blinked hard to push back tears. She ground the heel of her hand into her eyes as if she could hold her melancholy at bay.

He gazed at her attentively, then frowned. "We can leave," he said, concern edging his voice. "Find our entertainment elsewhere, or return home. Wherever you're happiest."

The melancholy dissolved, like the fog from the Gulf burning away as day progressed.

"Your concern is appreciated," she said truthfully. How long had it been since someone other than Kitty or Elspeth had cared about her feelings? "But the weather's so fine and pleasant, and," she added, cheeky, "the company is tolerable."

A corner of his mouth turned up, and his look was warm. "Couldn't ask for a lovelier day or companion, even if she is an insolent wench."

The fair bustled around them, yet she lost herself in his eyes. Was it possible to feel one's heart growing larger and larger? Was it not a machine that remained fixed in size? Yet hers seemed to swell, as though it could fill her body.

"Ample warning," he said as he led her toward a booth selling ribbons, "I'm determined to spend a disgusting amount of money on you today."

Giddiness flipped in her belly—for all that she prided herself on self-sufficiency, the idea of a gentleman showering her with pretty things was tantalizing.

Still, she said on a laugh, "I've no need of trumperies and gewgaws."

"They are utterly useless," he said with a nod, "and yet irresistible." He smiled at the woman manning the booth. "We seek trinkets, madam."

The woman held up one arm draped with ribbons.

"Finest satins for the lady. Or perhaps lace? These embroidered trimmings are exceptionally outstanding." As she spoke, she displayed different lengths.

Lucia could not resist, and stroked each ribbon lovingly. Such things were entirely frivolous, yet the colors and textures were utterly delightful.

In Napoli, there had barely been enough to keep her clothed in rags, and she and Mamma would lie in bed at night talking of what sort of beautiful garments they'd wear, if only they had a bit of money. Mamma had died in her threadbare shift. Now, whenever Lucia slipped into a pretty gown, she did it for herself—and her mother.

"I do love to adorn myself," Lucia admitted.

"A bit of beauty nourishes the soul," he agreed. "Isn't that right?" he asked the vendor.

"Indeed, sir," the woman said at once. "If the good Lord didn't want us making ourselves handsome, why would He make so many lovely things? Like this aubergine silk. It would be so charming trimming the lady's bonnet."

"We'll take that, and anything else the lady wants. Make her eyes shine with joy, madam."

Lucia watched him as he examined a roll of emerald satin with the studiousness of a scholar. A few of her past lovers would sometimes bring her little baubles—cheap, glittering things—but they'd present their gifts to her in the hope of a fuck. They were objects with conditions: access to her quim for the price of a paste necklace.

Not Tom. He gave to her from his heart, no stipulations, no expectations.

Ten minutes later, they left the booth with promises to return later to pick up a sizable bundle. She already planned which member of the Orchid Club staff would get which ribbon, though she knew for certain that Elspeth would get the buttercup yellow and Kitty had to have the one covered in miniscule roses.

From stall to stall, they traveled, stopping to admire carved wooden toys—a soldier painted in jolly crimson was selected for Liam—and observing a man making beeswax candles as bees crawled over his hands and arms.

While she enjoyed her outings to the shops with Kitty and Elspeth, she couldn't recall the last time she'd allowed herself a day strictly for frivolous pleasure. Responsibilities and worries and burdens fell away, her step growing lighter with each moment, until she believed that if she didn't have her arm hooked into Tom's, she might soar up into the air.

She couldn't suppress a chuckle when Tom boomed with laughter as they rode a swing boat. They watched a puppet show with a throng of children, the performance followed immediately after by a quartet of brightly dressed acrobats leaping and jumping like fleas.

"You're enjoying yourself?" he asked after the last somersault had been turned.

"So much." Her cheeks ached from smiling. "I haven't had a day just for amusements in . . . I can't remember when." Gratitude welled up like so much wine in a cup, liquid and warm. *"Grazie."*

Tom grinned. "Your delight is mine, love."

Love. The word made her stop in her tracks. He'd said it so easily, as if the word itself held little significance—but she could not set it aside so readily. Could he . . . ? Might she . . . ?

Don't be a babbea. *It's an expression, and nothing more.*

Unaware of her thoughts, he patted his stomach. "Revelry stirs the appetite."

She blinked, bringing herself back to that moment, grounding herself with the scent of trampled dust and the sounds of merriment. "It does," she said as brightly as she could manage.

He hailed a man pushing a cart.

"Tasty sausages, sir," the vendor said as he opened the lid on his cart. "Made from the best Devonshire pigs."

They collected mugs of beer and pieces of fragrant gingerbread, and ate standing up while watching a troupe of dancers spin and wave kerchiefs. Seeing the performers, she fell back through time and crossed an ocean, back to the fairs in Napoli. She and the other children would twirl alongside the women dancing the tarantella for coins, all of them grasping at moments of happiness in between the daily struggle for survival.

I am here now. With this man, in this place. My life is my own, and I'm grateful for everything I have.

She had to keep telling herself that. She couldn't let herself wish for anything more. This day, with its indulgence and joy, was enough. Being with Tom now was enough.

Her attention strayed from the performance, her gaze lingering on Tom as he enjoyed himself. Each bite he savored, and every sip of beer was met with his hum of approval, all the while his eyes were bright with pleasure. When he caught her looking at him, he winked.

Her heart leapt in response. All he had to do was gaze in her direction, and she felt as though she spun like one of the dancers—giddy, reckless, free. So long as he was beside her, she believed she could do anything.

Oh, she was in danger with him. Yet she couldn't stop her headlong tumble into emotions she'd never believed she would feel. He made the impossible possible.

"RING-A-BOTTLE! Try your skill for a ha'penny!"

Tom would have been content to pass the game by—there were other sights to see at the fair, other amusements to bring a smile to Lucia's face—but she stopped and nodded toward the booth, where a tall, thin man stood, crying to the crowd.

"I want to give it a try," she said.

"Truly?" Tom eyed the game with suspicion. The man encouraged the crowd to throw wooden rings at weighted bottles lined up atop a bench. Poppets of different sizes were arranged between the bottles, most likely prizes for whomever managed to land the ring onto the bottles' necks. No one, with the exception of the barker himself, was successful, men walking away with their shoulders slumped.

Yet Lucia had already plucked a coin from her reticule and approached the barker with it.

"Ah," the man said with a knowing nod. "Want your chap to win you a prize?"

"I intend to win *myself* the prize."

Tom smiled to himself when the barker looked back and forth between him and Lucia with a confused look.

"Guv?"

"The lady intends to be her own champion," Tom said. "I, for one, will not gainsay her." He adored that about her, her determination, her need to succeed on the basis of her own strength and skill.

The barker shrugged, then held up a wooden ring. "Real simple, like. I'll show you." He lightly tossed the circle of wood, and it neatly fell onto the neck of the bottle. "Now you." He offered her another ring.

"I want that one." She pointed to the piece of wood he'd just thrown.

The barker's forehead pleated. "They're the same, ma'am."

"Perhaps so," she said levelly, "but I will use the one you just threw. And I intend to do it from where you are standing."

He opened his mouth to protest, but Lucia kept her expression perfectly smooth. Clearly, she would not be dissuaded. After the barker retrieved the ring and handed it to her, a nearby stocky man in a tall hat paused.

"That gentry mort won't make it," he mused aloud while Lucia took her position.

"A pound says she does," Tom said.

"I watched three coves give it a go," the man in the tall hat said, "and none of 'em got the prize."

"Then it's a guaranteed win for you." Tom pulled a shilling from his inside coat pocket. He glanced at Lucia, who watched him with wry amusement. "Let's agree to it."

"Awright." His opponent produced a bob.

"Have we settled the wager?" Lucia asked drily.

"Go ahead, love," Tom said.

Lucia studied the bottles as she held the ring. The barker watched her apprehensively from the other side of the booth, and it seemed that nearby vendors and members of the crowd had stopped in the middle of their activities to watch.

She pitched the ring with a careful underhand throw. Tom held his breath as it arced through the air, then caught the edge of the bottle neck. For a moment, it appeared as though the ring would bounce off. With a clatter, it swung around the neck of the bottle and settled into place.

She'd done it.

He grinned as pure delight radiated through him—as if she'd captured the moon and brought it triumphantly to Prinny, himself. And Tom was the lucky sod who happened to witness her triumph.

This trip to the fair had been an impulse, a way to distract himself from the looming pressures of life. But it was far more than that. It was an affirmation—of her resilience, and the joy that could be found tucked between the pages of the world's weighty tome.

He was *alive*. He and Lucia were alive together, shoring up the strength he needed to face the coming tempest. And it was coming.

"I'll take that one, please," Lucia said in a matter-of-fact voice, pointing to the poppet in a blue dress.

Not bothering to hide his smugness, Tom turned to the man in the tall hat. It served the blighter right for underestimating her. "And I'll have my shilling, sir."

Muttering under his breath, his opponent shoved the coin into his hand before storming off into the crowd. Never had Tom received a shilling with as much pleasure, regardless of how replete the dukedom's coffers might be.

When Tom turned back, Lucia approached him, cradling the doll in the crook of her arm. At her exultant smile, more warmth bloomed in his chest. He itched to put a crown of laurels upon her head and carry her triumphantly through the fair.

"Devious." Unable to stop himself, he kissed her—quickly. "Hiding your aptitude at ring-a-bottle."

"You've stumbled across my cunning plan to conquer England, one carnival game at a time."

"The nation should quake in terror."

His heart pounded. Hell, but he delighted in her. This obsession with her body and the pleasure they created together continued to transform, changing into something far more complex than lust.

"Hold a moment." Tom approached a small girl who'd spread a ragged blanket on the ground. Lying atop the blanket were a handful of whirligigs, assembled from scraps of paper that had clearly been scavenged from found debris.

"Whirligig, sir?"

He tucked his winnings into her tiny palm.

Her eyes went wide. "You can have 'em all."

"I'd rather you had this," Lucia said, handing her the poppet.

The girl didn't waste words on thanks. The doll tucked under her arm, she ran straight to a pieman without a backward glance.

As Lucia and Tom moved on, she said, "The odds were steep, and you wagered in my favor, anyway."

"Only a fool would bet against you."

Her dark, depthless eyes gleamed, and his body filled with surging energy, as though he could accomplish anything—scale any height, bridge any distance, and become more than himself. There were no obstacles when she looked at him like that. There was only possibility.

"Learn the future," a woman called out from her tent, breaking his thoughts. "I can see beyond time! Come and discover what fate has in store for you."

She sat on a cushion in front of a low table draped with a shawl, with another bright shawl around her shoulders.

Tom gave his head a tiny shake. "Prognostication is a skill, not a power."

"You sound very certain of that," Lucia said wryly.

"My friend Blakemere, he went to one of those soothsayers. Got everything wrong—including the fact that Blakemere had just come back from Waterloo." Tom clicked his tongue. "Turned out the fortune-teller was drunk and couldn't see worth a damn."

"The sight isn't here," Lucia said, tapping the corner of her eye. "It's here." She pointed to her forehead.

"Anyone with good eyesight—or listens well—can position themselves as a fortune-teller."

Lucia lifted a brow. "Sounds like a challenge. I think a demonstration of your abilities is in order." She nodded toward a man shepherding his family around the fair. "Tell me his tale."

"I can do better than that." A wild impulse gripped him, and before he could question it, he approached the mystic. "Please, go and have a cup of tea." He dropped a handful of coins into her palm.

Baffled she looked at him, then rose slowly to her feet. "Don't you want me to tell your fortune?"

"Sometimes, it's better to be surprised," he said, gazing at an amused Lucia.

The fortune-teller tucked the coins into a purse before strolling off toward a vendor selling mugs of hard cider.

"I think His Grace has descended into madness, like the king," Lucia said with a laugh as he settled himself down on the soothsayer's cushion. It was slightly lopsided from years of use, and much mended.

"Tomorrow," he said in a low voice, "I'm going to publicly sever the ties that have long bound my family to a man of great power. He won't take kindly to what he'll see as my betrayal and desertion. It might cost my sister the lad she loves." He squeezed his eyes shut as if he could hold back the impending disaster.

"Ah." She reached out and cupped his face, her touch profoundly gentle. "Mayhem tomorrow. A bit of play today."

The tension in his chest loosened, and he opened his eyes. Gratefulness for her understanding nearly brought tears to his eyes. She understood and accepted. The gift she gave him with that faith had no price.

Her hand slid away, but the warmth of her lingered in him.

He cleared his throat, and tried to speak brightly. "Might I have your assistance?" He waved to the front of the tent. "If you will be so kind."

She stared at him for a moment. "If this is what you want."

"It is." He'd left his wild impulsivity behind when

he'd become a duke. But here was a chance to reclaim a part of himself, if even for a brief while.

She didn't press him further. Lucia went to stand in front of the tent and clapped her hands together.

"*Uomini! Donne!* Do you wish to know what tomorrow brings?" Her accent was stronger, as though she purposefully let it come through. "What is your *destino*?"

Several people passing the tent paused, considering her words. She was a surprisingly adept barker.

Tom made sure not to look at the fairgoers, gazing off into the distance as though preoccupied with forces beyond the mortal realm. All the while, his heart beat giddily. It had been too long since he'd done anything quite this mad. Tomorrow would come regardless, but now was for him and Lucia.

"Within this tent is the Prince of Riesling," she cried. "*Aimé!* He's a man exiled from his kingdom by those terrified of his mystical abilities. His *disgrazia* is to your benefit! Sit before him and he will reveal your fate!"

A lad with a young girl on his arm stopped. They glanced at each other with curiosity before the girl shrugged, clearly torn.

"*Amici,* the Prince of Riesling awaits your pleasure," Lucia said.

"How much?" the lad asked.

Tom caught sight of the boy's worn boots, and the hem of the girl's gown, which had been let out several times.

"For you, no charge," he said in a thick Prussian accent.

"Can't refuse that price," Lucia said. She guided the couple into the tent. "Please. Sit."

The lad and girl nervously sat on more cushions arranged on the other side of the table. They held hands tightly, and whenever she looked at her beau, the young chap blushed. Behind them, Lucia watched from a discreet distance.

"*Willkommen,*" Tom said, striving to keep his outrageous accent moderately convincing. "Your right hands, please."

The lad laid his palm up on the table. Slowly, the girl did the same, revealing that her own hand was misshapen, and she only had three fingers.

Tom picked her hand up gently and studied it, muttering, "*Ach!*" and "*Ja!*" before setting it down and doing the same for the lad. They both had neatly trimmed fingernails, and while the girl's hand had a few calluses from a sewing needle, the boy's was thick with evidence of his physical labor.

After this, Tom held their chins as he examined their unlined faces lightly dotted with pimples.

They're little more than children.

Behind them, Lucia looked on, her expression soft as she seemed to also recognize the youth and inexperience of the couple.

"You have just begun an exciting time in your lives, *ja?*" Even as he spoke, the girl nodded, and the lad quickly followed suit. "It is exciting, but it also makes you nervous."

"We were married only last week," she said eagerly.

"*Ach,* of course!" Tom peered at them and they stared warily back. "*Und* now, you face some difficulty. From . . . a friend . . . or a family member."

"Her father," the lad said at once. "He didn't want me marrying Susie. Not this young."

"*Natürlich.*" Tom stroked his chin. "You were . . . his apprentice."

"At the woodshop, yes," Susie said. "Everyone said to wait until Bill got his own place. But—"

"You could not, eh?" Tom nodded at Bill. "A pretty *Mädchen,* how could you not ask her to be your bride?"

Pink crept into both Bill's and Susie's faces.

"*Ja,* the *Eltern,* they worry," Tom said. "And you worry, too, *ja?*"

The couple nodded.

Tom closed his eyes and placed his fingertips at his temples. "I look . . . I gaze into tomorrow . . . it is cloudy . . . but I see . . . yes!"

"What do you see?" Susie cried.

Opening his eyes, Tom said, "There will be obstacles, *nein?* It will not be easy, but," he added when her shoulders fell, "ultimately, you will triumph."

Smiles wreathed their faces and their backs straightened.

"And Bill will soon open his own shop?" she asked.

"Within the year," Tom said with a confident nod.

Tears shined in the girl's eyes, and Bill exhaled as though someone had removed a crushing weight. When the lad fumbled in his pocket for a coin, Tom waved it away.

"*Freunde,* I cannot take your money. Save it today, for soon, you will spend it on your *Kinder.*"

Lucia pressed her fingertips to her mouth, her own eyes glossy with tears as the couple got to their feet.

"Thank you, thank you," they said with bows and curtsys before hurrying away with light steps.

A moment later, the fortune-teller returned, and Tom ceded her tent back to her.

Lucia took Tom's arm, giving his forearm a squeeze. Happiness swelled within him at her touch, and the look of warm admiration in her gaze made him buoyant.

"A man of many talents," she said.

"Telling people what they want to hear isn't much of a skill." His voice was gruff.

Gently, she said, "You gave them hope for the future."

He led her toward the ribbon vendor's booth so they could retrieve their purchases before leaving. The shadows lengthened, the day cooled. Time could not be held at bay. Much as he wanted to linger here with her, it was time to return home. He needed to prepare for the next day.

Two worlds pulled at him, and he feared they'd tear him apart.

"That's all anyone wants," he said. "Hope."

"That's what hope is," she said, picking her way

around a juggler. "For a brief while, we believe that tomorrow will be better than today. When we receive hope, we're given something precious." She stopped and looked up at him, her gaze full of emotion, and his pulse rushed in response. "*You* gave them that—and they won't squander it."

As they continued on to the booth, he turned her words over in his mind. She had risen and fallen and risen again, refusing to surrender to the vicissitudes of life, and he drew strength from her words.

Tomorrow, the solid foundations of his world would crack apart. He'd tear asunder a long-held alliance— and face the dire consequences. He'd no idea what was to come, and a measure of fear worked its chill way through him to contemplate that unknown future.

No matter what came, he'd have this day to return to, again and again, giving him a precious moment of happiness. Because he knew that like all things, happiness was fleeting.

Chapter 19

$\mathcal{L}$ucia openly studied Tom while he sat across from her, watching the landscape wind by. His brow was lowered in thought, and he lightly tapped his fingers against the squabs in time with the rock of the vehicle.

He had to be thinking about tomorrow, and its implications. He was a man who felt deeply. It could not be painless, this shift away from the rigid principles of his father, and the expectation that he'd continue on in the same manner. There would be consequences to taking a stand—consequences that affected more than just himself.

There was darkness in him now, in the quiet after the controlled bedlam of the fair, when he could muse on what lay ahead.

In the past, she'd barely known her chosen lovers— on purpose. They had shared pleasure and little else. It had been a clean and simple economy.

Yet she'd seen the depth of Tom's heart. The kindness he'd shown the young couple at the fair had been extraordinary. He'd nothing to gain from his compassion. It hadn't been performative. It was done for its own sake, and she'd seen enough of the world to know acts of true humanity were rare, indeed.

Tom was a light burning in the darkness, drawing her forward, making her long for his warmth. With him, she ached in the way one hurt when thawing frozen fingers and toes. There was pain, but she leaned into it, welcomed it.

"In Napoli," she said in the stillness, "my mother and I lived in the Quartieri Spagnoli. Maybe long ago, it had been a fine place, but if it ever had, that time had passed."

Tom's alert gaze slid to her as she spoke, and she undid the ribbons of her bonnet to set it beside her.

"It was difficult to survive in the Quartieri Spagnoli if you were determined to lead an unsullied life. *Allora*, I did what I had so Mamma and I could endure. Sometimes it was a choice between theft and eating. Morals did not fill an empty stomach."

Tom looked at her, his mouth set in a grim line. "I'm sorry you had to lead that kind of life."

"Here," she said, pressing a hand to her chest, "where it mattered, that's where I was good. In any case," she added with a wry smile, "that's what my mother would tell me. *Cerchiamo di fare del nostro meglio, e ogni volta anche di più.* 'We do the best that we can, and we always try harder.'"

"She sounds like a remarkable woman."

His admiration warmed Lucia. "She'd be the first to insist she was a humble woman of unimportant birth. But yes, she was remarkable."

"As is her daughter."

Lucia looked down at her hands folded in her lap, before turning her gaze back to him. "Tomorrow will come, and you'll survive it. So will your sister."

He grimaced, and he rubbed his hand in the center of his chest. "That's the part that pierces me like a knife—what all of this will mean for Maeve."

"What does she have to say about it?" Lucia asked gently.

"If I'm a warrior, she's my shield bearer, ready to fight with me." A corner of his mouth turned up and Lucia wanted to touch her fingers to it. "She'd adore you."

"She sounds like the sort of girl I'd like very much." But she and Lady Maeve would never meet. They couldn't.

He seemed to realize this at the same moment, and they both fell silent.

She reached across the narrow space of the carriage to take his hand. Their fingers wove together immediately. "All of this is to say that it might be frightening, these steps you're taking, but you'll do your best."

"*And* I can do better."

She gave him a soft smile. How readily they fell into this rhythm together, its give-and-take. "*Certo.*"

He lifted her hand to his mouth and kissed her knuckles. "You give me the strength to move forward."

The thought made her pulse skip with both terror and pleasure. "I'm merely a diversion, Your Grace."

"You're far more to me than a diversion." His gaze was hot, and it coursed through her with drugging intensity.

She was falling, falling, and couldn't stop herself.

He turned her hand over so it lay palm up, and pressed burning kisses upon her sensitive flesh. Each touch of his lips teased her to life, sparking arousal in flares along her body. He kissed her wrist, his tongue flicking out to trace across her skin. She pressed her thighs together to soothe the ache he created.

When he gently tugged her closer, she went willingly, crossing the interior of the carriage to sit on his lap. They kissed deeply, her fingers threading into his hair to obtain the perfect angle, his hands sliding up her waist. He tasted rich and potent, and she devoured him eagerly as she sank into his touch. His hands cupped her tight, sensitive breasts, making her moan.

They panted into each other's mouths, and she strained against his lean, solid body. The position frustrated her—she wanted more. In a moment, she straddled him, and they both groaned when the thick column of his cock nestled between her legs, curving hotly along her quim.

His hand delved beneath her skirts, and his fingers dipped down into the opening in her drawers. She cried out in pleasure when he stroked against her slick folds. He rumbled when his fingertip lingered on the ribbon attached to the sponge she'd had the good sense to insert earlier.

"Sweet Christ," he growled. He pulled back just enough to close the curtains before returning to caress her.

Rocking with the motion of the carriage, they both worked at the fall of his breeches to free his cock. It rose up in a curve, a gleam of moisture already shining in the slit.

She lifted slightly, bracing her hands on his shoulders, felt him align the head of his cock with her entrance. Then he sank into her.

"Yes," she said on a moan. At the same time, he made a deep, rough sound of pleasure.

His hands gripped her hips to thrust into her. She moved with him, and she lost herself in the bliss of their bodies, in the intimacy they'd made and the desire that burned so fiercely between them.

Their growls and moans filled the confines of the carriage, the air heavy with the scents of arousal. She watched the play of hunger and pleasure on his face, his eyes heavy, his jaw tight, and the sight of him lost to sensation stoked her excitement higher. With unerring skill, he angled himself exactly right so that every time she sank down, he hit the spot deep within her. He brought one of his hands down to rub her clit.

Release beckoned and she chased it, moving like a woman possessed.

"That's it, love," he rasped, driving harder into her.

"I—" Her words were lost as she keened with the force of her orgasm. On and on it went, cresting and receding and rising up again.

"Ah," he rumbled, then stiffened as he climaxed. "Yes."

An eternity later, they collapsed against each other, bodies heaving, clothed yet intimately joined.

Leaning forward, she rested her head on his shoulder, and his arms encircled her to hold her tightly. He murmured softly to her in a language she didn't know, but she understood him just the same—she was beautiful, perfect. Her eyes closed, she drifted on the feel of him still within her and the movement of the carriage.

She had played the game of survival very carefully, taking calculated risks, finding and exploiting opportunities. Always, she knew her objectives and how to reach them. But he . . . he was an unknown. A wild need that she chased recklessly, unmindful of the dangers he presented. Should he want, should he desire, he could devastate her with just a handful of words.

Pushing him away would be wisest, and insisting that they adhere to safe, circumscribed roles.

But she could not be wise. Not where he was concerned.

Chapter 20

$\mathcal{B}$eneath his clothing, a trickle of sweat ran down Tom's back. The sensation hurtled him back to the time, well over a year ago, when he'd stood in a field in the middle of the night, preparing to shoot a bottle of wine in order to win a wager. He barely remembered why he'd agreed to such a ridiculous, wasteful endeavor.

Instead of standing in a foggy field at midnight, he now sat in the House of Lords, preparing to vote on a new bill supported by Brookhurst. This latest bill was in favor of building more prisons.

Greyland sat beside Tom, and his unshakable presence served to anchor Tom to his seat rather than shoot around the chamber like a screaming rocket.

From his position on the Woolsack, the Lord Speaker called out, "Members of that opinion will say, 'Content.'"

Half the Lords—including the Duke of Brookhurst—said loudly, "Content."

When Tom did not join their number, Brookhurst whipped his head around to stare at him in disbelief.

"To the contrary," the Lord Speaker continued, "'Not content.'"

Tom's mouth was dry and his palms damp, but he added his voice to the chorus of, "Not content."

He deliberately gazed at Brookhurst as he spoke, so there would be no confusion as to Tom's vote. The duke glared at him with a mixture of shock and outrage.

Dimly, Tom felt Greyland giving his back one solid thump of approval. The rest of the proceedings sped by in a blur—the bill to build more prisons had been defeated—until everyone was dismissed by the Lord Speaker. Tom filed out with the rest of the lords, his head buzzing and his heart strangely light.

He'd done it. Stepped away from his father's well-worn path, and moved into unknown, untrodden territory. God help him and his family.

In the lobby, Greyland once again slapped his back as other progressive members gathered around, including the Earl of Ashford and Viscount Marwood.

"Nicely done, Northfield," Greyland said with an approving nod. "Good to have you amongst our numbers."

"Never thought to see the day when the Duke of Northfield took a stand for evolution," Ashford said.

"In time, all things are possible." Marwood grinned, but Tom couldn't quite make himself return the smile.

He felt his body poised in readiness, as though anticipating a blow, all the while, his pulse hammered. Yet there was a certainty in his turmoil. What he'd done was right and just, no matter the cost. And he'd face the consequences knowing he had made the right choice.

Angry footfalls echoed in the lobby as Brookhurst stalked forward. His face was ruddy and his mouth formed a hard, slashing line.

Here it comes. Tom straightened to his full height, preparing himself.

"Explain yourself, Northfield," Brookhurst said hotly.

Steadying himself, Tom lifted his eyebrow. "You are not entitled to an explanation."

"I should say I am."

"Sirrah—" Greyland said, his voice tight, but Tom held up his hand.

"Despite your belief," Tom said levelly to Brookhurst, "I am *not* my father. My votes shall henceforth be cast according to my own beliefs. Not his, and certainly not yours. Further, I decline the investment opportunity you presented to me."

"There are consequences to your actions." Brookhurst's cheeks darkened further, while his tone had risen in pitch. "Either today's vote was a singularity, and you *will* back the canal venture, or you and your family will face those consequences."

Tom narrowed his eyes, his anger surging. "Threats are unbecoming to a peer."

"Threats have the possibility of not being carried out. However, what I speak of will come to pass."

"Then end this wearying conversation and be about your business."

The lords observing the exchange between Tom and Brookhurst murmured with distress and disbelief, though Greyland watched it all with an unreadable expression.

Brookhurst pointed a finger at Tom. "The marriage between your sister and my son will never occur. Rely on it."

The room spun around Tom, but he kept his footing. Fury gave him balance and steadied him. "Lady Maeve would rather have a brother who conducts himself honorably than a bridegroom who is his father's puppet."

"Outrageous." The duke took a step back. "Resign yourself to ignominy, *Your Grace*."

Brookhurst swung around, then marched off, a miasma of fury trailing in his wake.

Tom let out one long exhale. There. It was done.

"I cannot believe Brookhurst has reduced himself to threatening a fellow duke," Ashford said in astonishment.

"The word *no* is an abomination to him," Greyland replied. "He makes certain that he never hears it. What do you think he means to do, Northfield?"

The reverberations of anxiety and anger still hummed through Tom's body. If someone asked him to hurl a boulder weighing three hundred pounds, he could do it. "I can't say. Whatever it is, he'll find me no easy target."

The men surrounding him murmured their approval. If only Blakemere had returned from Cornwall. Tom's friend had been a soldier, and could give him much-needed guidance when it came to readying for battle. Because a battle was coming, and Tom had to be prepared to ensure that those he cared about survived.

LUCIA had been in her room, reviewing the ledger for her personal finances, when Elspeth appeared in the doorway.

"You're wanted downstairs." Her friend wore an inscrutable smile.

"The sugar delivery's here already?" Usually, Mr. Kapoor came later in the day, but he was the only vendor she expected on Mondays.

"Our visitor *is* sweet, but he's not Mr. Kapoor."

At once, Lucia knew who awaited her. She rose and hurriedly shelved the ledger before smoothing a hand over her hair and tugging on the bodice of her dress. It had only been a day since she'd last seen him, but that time had passed with agonizing slowness.

"Oh, leave off that," Elspeth said with a wave. "In his eyes, you're encircled by rainbows and he hears the strum of fairy harps."

"It's not like that." Lucia hastened from her room, with her friend following.

"And what if it is? Would it be so terrible?"

Lucia feared the answer, much as she craved it. She'd done what she could to shelter and protect herself, but Tom snuck past her defenses. The mere thought of him brought a smile to her lips and a buoyancy to her heart.

She found him in the foyer, standing beside a large trunk. At her approach down the stairs, he gazed up at her, nearly making her stumble with the sheer joy in his glance.

"You see?" Elspeth murmured behind her. "Rainbows and fairy harps."

Yet as Lucia neared him, she saw the brackets of strain around his mouth, and the tenseness of his shoulders.

His first oppositional vote had been cast today. But he spoke before she could. "I've brought you something." Like a magician casting a spell, he waved to the trunk at his feet. "In truth, it's for the girls. But I hope it pleases you."

Heart thumping, she sank down beside it and undid the latch. With a shove, she pushed the top open. The scent of paper and leather rose up, and her hands flew to her mouth.

The trunk was full of books. She picked up one and read the spine. *A Child's Guide to Geography.*

Elspeth took another book and opened to the title page. "*The History of Europe and Asia For Young Readers.*"

Lucia's gaze rose to his—while her heart felt ready

to tear from her chest and throw itself at his feet. "These are yours?" she whispered.

"Some." He moved into a crouch beside her, and examined one of the books before setting it down. "The rest I purchased from McKinnon's. I asked McKinnon himself for his finest books for eager young minds."

"Oh, Tom." Her fingers brushed over the books, as though she could feel the knowledge they contained. Each one was a key opening a door to new worlds. Tears prickled her eyes.

The cost of books was not inconsequential. It had taken her months to save up for half a dozen texts for her students, and what this trunk contained surely cost over fifty pounds.

Awed, delighted, she cupped her hand over his jaw. He pressed a kiss into her palm.

"I believe I hear Kitty calling for me," Elspeth said, though Kitty was, in fact, out with Liam, visiting a friend.

A moment later, Lucia and Tom were alone. She gazed at him, knowing full well that her heart was in her eyes, yet she didn't fear showing him her vulnerability. If there was anyone she could trust, it was him.

"These can be part of the library for the girls' home," he said, almost shy. "I can bring more, but this seemed like a good start."

Her pulse throbbed, and she had to swallow hard to find her voice. "This is the finest gift I've ever received."

He—the consummate rake and libertine—blushed. "Glad you like it," he said with sudden gruffness.

"It's truly wonderful." Words seemed so paltry, so inadequate. Given time, she might be able to articulate her gratitude. What he'd done for her, for the girls, was bigger than any phrasing of thankfulness. But seeing the tautness of his jaw reminded her that today, he'd made a difficult choice. "How was—"

Tightly, he said, "Purchasing these books was an antidote to the ugliness I experienced today." He shook his head. "We'll talk of that anon. Did I interrupt you in the middle of anything important?"

She rose, and he unfolded himself to stand. Though she burned to know what had happened in Parliament, she had to respect his request.

"Your timing is impeccable. In half an hour, I'm to tour an empty house in Spitalfields to see if it will suit for the girls' home. Will you . . ." She swallowed. "Will you accompany me?"

Lucia had never before invited anyone along with her on a property tour, not even Kitty or Elspeth.

"It will likely be exceedingly dull," she continued. "I have to inspect rooms for signs of vermin, make certain there's no mold in the walls, check the plumbing and—"

"Lucia." His voice was low and velvet, achingly tender. When she silenced, he stroked his fingers over her collarbone. The jangling nerves within her quieted at his touch. "I'm honored."

She dipped her head, unable to form words. This was entirely new—a man at her side, supporting her, seeking nothing but her company.

"My carriage is in the mews," he said in a matter-of-fact tone that seemed specifically selected to calm her.

"If the landlord sees it," Lucia said, striving for a straightforward manner herself, "she'll charge me three times her asking price, thinking she's got a rich pigeon in the net. A cab will suit us well enough."

Though it would be beneath a duke to ride in a lowly hired cab, he merely said, "As you wish."

"Let me fetch my reticule, and we'll be on our way."

"Before you go—" He drew her close, and she inhaled his scent as she pressed herself to him.

When he tipped her chin up, she rose onto her toes, her mouth finding his. There was urgency in his kiss, as though he wanted to lose himself in her and never be found.

"Was today as bad as all that?" she whispered. "Tell me honestly."

He exhaled, his forehead pressed to hers. "Brookhurst made it quite clear there would be repercussions for my defiance. I've no idea what he plans, but nothing is outside the realm of possibility."

"Then we fight back."

"You make it sound simple," he said wryly.

"It won't be. But the alternative is to meekly accept whatever he doles out. And I can't be meek."

"*That,* I know. Now," he said after one more kiss, "let us find a home for your dreams."

She quickly climbed the stairs, and would have soared up even higher, had it been physically possible. *Dio* knew that her heart was up in the firmament.

Chapter 21

❧

The property Tom and Lucia toured had not been quite right for her needs—there weren't enough bedrooms for the girls, and the chambers on the ground floor were too small to serve as classrooms—but she'd been determined to keep looking until she found something perfect.

They'd returned to Bloomsbury and, in the sanctuary of her room, abandoned themselves to shared pleasure. Afterward, they lay together in her narrow bed, bodies snug and damp. She drifted into sleep and he held her, his gaze tracing over the cracks in the bedroom ceiling while his thoughts paced like captive creatures.

Time slipped away from him. Somewhere, hidden beyond the horizon, lurked Brookhurst's retribution. But there was no way of knowing what the duke planned. All Tom could do was balance nimbly on the balls of his feet, awaiting the strike.

Until then, he cradled Lucia with the care she deserved. Her breath feathered over his chest, her hand splayed atop his heart.

Make the world stop. Let this moment last forever-more.

But it could not. He was expected home for supper, and then he'd rise early the next morning to return to Parliament.

"Love," he murmured against the crown of Lucia's head. Her hair held her scent, and the slight tang of perspiration, and he inhaled it deeply. "I've got to go."

"No." Her voice was thick with sleep—she wasn't fully awake. "Don't you leave me, too. *Rimani.*"

His chest contracted painfully. Yet he couldn't linger.

"I'm so sorry, my love. I must be off. I've obligations."

A brief silence, and then she gave a long exhale while her body lost its slackness as she came fully awake.

"Yes, of course." She sat up, the blanket pooling around her waist, and rubbed her knuckles against her eyes. The room had darkened as evening had fallen. Though he couldn't see her fully in the shadows, his gaze moved over her greedily, taking her in.

She slid from the bed to pull on a robe before lighting a candle and seating herself at the table. In the candle's flickering illumination, he dressed, hating the feel of his clothing against his skin. She felt so much better contacting his flesh.

"When . . ." She cleared her throat. "When will I see you again?"

"If I had my choice—tomorrow. Better yet, I wouldn't leave and you'd be the first thing I'd see upon waking."

Pink washed over her cheeks, and he took delight in making an experienced woman blush.

She murmured, "Barring that . . ."

"Not until Thursday." He growled as he tied his neckcloth, frustration taut along his limbs. "Too many commitments."

"It is the way of life," she said in a voice that sounded desperately offhand. She gave a slight shrug.

He wouldn't let her retreat, not when they'd both bared themselves to each other. He bent so their faces were level, and said fiercely, "Know this—when I'm apart from you, you occupy my every thought."

"I think you mean to destroy me." She blinked hard, but he saw how her eyes turned liquid.

"No, love." Ferocity ebbed, leaving tenderness in its wake, and he kissed her. "I mean to build you up. Higher and higher until you can look down at the stars."

*B*rookhurst kept his distance when Tom returned to the Lords the next day. Tom observed the duke warily, yet all that day and into the next, things remained chilly but relatively cordial. It helped that Tom's schedule kept him occupied so he hadn't time to brood.

However, the correspondence between Maeve and Lord Stacey stopped. Tom only knew of it because his sister quizzed the footmen several times a day for the mail.

"I'm so sorry, little bird," Tom said to her as she sat moodily by the parlor window.

She gave him a wry, sad smile that broke his heart. "I had hoped Hugh would be better than this. But it seems he's not the man I believed him to be."

"Bastard," Tom growled. He could ride to Brookhurst's home in a matter of minutes and beat Lord Stacey into a pulp of muscle and bone.

Maeve looked down at her hands, a shadow crossing her face. "Sadly, that's the problem—he isn't a bastard. He's very much the Duke of Brookhurst's progeny."

Tom hurt for her, wanting to gather her close and sing her nonsense songs as he'd done when she was a little girl. But she was a grown woman now. There had to be other ways to comfort her. "Shall we go out? Break away from mourning and go to the theater? I hear Lady Marwood has a new burletta at the Imperial."

Maeve's face brightened briefly, and then she shook her head. "I haven't the strength to face the world just yet."

Goddamned Lord Stacey. "Should you change your mind—"

"You'll be the first I tell."

WEDNESDAY night found him climbing down from his carriage outside the Earl and Countess of Garsdale's home in Marylebone. He permitted himself a weary sigh as he mounted the stairs. Another dinner party, and more political maneuvering.

Lord Garsdale helped broker alliances amongst progressives. Gatherings such as this one were crucial, and so here Tom was, giving his hat and coat to a footman before going up to the drawing room.

The chamber fell silent when Tom entered. He stood in the doorway as a score of faces stared at him with inquisitive, scandalized expressions. A lady whispered to another from behind her fan. Someone audibly gasped.

The hostile expressions on the other guests' faces were easier to tolerate than the ones whose faces resembled frozen lakes, chilling him to his marrow.

Even Lord Garsdale held back, the look on his face pained, as though Tom had entered the room holding a pig head dripping blood onto the polished floor.

Whatever was happening, a tactical retreat was the wisest option. He could assess the situation and formulate a strategy. Tom turned to leave, but Greyland intercepted him and they both stepped into the corridor.

"He's done it," Greyland said in a low voice.

"Who has done what?"

"He hasn't gone to the papers," Greyland said tautly, "but he's been spreading the news in White's, and now everyone knows—your ownership of the Orchid Club, and your affair with the proprietress."

The room spun. Tom braced his hand against the wall. "Brookhurst is a sodding maggot," he said in a rasp.

Greyland exhaled through his nose, his expression grim. "Bastard must have had you followed."

"Fuck." It was a paltry word, one that couldn't begin to touch the rage that poured through him. "Half the sodding *ton* goes to the Orchid Club."

Greyland moved them farther into the hallway, away from the curious guests who hovered near the entrance to the drawing room. "But only you own it. Only you are sharing a bed with its manager."

Tom pulled a hand through his hair.

Oh, hell. Maeve, his mother. The scandal would seek them out, poisoning their social standing. Maeve hadn't just lost Hugh—she'd be unable to marry anyone else.

And Lucia . . .

Fury turned his stomach. Notoriety might help the Orchid Club—or it could ruin the establishment and smother her dream of opening the girls' home. Saints preserve him, but the moment he'd turned his entranced gaze to her that very first night, he'd become the agent of her destruction.

TOM's knuckles turned white as he gripped the carriage window. Impatience and dread gnawed at him for the drive to Bloomsbury. When the vehicle pulled into the mews, he raced to the front door. He had just enough presence of mind to don a mask before entering.

Elspeth let him in, the foyer deafeningly quiet.

"A good night?" he asked, distracted.

"You'll see it for yourself," she said grimly.

When he moved deeper into the club, half-empty rooms met him. Just over a score of guests milled uneasily. No one abandoned themselves to sex, instead drifting agitatedly from here to there. Without the many energetic bodies, the air held a slight chill, and the music was overloud.

There was no sign of Lucia in the main chambers. He went quickly into the corridor, and nearly collided with her as she carried a bottle of wine. Tom clasped her upper arms, needing the feel of her.

"I can't fathom it." Her mask couldn't hide her bewildered expression. "We turned guests away the night of the performances. Ever after, we hosted capacity crowds. Now . . ."

Her words died away as she looked up into his face. Without speaking, she handed him the wine. He drank directly from the bottle before handing it back. Her gaze pinned to his, she also pulled from the bottle.

Taking her hand, he led her into an unused small parlor. Light seeped in beneath the closed door, but it wasn't enough. He needed to see her—tonight more than ever. He stalked to a candle and lit it. Only then did he see how disordered the room was, serving as a storage for cracked knickknacks and worn furniture.

He pulled off his mask, then started to remove hers.

She stayed his hand. "Business hours."

"We won't leave this room unmasked." His words verging on desperate, he asked, "May I see your face?"

After a moment, she undid the ribbons, revealing herself to him. Ah, hell, but looking at her was a pleasure. His hands clenched and unclenched.

"The Duke of Brookhurst played his hand." Tom snarled. "Everyone knows—about the fact that I own the club. About us, our affair."

What a flimsy word, *affair*. It spoke of furtive caresses and sly looks. Nothing at all what he felt for her.

Her eyes went wide. "*Dio ci aiuti.*"

His gaze ricocheted around the snug chamber but found no solace in the jumble of furniture and chipped china figurines. His fingers itched to grab one of the little statues and throw it against the wall.

"Society now dines upon the feast that is a duke's ownership of a clandestine sex establishment." His mouth was dry. "And that the woman who operates it is my lover."

Her throat worked as she swallowed. "Thus I lose half my clientele. No one wants to be implicated in the scandal." She squeezed her eyes shut. "Half our revenue, gone. Which means . . . we can't afford to stay in business." Opening her eyes, she frowned deeply. "There's only one thing to do."

"No," he said hotly.

Yet she nodded, her expression bleak. Voice hard, she said, "Close our doors. Permanently."

"No." He could only repeat the word over and over until somehow he could push back the tide of disaster.

"Your reputation's in pieces," she said flatly. "The Orchid Club closes, and perhaps some of those injuries can heal."

"The home for girls," he said. Simply. As one drops an incendiary device.

"With no income for me, it can't happen."

He reached for her. "Lucia—"

She slipped away from him, her expression shifting from despair to anger. "I knew," she said on a whisper. Louder, "I *knew*." Her gaze turned to him, and it burned with fury. "I kept away from you for a reason. Said to myself, 'Lucia, don't be a fool. Don't open yourself to him, to how he makes you feel.'"

"Stop," he ground out. Each word she spoke was an agony.

"I should never have involved myself with you," she said, voice hard with anger and recrimination—for herself and for him. "But I was an *idiota,* and it cost me everything."

Mortal wounds didn't always come from bullets and bayonets. He saw that now. He rasped, "I'll find a way to fix it."

She stared at him, her features a brittle veneer. "There's nothing to be done. It's over. *Finito.*" As quickly as it had come, the anger burned itself out, leaving behind a burned husk that resembled Lucia. When she spoke, her words were hardly above a whisper. "You and I—"

His pulse roared in his ears, threatening to drown out all sound. He'd laid waste to her world. He had anticipated what Brookhurst might do to him, to Maeve, but never considered the duke would hurt Lucia. How fucking naïve.

Tom swung away from her, as though putting distance between them might somehow keep the truth away.

"Go," she said simply. "We'll not see each other again."

The worst of it was that she was right. He'd sworn to destroy anyone who harmed her—and that harm came from him.

He turned back and stared at her. She had her arms wrapped around herself.

Touching her was an impossibility. Soon, he'd have to rely on memory alone to conjure her. Empty hours and days and years would crawl past with only remembrance of Lucia.

"Please," she said brokenly. "*Lasciatemi*. 'Leave me.'"

"I am so sorry."

Her gaze met his and he saw hopeless despair. Yet there was nothing he could do to change it. There was nothing left to say.

He strode quickly from the parlor, moving sightlessly through the club until he was outside.

Tom tore off his mask and threw it into the gutter. There'd be no further need for disguises.

But he'd spoken honestly. He would find some way to make everything right for her, though they could never again be together. He would discover what it meant to go through the motions of living when his heart had been torn from his body.

It was hers. It would always be hers.

His mother stared at him, face ashen, while Maeve's mouth hung open. They sat across from him in the small parlor his mother liked to use in the morning after breakfast. But the sunny yellow walls and fire cracking cheerfully in the grate did nothing to dispel the constricting weight of the Powell women's silence. A clock ticked, counting the thick moments that followed his confession.

Tom fought to keep from surging to his feet and pacing. He owed his mother and sister the fullness of his attention, and so he kept himself where he was, arms braced against his knees as he leaned forward.

His father's death. His loss of Lucia. Now this—telling his mother and sister that their reputations were ruined, because of him.

He wanted to rage, to howl. But that would do nothing to ease his torment. It felt as though his bones were made of iron heated to white hot, searing him from the inside out.

"Please," he said tightly after minutes passed, "say something."

"What do you want me to say, Tom?" It was a measure of his mother's distress that she didn't call him Tommy lad. "Shall I congratulate you on your business endeavor?" Her mouth tightened. "A club for . . . fornication."

"A place for freedom," he said gently. "And the establishment employs so many, giving them a good wage."

"That makes it so much better," she snapped, then pressed her lips together. A sheen of tears filmed her eyes. "God above, Tom, what were you thinking?"

He raked his hands through his hair. "I'd hoped no one would ever learn of it." Thank Christ Brookhurst hadn't discovered that Tom's father had been the operation's founder and original owner. But that was a small consolation. It had been Tom's choice to keep the Orchid Club open, and now he had to face the agonizing consequences.

"But they did," Maeve said quietly. Her hands fisted in her lap.

He ached with the need to hold her close, to comfort her, but from the rigidity of her spine, he saw that she'd refuse his touch, so he stayed where he was.

"Will anyone receive us now?" Maeve whispered.

He had to be honest. "I . . . don't know."

His sister rose from the sofa and drifted to the fire, where she watched the flames move in a taunting dance.

"How?" his mother asked in a hoarse voice. "How have I failed as a mother that would lead you to *this*?"

"It wasn't *your* failure, Mam." He reached for her

hand, but she pulled away. Anguish cleaved him to be rejected by his own mother. "'Twas mine alone. And all of us pay the price." He looked back and forth between his mother and sister. "An apology cannot remedy this, and it's an insignificant thing, but I do apologize. I'm sorry." His voice cracked as he tried to speak. "I'm so damned sorry."

His mother's expression remained stony. But she did not leave the room, and he clung to the minimal consolation this offered.

"And this was the Duke of Brookhurst's doing," Maeve said, turning to face him. "The dissemination of this . . . news."

"He did not take kindly to my opposition." Tom stood and moved to her, carefully testing the tension between them. He silently exhaled when she did not walk away from him.

"The bastard," Maeve spat.

"Language, Maeve Georgiana!" their mother snapped.

Maeve looked past Tom, her gaze hot as she glared at the duchess. "Beg pardon, Mam. I ought to be more civil when discussing the man who decimated our lives because he felt *slighted*."

"If you had only done as he'd wished, Tom," their mother said despairingly. "A vote here or there. What would it matter?"

His jaw firmed, and it was a relief to feel the purity of anger. "It matters, Mam. Because you and Da raised me better than to pander to someone simply because it was the easiest and most self-serving thing to do."

"Do not dare lay the blame at my feet, child," their mother said tightly.

"I don't," he returned, hot, "and I'm not a child. I'm a man, and I take responsibility for my actions. That includes taking a stand for what I believe is right."

She stared at him a moment, and the air between them strung taut as a garrote. Slowly, incrementally, the fury left her eyes, and her shoulders sagged.

God above, but he never wanted to see his mother so disconsolate—and it was made worse by the fact that he was the one to bring her low.

"But the cost, Tommy lad," she breathed, and brought her hands up to cover her face.

In an instant, he was beside her, his arm around her shoulders, and gratitude surged when Maeve hurried over to also embrace their mother.

"A steep one, to be sure," he murmured. "But all of us—you, me, Maeve—we'll endure. We'll find a way to keep going."

"We have each other," Maeve added, bending her head low so that she looked their mother in the eyes. "And we're just contrary enough to persist despite whatever that rat-faced Duke of Brookhurst throws at us."

He heard his sister's defiance and a gleam of hope shone within Tom that perhaps there would come a day when their family healed from this terrible wound. Yet he'd never excuse himself—he'd perform penance for the rest of his life.

Their mother sniffed. "What of Lord Stacey?"

Maeve's lower lip trembled. "He's said nothing. Not a letter or note, and mine to him have gone unanswered."

"That whole family is a quantity of bastards," Tom snarled. He braced himself, waiting for his mother's remonstrance of his crude language.

"They are," she said instead. "Quite a collection of bastards."

The three of them chuckled softly, breaking the strained atmosphere. He reached once more toward a spark of hope that they could recover from this trauma. Thank God for his family. They would find a means of healing, standing side by side to face the ostracism that had already begun. He'd shelter them as best he could, and all of them had an abundance of strength to withstand further blows. That was something.

But it wasn't enough. Because he had lost Lucia. He'd torn her life apart, shattered her dream, and could not help her reassemble the pieces.

Chapter 22

❧

How am I to do this?

Lucia stood in the hallway outside the tenement room in Bethnal Green, having left off from packing up the Bloomsbury house for a few hours. The books in her arms weighted her down more than they ever had, as if they were made of stone, not paper. She clutched the books tightly to her chest—these last gifts from Tom—squeezing her eyes shut. The girls had to be told, but *Santo cielo,* she didn't want to.

Yet this was a task she *had* to complete—alone.

For a brief while, she hadn't been alone. Tom had been beside her, lending his strength and support in a way that Kitty and Elspeth could not. He'd given her the fortitude of his heart, the steadiness of his presence, and the joy of his body.

I miss him.

Her eyes burned, and when a lone tear traced down her cheek, she juggled books from one hand to the other so she might brush it away. A tear could disappear in a moment, wiped off, but the pain remained.

"Miss Lucia?"

She opened her eyes to see Mary looking up at her, a crease of worry between her small brows.

"Hello, Mary," she said with an attempt at cheer. "Will you help me with these books?"

When the girl nodded, Lucia handed her a few volumes, and together they walked into the room. Her heart seized as she beheld the half-dozen faces gazing at her, eager to begin the day and their lessons.

"We've a treat today," she said sunnily. "New books."

The girls exclaimed in wonder.

"Where'd they come from, miss?" "They *do* look new." "If there's one about plants, I want that one."

Lucia moved through the room, distributing the texts quickly, as if she wasn't handing out pieces of her heart.

"That gentleman from the other week," she said. "These books are a gift from him. And they *are* new, so treat them with respect."

Reverently, the children opened their books, their fingers tracing above the pages to preserve their cleanliness.

"I liked him," Mary announced as she took her seat at her desk. "He was handsome and smelled nice."

A broken laugh escaped Lucia. "He *did* smell nice." Like spice and coffee and leather, and she longed to inhale him deeply and draw him into herself. Anger at herself bubbled up caustically. She didn't want to want him, not after all that had happened and her foolish belief that she could put herself before others. "He's not coming back."

The girls nodded, and the looks of resigned acceptance on their faces nearly made Lucia's knees buckle.
They were too used to people coming and going, too
familiar with abandonment.

She stood in front of the desks and exhaled jaggedly.
"*Bambine,* before we begin today's lessons, there is
something I must tell you."

Her students gazed at her in expectation.

"Do you remember how I told you about a place,
a place that was warm and dry and there was enough
food and books for everyone?"

"And no rats running over our feet at night," curly-
headed Dora said.

Lucia prayed for strength, when all she wanted to
do was run away and hide herself in some dark place
where she could weep and scream and feel the fullness of her grief.

"Yes, that place," she said. "It *will* happen. I promise you that. Only . . ." She swallowed. "It's going to
be a little while longer before it exists."

"How long?" Mary demanded.

Lucia owed them the truth. "I don't know. Six
months . . . a year? I wish I could say, but I cannot."

Again, the expressions of calm resignation on their
young faces shredded her. It was as though they had
never fully believed that this special place for them
would ever exist. Another dream that had died before
it was born.

"But this won't change," she said, resolve firming

her words. "We'll still meet here every Saturday. I swear to you that our time together is safe." She placed her hand atop Dora's head, the texture of the girl's curls branding into Lucia's hand. "I'm not going anywhere."

A few of her students smiled and nodded, but Mary continued to regard her warily. From what Lucia had been able to piece together of the girl's history, her parents were long dead, and it was left to an older brother to take care of his siblings. But the brother could seldom find work as an unskilled laborer, and often disappeared for days. Mary knew hunger better than satiety.

"I promise, Mary." Lucia's voice throbbed with vehemence.

Slowly, the girl nodded. She opened her book and read, her lips silently moving.

Lucia forced herself to smile. She would persevere, she would make her dream happen. But, *Cristo benedetto,* she didn't know how.

Damn me. Damn me for loving him.

Tom climbed the stairs leading to his bedroom, his clothing clinging damply to his body. Despite the pugilism he'd practiced for hours that morning, fury and loss still sieved through him acidly. No matter how hard he threw his punches, no matter how many blows he took, he couldn't beat the sorrow away. It weighted him down and turned the whole world into a monochrome nightmare.

All the while, he imagined his opponent to be Brookhurst, and only when he'd knocked his sparring partner down with a vicious blow—causing the poor blighter's nose to bleed—did he realize how much he channeled his rage against the duke into each punch.

At the pugilism academy, he'd endured the stares and whispers of other gentlemen also there for a morning's exercise. Yet their muttering and pointed looks pinged off of him like so many pebbles thrown at a brick facade. They couldn't touch him. He didn't give a rat's arse what they thought of him. But Maeve, his mother—as women, they were more vulnerable to society's opinion.

His only consolation was that, in mourning, his mother and sister were not expected to venture out in public. Perhaps by the time they were free to socialize, the scandal might have dissipated. God help him, but he hoped so.

He reached his bedchamber and lumbered inside. The elegantly furnished room oppressed him, its carpet feeling thick enough to swallow him up, the dark blue walls the same hue as sky just before sunlight disappeared with darkness following.

Pulling off his shirt and dropping it to the floor, he strode to the bellpull to summon a bath.

"You should pick that up," Maeve's voice said behind him.

He whirled around before he could tug the bellpull. "Christ almighty, Maeve, you near gave me the apoplexy."

His sister bent down and gingerly plucked his soggy shirt from the carpet before flinging it at him. He snatched it before the garment could hit him in the face.

"When have you concerned yourself with how you discard your clothing?" he asked irritably.

"We aren't discussing how *I* treat my clothes," she said. "The subject at hand is *you*."

He deliberately dropped the shirt, defiantly glaring at her, then strode to his washstand and poured water into a basin. "I'm a sodding *duke*. It's expected of me to be heedless with my wardrobe." He splashed water on his face before dampening a cloth and rubbing it across his chest.

"That's true." She strolled to his bed and sat on the edge. "But I have heard it said that an untidy bed-chamber contributes to one's disordered mood. And clearly, your mood is disordered."

"It's rather evident why that might be the case," he threw over his shoulder.

"Except," she said with an expert air, "your mood has grown steadily more dour as time passes. You have been able to go out of the house, so while you might be experiencing some social ostracism, it isn't bad enough to keep you sequestered at home. Further," she went on, holding up a finger, "you might not be Mam's favorite person at the moment, but she's thawing to you. And clearly, *I* am here, favoring you with my presence—"

He bowed sardonically. "Much appreciated."

"—so I can only conclude that there is more troubling you than this situation with the duke of Brookhurst's calumny. Well," she added to herself, "it isn't exactly calumny, since it's true. But the idea is the same." She got to her feet and stood behind him. "Thus, I can only conclude that there is something else making you stomp around the house and punch things at the pugilism academy."

Unease prickling along his limbs, he set the washcloth aside. Here he was, thinking he'd been doing an admirable job of hiding his heartbreak, when in fact he had been as obvious as a snarling lion.

"So . . ." Maeve folded her arms across her chest. "Who is she?"

His stomach clenched. *Fuck.* Here was the trouble with having an astute sibling. Briefly, he considered denying it, but Maeve was tenacious, and she merited the truth.

Slowly, he faced his sister. "The woman who managed the club. She and I . . ." His words ground to a halt. Astute Maeve might be, but there was no way in hell that he'd divulge the details of his sexual life with her.

Yet she nodded with understanding. "You were lovers."

What a flimsy way of saying that Lucia had become everything to him. He'd delighted in her body, yet it had been the moments when they had simply been together that resonated like music. The happiness she'd given him had brought light into his life, and now that it was gone, there was no way out of the shadows.

"Yes," he said after a moment. "We were lovers. But," he continued, his voice roughening, "because of me, she lost her employment, and . . . her dream."

As a boy, he had climbed the stony exterior of the Kerry manor house, but he'd slipped and fallen. Fortunately, nothing was broken, but he'd sprained the hell out of his ankle. And how he'd howled—until his nurse Clodagh had quieted him.

There now, gasúr, she'd said, gathering him up in her sturdy arms. *Tomorrow, you might hurt a little, but 'twill be better than today. And the day after that will be even better, and so on, till the pain is gone and you can't imagine you ever felt it.*

Clodagh had been right. The pain had lessened, bit by bit, and within a fortnight, he had raced around the manor's grounds as if nothing had happened.

So he'd believed that all pain eventually faded until it disappeared entirely. Even his grief for his father, present as it was, didn't sink talons into him quite as deeply as it had. That hurt might never fully go away, but it eased.

That, he had believed, was the way of pain. In time, it lessened.

He was wrong.

Each moment without Lucia was a new agony, as if he was Prometheus eternally chained to a rock as a beast tore him open. Except with the titan, he'd only lose his liver. Tom continually had his heart ripped from his chest. Again and again.

"I see," Maeve said, breaking into his thoughts. "You love her."

Tom lurched like he'd taken a body blow. "I don't—" His denial ground to a halt.

Love. Was that what he felt? This constant demand to be in Lucia's presence? This need to breathe her in as though she was air and without her, he'd die? She was . . . she was everything. Life had no savor without her. It was flavorless and devoid of color. The thought of ever touching another woman repelled him. He wanted her. Only her. Now, and for the rest of his days.

"I do," he finally said. "I do love her. So much."

Just speaking it aloud confirmed what he already knew. He loved Lucia, and if he could, he'd devote all his energies to making her happy. Her joy was his joy.

"I'm glad," Maeve said, a bittersweet note in her words. "I'm glad one of us can be in love."

He reached for her hand and gave it a gentle squeeze. "I am so sorry about Lord Stacey."

She blinked back moisture in her eyes. "Me, too. I'd hoped . . . but I was wrong." His sister shook her head, as if to dispel her sorrow. "Let's talk of your lady. Does she know how you feel?"

"It doesn't matter," he said bleakly. "As I said, I cost her not only her employment, but her dream."

"What is it you want from her?"

"*From* her? Nothing. But I would give her everything if I could."

"Everything?" Maeve regarded him. "Even your name?"

Could he? Marry a woman with no connections, no family. A commoner.

Having her with him always—that's what he desired. He blazed with the need to spend every moment with her, to journey through life beside her. Raise a family with her. Grow old with her.

To bind himself to her for all of this world, and into the next.

But she would not have him—the last words from her lips had been to send him away.

Devastating weight pressed down on him, and he couldn't find the means to push back against it. He didn't want to. It would forever be his sacrament.

Maeve frowned in thought, tapping a finger of her free hand against her chin. "What if . . . you could make her dream come true?"

He rocked back on his heels.

A solution presented itself with sudden clarity. If the club was closing, it meant the house in Bloomsbury now stood empty. It belonged to him. He could do anything with it. Including transform it from a site of illicit pleasure into a place of learning. The school Lucia had dreamed of would live. He could make it happen for her, for the girls she wanted to help.

Could he—? Might it be possible?

He was a goddamned duke. He could make anything happen.

Or so he hoped.

"I know what I have to do." He straightened, gently tugging his hand from Maeve's. "I know how to fix everything."

Step one. Give Lucia her dream—a home for girls.

Step two. Find a way to alter the facts so he could prove Brookhurst wrong, and restore the Powell family's reputation.

Step three.

Oh, God. *Step three.* The most terrifying step of all. But worth the risk.

Step three. Ask Lucia to marry him.

The very idea struck him with blinding force. For all his years, he'd believed that when he did marry, it would be a strategic alliance with a woman of rank. Love would never be a part of that union. That was the way of it for dukes and other aristocrats. Duty before heart.

Wedding a commoner, and one not fully English, presented a massive break with tradition. Of a certain, doors would close to them, despite his rank. But he had allies, and the might of generations of Dukes of Northfield behind him. He would find a way to ensure Lucia got everything she wanted, everything she deserved.

He loved her—he prayed that she loved him, in spite of everything—and if he offered himself permanently to anyone, it had to be her. Only her.

"I have to go." He paced to his wardrobe and pulled out a fresh shirt.

"You haven't bathed," Maeve noted.

"So, I'll stink." He pulled on his shirt and rooted around for a waistcoat and coat, but draped them over his arm rather than actually put them on. Urgency pushed him. He didn't have time for niceties like being bathed or fully dressed. There was so much to do.

He stalked toward the door of his bedchamber. Then stopped and strode to Maeve.

He kissed her cheek. "Thank you, little bird."

She looked up at him, her eyes full of love. "I expect repayment in trips to Catton's."

"Every day," he vowed. He glanced toward the door.

"Go," she said gently.

He went.

Chapter 23

❧

$\mathcal{I}$t was surprising how a life could condense into a few boxes.

Lucia had, by design, kept her possessions to a minimum. Always lurking in the back of her mind was the idea that everything was temporary, and soon, the world would fall apart and she'd have to pick up and start over. Again.

But she'd hoped, when she had moved into what had been Mrs. Chalke's bedchamber above the Orchid Club, that she might be there for some time.

Instead, just a little over a year later, she'd had to pack up everything and decamp. Though Tom owned the building that housed the establishment, and wasn't going to toss her and the staff on the street, if word was out that the Bloomsbury house was the club's home, they would attract the wrong kind of attention. The authorities could no longer feign ignorance about the operation's existence, and would move in to shut everything down—perhaps even arrest her and her workers. The safest thing to do was decamp speedily.

With the staff's assistance, it had taken three days to clear out the furniture from the Orchid Club. Most of it had been sold, though a handful of pieces were put into storage. The house in Bloomsbury was now vacant for the first time for almost two decades. Then, in a remarkably brief span of time, Lucia had found rooms to share with Kitty, Liam, and Elspeth.

It wasn't so bad.

She moved a stack of shifts from a box into the battered clothespress that came with the rented room, then stood back to survey her handiwork. That was the last of everything. This set of narrow little rooms in Spitalfields was now her home—for now, at least.

Her bedchamber faced a tiny courtyard, so she had a bit of light throughout the day, and she could watch a trio of children playing with a stubby-tailed puppy. The silk weavers at their looms made a pleasant click-ing sound, almost soothing in its continuousness. And there was a shop just at the end of the block that sold decent steak-and-kidney pies.

Truly, she ought to be grateful that she'd found a decent, safe place to figure out the next step in her life. She sank into a chair and put her head in her hands.

"What can we do, my dove?" Kitty asked as she came into the room with Liam on her hip. Elspeth was close behind, and both women wore similar expres-sions of concern.

Pasting a smile into place, Lucia looked up at her friends. "I'm merely tired. We've done considerable work in a short amount of time. But it's all come together nicely, I think."

Elspeth put a hand upon her shoulder. "Lucia."

Merely saying her name with such compassion shattered the brittle fortifications Lucia had erected around herself. Her shoulders slumped and she cupped her palm over her forehead.

"Before we left," she said in a low voice, "I walked around the empty building. All those rooms where there had once been life and pleasure. Now . . . They are vacant. Like it is in here." She pressed her hand to her heart. "The structure stands but there's nothing inside."

"It's all right to feel hurt and sad," Elspeth said.

"And angry," Kitty added.

"I don't want to feel *anything,*" Lucia said and growled in frustration.

"That's not how life works." Elspeth gave her shoulder a squeeze. "We feel things, good and bad, and that's how it's supposed to be."

Lucia rubbed her cheek against Elspeth's hand. "Dreadfully inconvenient things, emotions."

"They are." Kitty jogged Liam up and down, who giggled. "But without them, we'd be men, and who wants that?"

Elspeth grinned. "I surely don't."

An ache pulsed through Lucia to see the adoration in her friends' gazes. While the last few days had been a whirlwind of activity, she'd been able to keep thoughts of Tom at bay. Here, in the quiet and stillness, nothing distracted her. It was a brutal wound that cut her again and again.

Only when he was gone did she feel the cavernous space he left behind. She was half a person. By some marvel she kept standing and talking and breathing and doing all the things she was supposed to do to remain alive. Yet it wasn't fully life, just the rote motions of it.

"Oh, but we're being heartless with our mooning." Kitty looked apologetic.

"No. It's all right. I've had to let him go." Lucia made a motion of casting something aside, as if it was so easily done. Perhaps the more she told herself this, the more chance she had at believing herself. "And let go of the Orchid Club. But I'm not abandoning my dream. Somehow, I'll make the girls' home happen."

"And you'll have our help," Elspeth vowed.

Lucia pressed her fingertips to her trembling lips. How fortunate she was. How very lucky.

A knock sounded at the door. She rose to answer it, and started when she saw Will standing in the hallway. At once, she embraced him, which was not unlike hugging an oak. He patted her back with his enormous hands.

"*Mi dispiace,* Will."

"For what?" A puzzled look crossed his craggy face.

She pulled back. "I've cost you everything."

"A bit of an exaggeration, eh? I lost a situation, but I've got my other work, and besides, there's always more jobs." He shrugged as if it was hardly worth mentioning.

"But you were all counting on me," she said, aching with every word, "and I let you down."

He exhaled. "The world don't rest on your shoulders alone, missus. See here." He jerked a thumb over his shoulder. "Come on outside with me for a spell."

"What—"

"You going to argue, or just take a little walk?"

She gave him a rueful smile. "I'll be right down."

He trundled down the stairs, the steps creaking beneath his mass, and Lucia followed. She heard Kitty and Elspeth behind her. At the front door, he waited, gesturing for her to precede him. She pushed the door open, and her breath left her in a rush.

The entire staff of the Orchid Club stood on the front steps and spilled into the street. Every single person the establishment had employed, from Jenny to Arthur to Peter, the groom. They all looked at her, wearing expectant expressions.

Her throat contracted. She'd tried her best to give everyone a personal apology and goodbye, but it clearly hadn't been enough—and she couldn't blame them. Her own foolish choices had led them to this sad state of affairs.

"*Amici,*" she said. "I am so sor—"

Jenny moved to the front of the throng. "None of that! We're not here to rake you over the coals."

"I've paid everyone their final wages." That was the only other reason she could imagine why they would gather in the street outside her rented rooms.

Jenny dug her elbow into Arthur's barrel-like chest.

"Oh, right!" He reached into his coat and pulled out a thick envelope, which he handed to her.

Lucia opened it, and the ground tilted beneath her. The envelope brimmed with cash, easily close to fifty pounds.

"What . . ." She tried to speak around the thickness in her throat. "What have you done?"

"We pooled our money," Will said behind her, "so we could rent a new location for the club."

"Bunch of us have been talking," Arthur added. "We know you need the blunt from the club so you can start up that home for girls. First we thought to just have the cash for the home, but then we got to talking and—"

"And why just give you a bowl of soup when we can pay for the pot?" Jenny said, her voice practical. "That is to say, better to have a steady source of blunt rather than one lump that mightn't last long enough."

"Oh, *miei cari.*" Lucia's eyes were hot and scratchy, and she felt the burning track of a tear trace down her cheek.

"You helped us, missus," Will said in a matter-of-fact tone, "now we're helping you."

"*Grazie mille.*" She looked behind her to see Kitty and Elspeth smiling. "Did you know of this?"

"Heard a whisper or two," Elspeth said.

Pressing the envelope close to her chest, Lucia fought a sniffle. Though she might not have Tom in her life anymore, and ached with a desperate loss, she would find a way to keep going. She had to.

"*Faring* all right, old man?"

As he and Blakemere stood outside the Palace of Westminster, Tom tried to smile at his friend. While he was glad to have Blakemere back from Cornwall, even the earl couldn't ease the pressure of the iron bands that wrapped around Tom's chest.

"Oh," he said airily, "I was only thinking that I should've done what any sane, reasonable man ought to have and simply run Brookhurst through with a sabre."

"They hanged the Earl of Ferrers, you know."

"Fifty years ago," Tom noted. His words were steely. "I might fare better in our enlightened age."

"This plan will come off." Blakemere tapped the side of his nose. "I've an instinct for strategy, and yours is sound."

"I pray your instincts are right." Tom inhaled deeply, catching the scent of tobacco from the MPs having a last puff of their cheroots before heading inside.

Years ago, at Oxford, he'd attempted to acquire the habit of smoking. It had seemed so sophisticated and manly, but all it had led to was Tom coughing so hard he vomited on the steps of the Radcliffe Camera. A similar nausea gripped him now as he waited to begin his plan that would, he hoped, set everything right.

He'd face any cannonade to ensure Lucia's happiness.

Including asking his mother and sister for help. They had listened to his plan for remedying the situation and decided they would lend their support. The unexpected gesture humbled him, and he'd kissed both his mother's and sister's hands before setting off this morning.

"We've assembled?" Greyland asked, approaching Tom and Blakemere. Two men strode behind him. "I've brought Lords Ashford and Marwood as reinforcements."

Tom shook hands with each of them. "You've been apprised of the circumstances?"

"I'm excessively looking forward to humiliating Brookhurst," Lord Ashford said grimly. "The man's an ass and his reign of terror in the Lords ends today."

"We oughtn't get ahead of ourselves," Tom said. "Nothing is certain, and if I'm not successful in this, it might taint your own reputations while utterly ruining mine."

"That's assuming we *had* sterling reputations to begin with," Lord Marwood said with a grin.

Tom lifted his hand, signaling for quiet. His whole body vibrated with tension. "That's Brookhurst's carriage."

"We're with you," Blakemere said, knocking his fist into Tom's shoulder. "Take the bastard down."

The elegant vehicle rolled to a stop, and a footman leapt down to unfold the steps and open the door. One of Brookhurst's polished shoes appeared before the entire man emerged. The duke brushed at his cuffs and adjusted the brim of his hat.

The time was now.

Feeling the gaze of dozens of MPs on him, Tom strode to Brookhurst. He drew up in front of the duke, fighting the urge to plow his fist into the son of a bitch's face.

"Northfield," Brookhurst said icily. He didn't offer even a cursory bow.

I'll fucking kill him.

"You have spread baseless slander about me," Tom said in barely more than a growl. "Because of you, the *ton* believes me to be a panderer, and the resulting ignominy has tarnished the honor of my family."

"Are you calling me a liar?" Brookhurst flared his nostrils in affront.

Low muttering rose up from the observing crowd.

"Everything I said was true," the duke added. "That is undeniable."

"I do deny it," Tom said bitingly.

Brookhurst looked over to see their audience. Distinguished MPs watched with open fascination, and at the sight of them, Brookhurst smirked. "You cannot prove that."

"I can and I will," Tom said. "We will go there now. This very moment."

"Now?" Brookhurst frowned.

"Yes, this very moment." Tom pointed at Brookhurst's footman. "Distribute the address of the place to whomever desires it. We'll form a caravan. Then, the truth will be discovered."

The duke narrowed his eyes, as if trying to find the flaw in Tom's plan. Finally he said, "As you like. You and I shall go together." Brookhurst made a show of opening the door to his carriage. "It would be my pleasure and privilege to transport you there myself."

He climbed into his carriage.

Tom glanced at Blakemere. The moment had arrived, everything moving as it was supposed to.

His friend nodded. In a trice, Blakemere had gotten into his own waiting carriage and driven off. Meanwhile, other MPs had been given the address of the Orchid Club—no doubt pretending that they didn't already know where it was located—and were climbing into their own vehicles to witness what promised to be a spectacle.

"I await your pleasure," Brookhurst called smugly.

After nodding at Greyland and the others, Tom took a breath, then got into the duke's carriage.

"I was concerned that today was going to be tedious," Brookhurst said as they drove toward Bloomsbury. "Clearly, I was mistaken."

Tom said nothing, lest he show his hand too early. Now there was nothing to do but wait.

Chapter 24

House available to let—commodious lodgings with four bedrooms and two spacious parlors located within Clerkenwell and within a short distance from Sadler's Wells. Excellent kitchen. Serious enquiries welcome.

Though the property sounded a bit small as a location for the new club, Lucia used a pencil to circle the advertisement. The longer it took to find a site for the next establishment, tentatively named The Lily Club, the longer her staff would be out of work, and the greater the amount of time before Lucia could establish her girls' home.

The amount collected by the staff would cover a deposit as well as several months' rent. It was a good start, provided she found a location quickly.

Noises from the traffic outside echoed up into the warren of tiny rooms in which she sat. Kitty and Elspeth had taken Liam out for some air—admittedly in shorter supply here in Spitalfields than in Bloomsbury.

The next chapter in her life beckoned, but summoning excitement for it proved a challenge. Moving her body, heavy with loss, proved a barely surmountable obstacle. Finding enthusiasm felt too great an endeavor. The world became distant and gray, a shadow of itself, and, drained of life, she could only watch.

It had been far, far too long since she'd last seen Tom.

She had to find a way to move on. She *had* to. And yet the prospect of being without him leeched away all pleasure.

Hopefully, he'd found a way to weather the scandal. But if he did, she would never know. And that not knowing—just as she'd never again know his smiles, his wit, the warmth of his gaze—formed a grievous injury that could not heal.

A knock sounded at the door, and she surfaced from her grim thoughts. She stood, shook out her skirts, and went to see who it was.

Standing before her was a footman in gold and scarlet livery. A liveried servant wasn't often seen in Spitalfields, and she didn't recognize the colors of his uniform.

His posture impeccable, he held out a square of folded paper. "Madam."

She took it from him and read.

My love,
A carriage awaits you downstairs. In it, you will find my friend the Earl of Blakemere. I ask that you accompany him. The gamble you

*and I take could secure our future happiness,
so I ask you to trust me.*

*Your servant, &c.
T.*

For several moments, Lucia could only stare at
Tom's note. The wisest thing would be to refuse and
stay here, hiding in her rooms. Caring for him had
already cost her so much.

I ask you to trust me.

Did she? Could she? She balanced on the edge of
her wariness. A moment passed, and then another. She
drew in a breath.

"Let me fetch my hat and wrap," she said to the
footman.

"I will await you downstairs, madam." He bowed
and strode away. Other tenants poked their heads out
of their rooms, watching him go.

With shaking hands, Lucia draped a shawl over
her shoulders and tied the ribbons of her bonnet. She
glanced into the looking glass propped atop the man-
tel. Her wide gaze was reflected back at her, but at
least the aubergine ribbon tied beneath her chin gave
her face a hint of color.

You're stalling.

She steadied herself. With a final breath, she went
into the hallway, closed and locked the door behind
her, and took the steps down to the ground floor.

An elegant, but unfamiliar, carriage waited outside. Children clustered around it, peering into the windows. A gentleman's hand emerged, handing each child a coin, but the hand was unknown to her.

The footman opened the carriage door, and the gentleman inside peered out at her. He had sandy hair and an open, lively expression. Something about him seemed familiar—a not uncommon feeling for her, given the nature of managing a clandestine club.

"Miss Marini?"

"Yes," she said cautiously.

"I'm Blakemere, your escort. Please." He gestured to the interior of the carriage.

"Where are we going?"

He motioned for her to come closer, and she did, but she didn't climb into the vehicle. Tom had asked her to trust him, but that trust only extended so far.

"Northfield has made substantial changes to the Orchid Club," Blakemere said in a lowered voice. "He needs you there right away."

Anxiety tangled in her belly. "Is that safe for him?" Their association had cost him—and her—dearly.

"He's taking a chance, but it could pay off." Blakemere's gaze was surprisingly steely, as though he'd done and witnessed a great many things.

She shook her head. A lifetime of caution could not be discarded in an instant like a soiled handkerchief. "Please, tell me what I'm to expect."

The earl shifted from resolute to charming as he

offered her a crooked smile that no doubt enchanted many.

Not her. Not today. She stared back at him with the same unbending expression she used to quell unruly guests.

"I believe Northfield would like to surprise you," Blakemere said at last. "But I do advise you strongly, no matter what you see there, it's critical that you do not appear at all astonished. It's all part of his plan. You'll see."

Doubt gnawed at her. What the earl asked, what Tom asked, required considerable faith. Could she trust him? She'd brought him into her heart, her world, opening herself to him as she had to no other.

She could not blame him. She had to own her responsibility in all this. With open eyes, she'd taken the chance to be with him. The fury she'd felt toward him was meant for herself.

If she went with Lord Blakemere, she might make the same mistake of giving in to dangerous feelings. But if she didn't…she would always wonder, *What if?*

"Will you come with me now?" Blakemere asked.

She hesitated. At the least, she could tell Tom that she'd been wrong in the placement of her blame. She couldn't undo the damage of her anger, but she could offer him an apology. If he could not forgive her…she would live with the aftereffects of her rage, hoping that the injuries she'd caused him would one day heal.

Lucia allowed the footman to help her into the carriage. The door closed behind her, the vehicle rocked from the footman climbing onto his perch, and then they were off.

"Forgive me if I'm not much for conversation," she said to the earl as they sped down Brushfield Street.

"That's perfectly agreeable. I can prattle enough for the both of us."

Lord Blakemere was true to his word, filling the silence with a steady stream of cheerful talk. He explained to her that he and his wife had just come from Cornwall, and were weary but exhilarated by a considerable amount of work that came with fixing up not just a manor house but an entire village. He didn't seem to mind that Lucia only half listened. But his chatter did give her something to focus on rather than stewing in a morass of nerves as they neared Bloomsbury. Or rather, she *attempted* to focus on his talk. Inside, she trembled and quaked. She pressed a hand to her chest as if she could somehow gentle her thudding heart, but it went on fiercely pounding.

"And now, here we are," the earl said, at last.

She crossed herself. *Dio, dammi la forza.* "God, give me strength."

The carriage stopped, and Lucia was helped down onto trembling legs. She frowned in confusion to see an array of expensive coaches lined up on the curb outside the Orchid Club's former home. Even at the height of the establishment's popularity, vehicles chose to use the stables located discreetly behind the house, rather than advertise their presence. Yet here they were in the bright light of day. The door to the house itself stood open.

Her stomach clenched, but she didn't wait for Lord Blakemere. Shouldering aside her anxiety, Lucia marched up the front walkway and stepped inside.

Over a dozen aristocratic men stood in the foyer but none of them wore masks. They all turned to stare at her, their collective gazes sharp as stilettos. A tall, lean gentleman with a full head of snowy hair glared at her with so much fury and hatred, Lucia almost recoiled.

"Here she is," Tom said, coming forward through the crowd.

Forgetting the white-haired man, her gaze devoured Tom. He looked appallingly handsome and quite ducal, if not a little thinner, his eyes ringed by dark circles. The urge to go to him and throw her arms around him—inhale his scent and then absorb the solidity of his body—was strong, but she forced it back.

His gaze flashed when he beheld her. Yet he didn't reach for her, despite the need in his eyes.

"Miss Marini." Tom bowed. He addressed the noblemen. "These gentlemen are here to observe your good work."

"I . . ." She tried to smile as Lord Blakemere had advised, but her bewilderment made it almost impossible. For her and Tom to be seen together, *here,* endangered him.

Just then, a black-haired girl in a crisp smock and carrying a sheet of paper ran through the group. She didn't seem to care that the men she hurried past represented half the wealth in England. But she stopped when she saw Lucia.

It was Mary, her student from Bethnal Green. Her clothes were clean and free of holes, her boots shiny and new, and she proudly held up the paper.

Lucia nearly wept to see the child looking so well—but her astonishment at seeing Mary *here* stopped her tears.

"Miss! I'm to read a report on toadstools," she announced grandly. Then, more shyly, she added, "Will you come listen?"

Lucia's mind could not catch up with what her eyes beheld. Distractedly, she murmured, "In a moment, Mary."

The girl nodded and sped off into the room that had been the parlor. Lucia refrained from casting a puzzled glance in Tom's direction, but Heaven above, it was a challenge. Confusion made her dizzy. It was as if she'd been thrown into the sea but could suddenly breathe underwater.

"Let's move on, gentlemen and lady." Smiling, Tom motioned that they should follow Mary.

Move on to what?

Lucia walked down the corridor she'd patrolled countless times, but never with an unmasked audience comprised of noblemen. That's clearly what they were—

from their stiff bearing to the cut of their clothes, everything about them proclaimed their wealth and privilege.

She reached the parlor and barely contained her shock. The room had been completely transformed. At one end, a slate hung from the wall, and was covered in chalk writing and diagrams. Before the slate stood a woman in spectacles, who was reading aloud from a book.

Arranged in front of the slate were twelve desks, and at each desk sat a girl with her own book. They looked up at the bespectacled woman, their expressions attentive. Lucia recognized half of the girls from her tutoring but the others were new to her. In a corner, an orange tabby cat dozed on a patched cushion.

It was a school. Here. In what had once been the Orchid Club.

Heart hammering, she turned at Tom and the other men's approach, yet she schooled her features to make it seem as though seeing a sex club transformed into a home for girls was an everyday occurrence.

"Miss Marini has provided the girls here with everything they will need," Tom said to the noblemen. "There are more classrooms, a refectory, dormitory rooms, and an abundance of supplies, some of which I have financed, and others that receive funding from private donations."

"And what do these students learn?" one of the men asked.

Tom looked expectantly at Lucia.

Madonna! "Mathematics," she stammered. "Grammar, literature, the sciences."

"What of sewing, cooking?" an older gentleman prodded. "Anything *useful*?"

A steadying bolt of anger anchored her. She straightened. "The subjects they study *are* useful. The enrichment of their minds is valuable enough, but their fluency in these subjects will, at the least, ensure they can be employed as teachers and governesses."

"Which is highly respectable employment," said a young woman with reddish-brown hair and dressed in black, coming forward. She looked to be in her late teens, and the vivid blue of her eyes matched the hue of Tom's. Beneath her arm, she carried several hornbooks. Her smile was warm as she nodded at Lucia—but Lucia was certain she'd never met the girl.

"Ah, my sister, Lady Maeve." Tom wrapped an arm around the young woman's shoulders. "She assists several days a week."

Of course. The girl had Tom's striking looks, her gaze sharply intelligent.

"Are you not in mourning, Lady Maeve?" the angry-looking man demanded.

"There's always an exception for good works, Your Grace," the girl said with barely hidden fury.

This was the man who'd ruined Lucia, and trampled Tom's reputation. The man who'd taken everything from her.

It was all she could do to keep from springing forward and ramming her fist into his stomach.

An older woman, her dark hair threaded with silver, her bearing regal, came forward. When she spoke, her works were musically inflected with an Irish accent. "As her mother, the decision as to whether or not her activities are suitable is entirely mine."

The men bowed, and Lucia, setting aside her anger, quickly bobbed a curtsy.

"I believe many of you know the Duchess of Northfield," Tom said to the group.

Cristo in cielo, this woman was his mother.

The duchess nodded at the men, and when she looked at Lucia, her gaze wasn't entirely friendly.

"Your assistance here is greatly appreciated, Your Grace," Lucia said.

"I am here for my son," she said primly. "And for the girls."

"*Certo.*" Lucia swallowed around the lump in her throat. She'd seen all walks of life in her establishment, and knew that beneath everyone's clothing, they were merely human. Long ago, she'd gotten beyond feeling intimidated by someone from a higher social class—but the Duchess of Northfield made Lucia feel no bigger than a spool of thread.

"Hugh!" the Duke of Brookhurst's eyes went round and color drained from his face. "What the blazes?"

Several of the men nearby coughed at the Duke of Brookhurst's language.

Lucia followed the Duke of Brookhurst's gaze. An exceptionally handsome young man, likely no older than his early twenties, appeared. He had sandy hair and hazel eyes, and the pristine cut of his expensive clothing revealed his rank.

Lady Maeve stared at him, adoration shining in her face. "Hugh."

There was so much love in that look, so much joy, it was like being in the presence of something holy. Lucia almost shielded her eyes.

"I've brought more ink," the young man said. "Cleaned out the stationer's shop." He held up a box that contained numerous bottles. "Brought some quills, too." When he looked at Lady Maeve, his expression brimmed with devotion.

"Lord Stacey." Tom tipped his head in greeting.

"How good of you to assist us," Lucia said with a grateful smile.

Hugh—Lord Stacey—gave her a bright grin. "A good cause, of course, and when His Grace, the Duke of Northfield, told me of the place, well, naturally I offered my services."

A choked sound came from the Duke of Brookhurst, his gaze fastened on his son. The pallor had left his face, replaced by a hectic flush.

"As you can see, gentlemen," Tom said to the assembled crowd, "I am not, in fact, the owner of an illicit club. I am the patron of this home, and Miss Marini is the headmistress. Your Grace," he said, turning to the sputtering duke, "I do believe that your accusations were inaccurate."

"Quite inaccurate," Lucia said coolly.

A dark-haired man with a striking and stern countenance moved to the front of the group. "You've made serious allegations against a fellow peer. Allegations that have been proven false."

Mutters rose up from the crowd.

". . . Brookhurst went too far . . ."

". . . lies . . . slander . . . against a duke's *charity* . . . his own political gain . . ."

The Duke of Brookhurst glanced toward a trio of older men, clearly seeking their support. But their faces were stony with condemnation.

"Leave now," Tom said, his voice brutally flat. "Or else you and I shall meet each other at dawn."

"He's a very good shot," Lord Blakemere added sunnily from the back of the crowd.

Tom stared at the Duke of Brookhurst with the patience of an executioner. He took a step toward the duke. Brookhurst recoiled. Tom kept moving forward, and the duke scurried backward.

"Hugh," he said, his voice a rasp, "come with me at once."

A pause followed. Tom's sister looked back and forth between her beau and the young man's father, her eyes round with apprehension.

"I'm staying with Lady Maeve," Lord Stacey answered flatly.

If Lucia didn't hate the Duke of Brookhurst, she might have summoned pity for him as he registered his son's betrayal. His face crumpled.

The crowd parted and with a guttural sound, the duke scuttled away and sped through the door. The moment he was gone, Lady Maeve rushed to Lord Stacey, and they embraced tightly.

One of the older men approached Tom, his hand extended. "Apologies, Your Grace. I believed Brookhurst's slander, which discredits me." He turned to Lucia and gave a small bow. "I pray you accept my sincerest regret."

"*Scuse accettate.*" She made herself nod with the air of a tolerant goddess. "'Apology accepted.'"

Before Tom, no nobleman had ever offered her a gesture of respect, but the crowd of aristocrats followed the man's lead and also bowed.

Surely I'm dreaming.

"I hope this clears up any and all misunderstandings," Tom answered.

"Without doubt," the other man said readily. "And I shall personally ensure that word disseminates, exonerating you and Miss Marini of any illicit behavior."

"Much appreciated," Lucia said with as much regal hauteur she could muster.

"Now that's settled . . ."

Tom drew in a shaky breath as he faced her. Deliberately, his gaze on hers, he lowered himself down, until he knelt on one knee.

Lucia had never once fainted in her life. Not after enduring punishing hunger or intense physical pain. Yet now she grew light-headed.

"Miss Marini," Tom said, his voice thick as he took her hand. "Lucia," he added in a low, urgent whisper for her alone. "I love you. Will you be my wife?"

She could not have heard right. It was impossible. And yet he looked at her with such heated reverence— there could be no doubt.

Lady Maeve gasped, and there were mutters of both pleasure and outrage from the onlookers.

". . . a commoner . . ." ". . . *foreign* extraction . . ."

Before Lucia could even begin to consider how she might answer, the duchess cleared her throat.

"Miss Marini," she said in a frosty tone. "A word. Alone."

Tom tensed beneath Lucia's hand, and she felt her own body go taut in readiness. Mamma used to glare at any lad who looked too long in Lucia's direction. Surely the mother of a supremely eligible, highly sought bachelor might growl in warning at a woman who might be predatory.

After all that had transpired today, the hazards Lucia had faced, a quiet chat with Tom's mother shouldn't frighten her. *Shouldn't,* but did.

"Of course," Lucia said with far more serenity than she felt. She gave Tom a fabricated reassuring smile. "There's a small chamber just down the hall."

Her head high despite her anxiety, Lucia walked

toward the room that had once held intoxicated guests. Now a trio of girls sat on a sofa and read a book aloud.

"*Scusate, care*," Lucia said to the girls. "May we have some privacy?"

The children stared at the duchess with awe as they got to their feet and filed out.

Despite the sofa, Lucia remained standing. In case she needed to run.

"I learned only this morning that he loved you." The duchess faced her, and in the beautifully sculpted lines of her face, Lucia saw echoes of Tom. "He doesn't favor me with a single word about his feelings for you, a woman of common birth, and today he tells me he intends to offer matrimony."

"It was equally surprising to me, Your Grace." Lucia could not yield or show any fear, but taking a defensive stance would set a tone that would resonate for years to come.

"I tried to talk him out of it," the duchess said bluntly.

"Understandable," Lucia answered.

"But he would not be dissuaded," the older woman went on. "He insisted that he would ask you, and await your answer."

"That's . . ." *Astonishing. Wonderful. Impossible.*

"What is your answer?" The duchess lifted her eyebrow.

"I don't know," Lucia said honestly. She looked straight into the duchess's eyes. "I have learned a great many difficult lessons over the course of my life, Your

Grace. Above all, I learned to protect myself, to be cautious. Especially," she said, "where my heart was concerned."

The duchess regarded her thoughtfully.

"When it comes to Tom," Lucia continued, spreading her hands, "I have no caution. His burdens and sorrows are mine. His happiness is my happiness. His heart," she said, her throat growing tight, "is my heart." She dipped her head as understanding filled her. "I know you think me a scheming opportunist, Your Grace. If there was a way for me to have Tom but never become a duchess, I'd take that option without hesitation. I want the man, not the title."

For several moments, the duchess gazed at her.

Then, she opened her arms.

Lucia stared at the older woman. She took one step, and then another, and then she was clasped in the duchess's embrace.

So long. It had been so long since a mother had held her. The duchess smelled of roses and tea, and Lucia drew the scent deep into her lungs. Only through sheer determination did she remain standing. Yet she clung to the duchess, squeezing her eyes shut to keep the tears from falling.

"There, lass," the older woman murmured. "Forgive an old bear for guarding her cub." She stroked a gentle hand down Lucia's hair. "All mothers dream that someday, someone will love their child as much as they do."

"I love him so very much." Saying the words aloud, she saw how true they were. That all the things she had been feeling, all the joy, the pain, the need to be beside him every moment of every day—it was love. Love at last.

"And he knows it, too. But he needs to hear it from your lips." The duchess slowly released her. "I'd wager he's out there, dying a hundred deaths to have us in here alone together. Shall we end his suffering?"

Lucia dashed a knuckle across her eyes. "It's the humane thing to do."

When she and the duchess returned to the corridor, they did so arm in arm.

Looking hunted, Tom paced in front of the assembled crowd. He stopped in midstride to see his mother and possible future wife walking together like the dearest of friends. The smile that spread across his face made Lucia's heart soar.

As Tom came cautiously forward, the duchess slipped her arm from Lucia's and removed her left glove, tugging at one of her fingers.

"Hold out your hand, Tommy lad," she said. When he did so, she carefully set something in his palm.

A ring. It gleamed, light reflecting on the large sapphire surrounded by diamonds. Lucia had never seen anything half so splendid, and it stopped her heart. *No. That could not be . . . not for me?*

"You know what to do," the duchess said.

His fingers curled around the ring, and he pressed a kiss to his mother's cheek.

Tom turned to Lucia. His voice rough, he asked, "Will you?"

A handful of the watching noblemen stalked off, but Lucia paid them no mind. She saw only Tom and felt only the pulse of love between them.

Yet—

"We're not equals," she said softly to Tom. Because she had to. Because he needed to know, fully, what this would mean for him, and their future together.

"We are. In every way." His gaze was the home she'd been seeking all her days. "What anyone says or feels, that doesn't matter. All that matters is you and me. Please. I need you in my life."

"I . . ."

He took so many chances for her. Risked everything— for her. Surely she could do the same. Surely love meant the possibility of devastation but also the prospect of measureless joy.

"*Sì*," she finally said. "*Ti amo.* 'I love you.' Yes."

His throat worked as he swallowed, and his heart shone from his eyes.

The crowd had grown to include many girls in pinafores, Mary amongst their number, and several women Lucia took to be teachers. At the very back of the throng, Lucia spotted Kitty, Elspeth, and Liam. Her family.

"Hold out your hand, dear," Lady Maeve said *sotto voce*.

Lucia did so, and Tom took her bare hand in his. Warmth cascaded through her as he slid the ring onto her finger.

The onlookers broke into applause.

Tom's face lit with happiness, and her heart pounded in response. Still holding her hand, his gaze lingered on her mouth.

"Later," she whispered.

"And all the days and years after," he said.

Epilogue

*L*ucia barely felt the midnight chill as she stood on Newcombe's high street. She waited with the Duchess of Greyland and the Earl and Countess of Blakemere as Tom and the duke completed their New Year's duties here in the snug Cornish village.

Holiday visitors strolled along the lantern-lit streets, and laughter tumbled out of the taproom and restaurants. Up the hill, lights blazed in the windows of the veterans' home as the men celebrated the turning of the year. Hard to believe that not long ago, this town had been hovering at the edge of disaster, reliant on smuggling to keep its villagers housed and fed. At supper, in the newly refurbished manor house on the hill, the countess had proudly announced that the hotels were at capacity, regardless of the trouble associated with winter travel.

And, in keeping with the holiday's tradition, Tom and the Duke of Greyland crossed the threshold of every villager's home.

"Don't see the good luck in a dark-haired man stomping through your door," the blond earl grumbled good-naturedly. "Everyone knows you can't trust blokes like that. Shifty. Underhanded."

The duchess laughed. "No one would ever use those words to describe Alex. Me, perhaps," she acknowledged, "but never my husband."

"Wasn't precisely an upstanding citizen, myself," the countess said wryly.

"None of our husbands married women of sterling morals," Lucia said, shifting the basket she carried. It was a chance, bringing its contents along as she and Tom accompanied his friends on a midnight ramble through the village. Yet if there was any group of people who'd appreciate her offering, it was this assembly.

"Perhaps therein lies the secret to happiness," the earl said, beaming down at his wife. "Wed a woman of suspect character, keep the passion alive."

The countess rested her head on her husband's shoulder. "It helps to take a rogue as a husband."

Tom and the duke appeared, and while Greyland scowled without ire, Tom smiled warmly. Both he and the duke immediately went to their respective wives.

"Greyland and I earned our wine tonight bringing everyone coal, bread, and coins." Tom wrapped an arm around Lucia's waist to draw her close.

"Surprised you're not drunk on kisses," Greyland

muttered, though a smile tugged at the corners of his mouth. "All the ladies of the house insisted it was good luck to give you a buss on the cheek."

"They would've kissed you, too," Tom said, "but you're so bloody ducal, they were intimidated."

"Poor, imperious duke," the Duchess of Greyland cooed. She patted her husband's arm. "Later, I'll give you all the kisses you didn't get."

"Why wait?" Greyland swept her into his arms and pressed his mouth to hers.

Tom, Lucia, and the others hooted. The duke, without breaking the kiss, threw them a rude gesture.

Lucia clapped, all the while conscious of the letter in her pocket. She intended to share its contents with Tom anon. Though Kitty had been careful to keep any potentially scandalous elements from the missive, in case it should fall into the wrong hands, she'd reported that under her and Elspeth's leadership, the Lily Club had become the city's latest sensation.

The home for girls thrived, and upon her return to London, Lucia planned to scout another location for a second establishment.

"Time for our New Year's treat," she said when at last the duke and duchess broke apart. From her basket, she produced six small bundles, which she handed to everyone and kept one for herself. "In Napoli, we give each other figs wrapped in laurel leaves."

"How lovely," Lady Blakemere said.

"And we say, *buon anno.*"

Everyone unwrapped their figs and bit into them.

"Delicious," Greyland said after taking a bite.

"Our gratitude for sharing this with us," the duchess added.

Tom gently stroked a thumb down Lucia's cheek, and only when she saw the gleam of wetness there did she realize she wept.

"Why do you cry, love?" he murmured to her. Worry creased between his brows. "Something saddens you?"

She looked at all the faces of Tom's friends—her friends, too, now—and thought of Kitty's letter, and what it meant. For so long, she had fought. Battle after battle. Always holding tightly to her heart, lest it suffer another agonizing wound. It was better that way, or so she'd believed. She had shared friendship with Kitty and Elspeth, but never fully opened herself to them. There was safety in her solitude.

But Tom had shown her what it meant to truly let someone in. He had proved to her that, in wagering on love, she had so much to gain. Friends. Family. A true home.

Courage meant more than fighting back with a sturdy sword and shield—it meant stepping into the light, naked and vulnerable.

"This isn't sadness," she said to him. "It's love."

He gazed at her, his handsome, beloved face filling with so much adoration, it robbed her of breath.

She gripped him by the lapels of his coat and kissed

him. In front of the world, she dared to show everyone that she loved him. When he kissed her back, wrapping his arms around her, she felt the world expand around her. It gleamed with the promise of everything new.